MW00935048

The Lost Medallion

The Lost Medallion

Bryan M. Powell

This book is a work of fiction. Except for the references to the biblical account of the Magi coming to Jerusalem and Bethlehem, all other references to historical events, real people or real locations are used fictionally. The names of characters, places and events are products of the author's vivid imagination. Any resemblances to actual persons, living or dead, and events or locations are entirely coincidental.

Fantasy - Fiction, Christian - Fiction, Young Adult – Fiction,
Historical - Fiction, Prophetic – Fiction
Cover design by Graphics_360 Arewa Olanrewaju
Photography by Amy McCarthy – photographybymccarthy@gmail.com

Manufactured in the United States of America
ISBN-13:978-1544264493
ISBN-10:1544264496

Cast of Characters

Balthazar, Melchior, and Gasper – With the medallion at large, their quest isn't over until it is found and destroyed.
Colt O'Dell – Glenn O'Dell's son learns that finders keepers isn't such a good idea.
Dr. Damian – Finds himself at a crossroads and has to make a choice.
Ty Huntley – His determination almost gets him killed.
Pastor Scott Wyatt – Once again his tested, but with wisdom and skill, he passes the test.
Angela Wyatt – Scott Wyatt's wife, always ready to serve.
Jacob Myers – Reconnects with a distant uncle.
Felicia Beauchamp – An exchange teacher from France fidgets her way into Jasper's life.
Simon Levi – Jacob Myer's uncle and curator of the Institute in Antiquities.
Former Sheriff Randy Baker – a man with one big secret and is willing to kill to keep it.
Sasha – A young Jewish girl whose changed Colt's life.
Layla Ali – Her past and presence were shrouded in mystic.
Glenn and Karen O'Dell – Had to come to grips with their carnal life-style.
Prince Argos – The prince over the US southern region.
Prince Leo – His silent presence often made the difference between victory or defeat.
Prince Selaphiel – Helper of saintly prayers.
Prince Uriel – The one who protects the saints.
Michael the Archangel – Ever the guardian angel oversees Israel during her next crisis.
Prince Azrael – Watches over his earthly charges, and sometimes gets too involved.

Prelude

Colt stood next to his bed fingering the inscriptions on the four-inch disc he found in the Witch's Cave. Ever since that day, he'd tried to decipher the inscriptions, but had not been able to break the code. Its engravings captivated his attention and he tried again. "Mon-e-may, ec-ta-ron, seekie-lay-mini." Tossing it aside, he flopped on his bed. Hands on his stomach, he muttered, "It's useless. I'll never figure it out."

But he did, he just didn't know it ...

A pair of green orbs peered through narrowed eyelids at the little boy. The demon's breath came in short, angry huffs. Drool formed in the corners of its gaping mouth and hung like froth from a tired race horse. Were it not for the Holy Spirit's seal which he placed upon Colt, the creature would have sunk its talons into Colt's head long ago. As it was, each time he attempted to read the engravings, he became more ill.

He'd found the ancient disc in the witch's cave several months earlier and ever since, guarded his secret from all comers. His parents, not even his closest friends, the wise men, were aware he possessed the relic. Something about the disc called to him, spoke his name and he spoke to it.

As a wave of nausea snaked through his stomach, Colt wrapped the disc in an old cloth, tucked it between the two mattresses and flopped in bed. He spent the next two hours in a dreamlike state ... caught between light and darkness ... caught between opposing forces. Shadowy figures with clawed feet and leathery skin attempted to grab him and drag him into the night, while bright, shining beings surrounded him, holding the raging creatures at bay. He stood atop the exalted pedestal overlooking the sacrificial chamber where swords clashed and the screams of dying men penetrated his ears. He was back in the Witch's Cave. The deep rolling echo of thunder shook the earth beneath him nearly knocking him from his perch.

All at once, excruciating pain shot through his head. He turned and saw himself standing a short distance away. His slingshot dangled loosely from his hand ... a wicked grin spread across his face. Seemingly in slow motion, he watched himself reload and fire again and again. His feet slipped.

Falling ... he was falling.

Voices ...

Bitter laughter ...

Fading light ...

The pounding grew louder.

He gasped for air.

Sitting upright, he threw off the covers which ensnared his feet and realized it was only a dream ... one he'd had before. One he feared he'd have again.

The knocking continued and he realized his mother was outside his door, calling his name.

"Come in," Colt said in a shaky voice.

His mom peeked around the door. "I heard you screaming. Is it your stomach again?" she asked. Placing her hand on his forehead, she gazed down upon him.

"Yes, Ma'am," averting his eyes. "Do I have to eat supper?"

Supper had been Colt's favorite meal behind breakfast and lunch, now all he wanted was dry crackers. He'd even lost interest in his *Gameboy*, and watching television was totally out of the question.

Karen's face shadowed with concern. "Colt Honey, I fixed your favorite ... chicken strips."

He groaned, flopped back down and tugged the covers

under his chin. "Can I eat them in bed?" he asked, his eyes closed.

***

After standing and watching her son drift in and out of sleep, Karen pulled her cell phone from her pocket and called her husband. "Glenn, Colt came home from school early ... again. I know we talked about it, and you weren't so keen on the idea, but I think I need to call the doctor and get an appointment. This is happening too often."

Karen listened and waited as Glenn procrastinated. "Okay, go ahead. I'm in a meeting with a client right now, and can't get free for at least an hour. When I'm finished, I'll call you. Is he awake?"

Karen glanced at him. His eyelids hung in a half-closed position, but she knew he was listening. "Yes, I'll give him the phone."

She pulled the sheet back and handed the phone to Colt.

"Hey, Dad."

"Hey buddy, I hear you're not feeling so hot. Did you kiss Melissa and get the cooties?"

A dry chuckle percolated in Colt's chest. "No Dad, I don't even like her."

"That's not what I've heard."

Colt rolled his eyes. "Mom's going to take me to the doctor. Will you be there?"

"No, not right away, but don't worry. I'll come as soon as I can. When they get done checking you, how 'bout we go out for a movie or ice cream."

A weak smile parted Colt's pale lips. "That sounds great, see ya." Handing the phone to his mom, he rolled over.

After making a call to the doctor, Karen bundled Colt up and guided him to the car.

Chapter One

Sitting on a padded chair in the examination room, Karen let her mind wander. The poignant smell of alcohol and antiseptic triggered painful childhood memories. She'd been a healthy child growing up, but after stepping on a rusty nail while running barefoot through the lawn when she was ten, she'd not liked going to the doctor. The experience in the doctor's office wasn't pleasant and left her fearful of doctors ever since. *Couldn't they make getting a tetanus shot less painful?* She hoped this visit wouldn't be as traumatic for her son as it had been for her.

She blinked away the memory and watched the doctor run through his routine; listening to Colt's breathing, inspecting his eyes, ears, nose, and throat. Finally, he stepped back.

"I think it's just a bug," Dr. Newbury said, pulling off his latex gloves, and patting Karen's shoulder.

She sighed wearily. "But this has been going on for months. It's beginning to affect his school attendance and grades."

Dr. Newbury peered over his wire-rimmed glasses. "The boy is tough. He'll probably sweat it out simply by running around."

"But that's just it, he doesn't run around, not like he used to."

The doctor checked the chart. His eyebrows notched up an inch. "I do see he's been in several times since the year began. Maybe we should keep him overnight and run some tests."

Eyes widening, Colt rucked deeper into the paper covered examination table.

Karen leaned over, brushed back his flaxen hair and kissed his warm forehead. "It will be all right, Honey. They just want to figure out what's going on. You want to feel better. Don't you?"

He nodded and took a tentative breath. "Yes, but I don't want you to leave me." A single tear inched down his cheek.

"I won't leave you, hon. I'm sure the hospital will let me stay with you." She glanced at Dr. Newbury who nodded his approval.

"We'll need to take some blood and run some tests."

Colt's jaw dropped. "Tests? I've missed so much school. I'm not ready for any tests."

The two adults exchanged smiles. After taking her son's hand, Karen gave it a gentle squeeze. "It's not those kinds of tests. I want you to relax and when we get you out, we'll take you to the ice cream shop and get you the biggest ice cream sundae money can buy."

Colt licked his lips. "All right," he said, pumping the air.

***

The following day, Glenn and Karen sat in Colt's hospital room listening to the doctor drone on about viruses, influenzas, and allergies when Balthazar, Melchior and Gasper strolled in. After exchanging greetings, the doctor led Colt's parents from the room and continued his analysis in the hall.

"We haven't been able to put our finger on the source of Colt's fever or elevated blood count. We have ruled out the major concerns, leukemia, lymphoma, even Lyme disease. What we're left with is mono or an allergic reaction to something in your house. My advice is to keep track of what he eats, wears, touches and where he goes."

The lines on Glenn's face deepened with concern and Karen fought back a sniffle. "But what about his fever?"

The doctor shifted his weight from one foot to the other.

"It's a low-grade fever. I'd say give him a low-dose aspirin daily, keep him hydrated and let's check him in a week or so."

His tone seemed too clinical for Glenn's liking, but he held his tongue. After shaking hands and thanking him, Glenn and Karen returned to Colt's room where he found him chatting with the wise men.

***

Colt's fingers played nervously with the sheet as he answered the wise men's question. "I noticed a shiny round thing fall from the witch as she flailed around. Someone stepped on it and I thought it wasn't important. But then, I saw the witch clutching at her neck and knew she missed it. Our eyes met and we both saw it under the scuffling feet. That's when I knew I had to act."

"You mean that's when you fired off your first stone and nailed her between the eyes." Gasper stated, a growing smile stretched across his face.

Colt shifted uncomfortably at the thought. "Yeah."

"Is that when you grabbed the disc?" Melchior inquired.

"No, Sir. The witch was still a threat and I knew she'd kill Gasper if I didn't do something fast. That's when I took my second shot. It was only after the witch was dead and gone, that I climbed down and picked up the medallion."

"But how? We would have seen you." Balthazar could hardly believe his ears. He'd been stepping all around the disc. Pools of blood and bodies littered the stone floor and yet, to hear Colt, a young adolescent, speak about treading through the carnage like it was a stroll through the park made him rethink the boy's capacity to flinch.

"You and Melchior were so relieved that Gasper was safe, you didn't even notice me. That's when I took the medallion and put the golden chain around my neck. Just as soon as I did, I felt a tingle of electricity run through my body. I felt like Superman." He said with enthusiasm. Then, like a balloon with a slow leak, his shoulders sagged.

"How do you feel now?" his mother asked, pushing past the three wise man and taking his hand.

"I feel like a thief … like I should have thrown the medallion down that black hole when I had the chance."

"So you think your health issues might be related to the medallion?" Balthazar voiced everyone's thoughts.

"Beats me," Gasper concluded. "I was under the impression it was lost when the cave collapsed."

Colt glanced between his parents and the wise men. Tears rimmed his eyes and he began to sob. "I'm sorry. Am I in trouble?"

Karen stroked his head. "Oh, Honey, don't cry. You're not in any trouble." Looking at Balthazar, she asked, "Is he?" Her voice ticked up a notch.

Balthazar exchanged worried glances with his friends, then returned his gaze to Karen. "We are not here to judge or condemn the young man," his sagged tone sounded conciliatory. "He's human like the rest of us. I would, however, caution him against keeping secrets; especially from his parents. But as to the disc, or medallion or whatever you call it, I'd dare say, it is at the root of his illness. You say he's been getting sick ever since Christmas?"

Karen nodded.

"Hmm, nearly six months ago."

Karen shuttered at the thought. "Yes. At first, we thought it was a stomach thing, but then it got worse. His grades started to fall and—"

"And what?" Balthazar asked.

Karen's shoulder slumped. "He got into a couple of scrapes with some of his classmates."

"A couple of scrapes?!" Glenn sprang to his feet. "And I'm just now hearing about it? Sounds like Colt isn't the only one keeping secrets."

"Glenn, keep your voice down," Karen said through clenched teeth.

"This is crazy. First Colt steals some worthless two-thousand year old relic, claims he has a belly ache, gets into a school-yard fight all the while you keep me in the dark."

Karen spun on her heels. "It's not like you've been around, lately. You've been spending so much time working. I've hardly had time to tell you anything."

As Glenn stomped from the room, Karen slumped on the bed. "I'm sorry you men had to see that. It's just that—" her statement melded into sobs.

The room settled into an uncomfortable silence interrupted only by Karen's sniffles and the occasional beep of a monitor attached to Colt's finger.

Ten minutes later, Glenn returned. It was obvious he too had been crying as evidenced by his swollen eyes. "Sorry fellas. It's been a rough couple of months. But I simply can't believe a worthless two-thousand year old relic could make someone sick."

"Hey, I take exception to that," Gasper protested. "I happen to think we, two-thousand year old relics, are quite valuable."

Hand on Gasper's shoulder, Balthazar tugged him back. "Uh, I think he's referring to the disc. That relic is just as potent as it always has been. If it falls into the hands of the wrong person, it could do great damage."

Looking at Colt, he continued. "You haven't tried to read any of the inscriptions ... have you?"

Colt took a big gulp and nodded. "Yes, Sir," his lips paled, "but I couldn't figure it out."

The lines on Balthazar's face deepened. "I suspected as much. You need to get rid of that disc as soon as possible." He turned and faced Karen. In a low tone, he said, "It is for this reason Colt is sick. I fear the longer he possesses it, the sicker he will get. My only hope is that we acted in time. He needs to destroy it if possible. If he can't, then he needs to bury it in the deepest hole he can find." His statement chilled the room.

"Can't you take it?" Colt interjected.

Balthazar shook his head. "No, I'm afraid not. Its existence is linked too closely to ours. It may be that if it is destroyed, we might cease to ..." he let his words trail off.

"But I don't want you to ... you know—"

Melchior, who had taken a stance near the window, pulled his gaze from the darkening sky. "Don't worry, my young friend. Our times are in God's hands. We need not fear the future. Let's get you well and we can talk about tomorrow ... tomorrow." His reassuring smile carried a hint of doubt, but he tried to put on a good front.

Chapter Two

The following day, after he'd been released from the hospital, Colt and his parents returned home. Once supper was over, he went to the garage and found a shovel. With the disc stuffed in his back pocket, he headed to the backyard and began digging through the Georgia clay. At first, rocks and roots prohibited his progress, but once he'd cleared the upper twelve inches of earth, the ground became easier to shovel.

With each scoop of dirt, the hole grew deeper and wider. After digging for thirty minutes he paused and gazed into a three foot hole. By now, sweat dripped down his forehead and into his eyes. He swiped his muddy hand across his face leaving long reddish streaks. Taking one last look at the medallion, he folded an oily rag around it and tossed it in the hole, then began replacing the dirt. Soon all that evidenced his evening's work was a fresh mound of dirt which he quickly covered with sod. Once he'd tamped it down as level as possible, he replaced the shovel and crept into the house. His mother relaxed in the living room, reading and his dad was sequestered in his home office. It was obvious neither missed him. Taking care not to make any noise, he climbed the stairs to his room, showered and went to bed. The nausea that had hounded him had returned and he was glad his night's work was over. Hoping his troubles would end; he pulled the covers over his head.

As sleep closed in around him, so did the images. Images

of ethereal beings fluttering like moths around a streetlight. Once again, he dreamed he fell into a big black hole and was buried with a thousand golden medallions. He woke, gasping for air.

Frustrated, he tried again. As his mind drifted, he saw himself thirty thousand feet above the earth. Everything looked so small, so beautiful, then the circular earth turned dark and morphed into the medallion. It spun wildly out of control and he feared it would send him spinning into the universe. Then a large winged creature swooped down and snatched him by the collar and carried him to a mountain where a majestic temple stood. The creature set him down and he gazed around trying to determine if it were real or imagined. Then, the doors of the temple opened and Mrs. White, the White Witch emerged followed by a host of foul looking bat-like creatures. Extending her hands, she began saying something, but he couldn't make it out.

Suddenly, the medallion appeared in his hand and she lunged for it. Fearing for his life, Colt tried to run, but his legs and feet refused to move. It was like they were mired in the Georgia clay. His dreams were interrupted by someone shaking him by the shoulders.

"Colt, Colt, wake up!"

His mother shook him. Worry lines tugged at the corners of her mouth. "Colt, you had a nightmare. I heard you calling out."

Colt wiped the sleep from his eyes. "It was terrible." After trying to recollect the images, he flopped back on his pillow. "I did what Balthazar said. I buried the medallion. Maybe that was why I had those nightmares. I heard it calling out to me."

Karen took a shaky breath. "I don't think an old relic from the past has the ability to do that. You're giving it authority in your life which belongs to God. That's called a stronghold and if Satan can get a stronghold in your life, he will try to establish more until he has total control of you."

"But Balthazar said Satan can't possess a Christian."

"Yes, that is right. But he can insert wrong thoughts into your mind and cause you to stumble."

Colt felt his forehead wrinkle into a question. "I don't understand anything about spiritual warfare. I only want the medallion out of my life and to get better."

His mom patted his arm. "Well, I hope you buried it deep enough that your dog won't dig it up."

Arms folded over his chest, Colt snuggled deeper into his bed. "Harley wouldn't do that, he knows better than to dig in the yard," he said with a yawn.

Karen stood and stepped to the door. "You want a night light on?" She waited, but by then, Colt was asleep.

***

The following morning, Karen stood in the kitchen preparing breakfast. Suddenly, her thoughts were shattered as a shriek cut through the air. At hearing her son's scream, she dropped a cereal bowl which struck the floor and shattered. Not caring about the broken dish, she dashed from the kitchen, her bare feet missing the threatening shards.

Glenn, who had been standing in the door, jumped out of the way as his wife plowed past him. Stride for stride, he followed her up the winding staircase to the second floor.

Panting, she burst into Colt's bedroom with Glenn seconds behind her. She stopped abruptly and sucked in a sharp breath. Colt stood holding the medallion in his trembling hand. A ray of sunlight danced off its rim, temporally blinding her.

"Colt, what's the meaning of this?" she demanded.

Colt gulped, too frightened to speak.

Glenn snatched up the medallion from his hand and eyed it with caution. "Colt, why did you scream?" His tone was etched with frustration.

Karen laid her hand on her husband's arm in an attempt to calm him down. "Glenn, I know you don't like holes in your yard, but Colt buried the medallion in the backyard last night.

As you can see, there it is.

Colt buried his face in his hands and began to cry. "I hope Harley didn't dig it up," his muffled words ached with pain. All at once, he glanced up. "How did it get in my bedroom and on top of my Bible? Do you think it's a sign?"

***

Glenn stepped to the window and peered through the double-paned glass. Near the fence in the back yard, lay Harley. A deep hole surrounded by a large mound of dirt marked the place where Colt placed the medallion. The dog appeared to be sleeping, but Glenn had a sick feeling he wasn't. He returned his gaze to the golden disc and began to inspect it more closely. "Mon-e-may—"

"Dad, stop—you'll start having nightmares too." Colt's sharp command took Glenn back and he stared at his son.

"Colt, what's gotten into you? That was very disrespectful." Karen said, snatching it from her husband's fingers. "Now, apologize!"

Stepping closer, Glenn placed his arms around the boy's neck and spoke in an even tone. "I don't think he meant any disrespect."

"Maybe not, it's just that ..."

"—that what?" Glenn interrupted, "that he's been hanging around Gasper too much?"

His angry words flew at her in rapid fire succession. His hand to his mouth, he slumped down. "I'm sorry, I didn't mean what I said."

Not giving his weak apology a chance to take root, Karen narrowed her eyes. "No, it's not because he's been hanging out with Gasper or any of the other wise men. At least he has someone to hang around with. You've been practically living at your office. Even on Sunday, you're gone almost the entire day at the golf course. As far as this medallion is concerned," she tossed it on the bed, "Balthazar was the one who suggested he bury it in the first place, and that's what Colt did. Now that it mysteriously reappeared, I don't know what to think. One thing is for sure, you shouldn't read its inscriptions."

Glenn picked it up and bounced it in his hand. His wife's accusations stung. She was right. Not wanting to make matters worse by defending himself, he shifted the focus. "Okay, right after breakfast, we'll box the disc up and send it across the country to an empty warehouse I own on the west coast. In the meantime," he said, pulling his cell from its clip, "let's get the mess in the kitchen cleaned up," he said as he scrolled through emails, checking for anything new.

Karen rolled her eyes and followed him down the stairs. Within minutes, she'd gotten the floor cleaned, breakfast served and coffee poured while Glenn sat, responding to several text messages he'd received while in Colt's bedroom.

His cursory breakfast prayer was brief, and they ate in silence. Once they finished breakfast, Karen stood, "Colt I want you to help me with the dishes before you and your father get involved in something else."

Colt nodded. Glenn remained focused on his phone.

She released a weary huff and turned to the sink.

A moment later, Glenn pushed back his chair and stood. "Oops, I gotta go. I forgot I have a ten o'clock appointment. If I don't leave now, I'll be late." Gathering his sports coat and briefcase, he gulped the rest of his coffee, pecked Karen on the cheek, and stepped back. "I'll probably be late for dinner, so don't hold up on my account," he said heading for the garage.

Karen gave him a weak wave. By then, he'd disappeared.

"But what about the medallion, I thought we were going to wrap it up and mail it to California." Colt's statement caught his mother off guard.

"Yes, you and your father were. I guess he has a lot on his mind. But since he left, why don't we just pick an address in some obscure town in Alaska and send it there with no return address."

A mischievous smile brightened Colt's face. "Let's do it."

Chapter Three

Standing between the celestial realm and the physical, Prince Argos eyed the vista before him. Despite his spiritual nature, the strain of keeping constant vigil over his domain tugged at the corners of his mouth. The lines around his intense, gray eyes had deepened over the centuries. He longed for the final conflict in which all evil would be banished and the kingdoms of the earth would become the kingdom of his God and of his Christ, there to reign for ever and ever. Until then, however, he held his post ... unwavering.

In the months since the incident involving the White Witch, things had been relatively quiet. But he knew as long as Satan and his emissaries were on the loose, and the witch's medallion existed, the people of North Hamilton, Georgia were not safe.

"News, my lord." Prince Leo stated with a crisp salute as he lighted on a cloud next to his commander.

Prince Argos shifted his stance slightly, his attention riveted on the distant horizon. He spoke in an even tone. "I have been keeping a steady eye on our four charges; Balthazar, Melchior, Gasper, and of course, Master Colt."

"And?"

"There have been the usual attacks by the world, the flesh and the evil one, but none that a little persuasion from my sword and the Word of God, couldn't handle."

Prince Leo shifted his stance. "You don't sound very convincing. Is there something else?"

Fingers stroking his chin, Argos gazed at his companion

with interest. "You're in rare form today. It seems nothing escapes your attention."

Prince Leo peered upward. "I only seek to understand."

Prince Argos crossed his arms over his massive chest and released a sigh. "Yes, of course. It's Master Colt."

"Master Colt?" Prince Leo repeated. "Is he well?"

Shaking his head, the mighty prince let his hair catch the updraft, making him look like the king of beasts. "I'm afraid not, and I am blind as to its cause." He returned his attention to the now setting sun.

Leo remained silent until the last tentacles of orange faded. In the gathering twilight, he asked, "And of the medallion? Any sightings?"

"My searching has been extensive, but fruitless, as has the former sheriff's."

"Maybe it is lost to the world. That would not be a tragedy, now would it?"

In the fading light, Prince Argos' eyes burned with radiant luminescence. "I fear it has not been lost. Although it was just a medallion with an ancient inscription, its presence still poses a threat. Like the false gods before it, like other icons, amulets, and talisman, they possess demonic powers surrendered to them by the faith of their human owners."

Leo's face blanched. "But how, my lord?"

"Faith in a false god is just as powerful as faith in the true God. That doesn't mean the Almighty can't overcome it. We have seen him do it on many occasions. The showdown on Mount Nebo between Elijah and the four hundred false prophets of Baal is one example. Their faith, though sincere, was founded on a false premise, but that did not stop them from believing and even cutting themselves until they bled. The problem with false faith is that it creates a world view. A world view is the foundation for thoughts, and thoughts ... actions.

If someone finds the medallion and deciphers the

inscriptions from the Book of Incantations they could unwittingly unleash a power greater than the one possessed by Mrs. White. In the murky spirit realm, there was always a demon vying for a higher station. That is the way of evil. Just like their father, the devil, who aspired to ascend to the very throne of the Almighty, so too, his minions are never satisfied with their position. They lusted for more ... more power, more authority, even to the point of open rebellion." Prince Argos stated ruefully. "I don't envy the dark Lord."

"What is that?" Prince Leo, his second in command asked, his forehead wrinkling, clearly interested.

Argos released a soft chuckle. "I'm afraid you caught me in one of my more reticent moments. I was just thinking how different our realms are."

"Oh? How so?"

Prince Argos laced his fingers behind his back and began to pace as if he were a scholar instructing his favorite student. His lifelong ally fell in step with him.

"Well, think of it. The realm of light is ruled and ordered by our willful subjection to the Almighty, all-loving God of eternity. It is with joy we serve his Majesty and in so doing, we serve each other as co-laborers. Yes, there are echelons of power; the greater are served by the lesser, but it is willingly, not by cohesion.

Compare that to the realm of the darkness. They lust and have not, they kill and deSire to have, and cannot obtain. They fight and war, yet they do not get what they fight for. They devour, but they are never satisfied and worst of all, they are in constant rebellion even against their master. He, like us, is a created being. His domain is limited to the earth and will soon come to an end. Whereas, our Lord's kingdom will never end. The only thing that unifies them is their hatred for our Lord, who is the blessed and only potentate, the King of Kings and Lord of Lords; Who only has immortality dwelling in the light which no man can approach, which no man has seen, nor can see: to Him be honor and power everlasting forever and ever, amen." For a golden moment, the two angelic beings stood in silent wonder as they mulled over his stark revelation.

Prince Leo squared his shoulders. "And what of the physical realm? Do they not share some of the traits of their father the devil?"

Prince Argos nodded slowly. "I'm afraid so. The only difference between them and the fallen ones is they still have a choice. It is our task to protect the children of light so they can tell the good news of redemption to those of Adam's fallen race. But I'm sure you didn't come to discuss the Master's plan for the ages."

Leo's features relaxed onto a smile. "No, I have news, my lord."

Prince Argos stopped to face his second in command. "Has there been any movement from the underworld?"

"There hasn't, but the former sheriff seems to have taken an inordinate interest in our charges, the wise men, and young Colt. I have had to intervene on several occasions to keep Mr. Baker from harming the wise men. As to the young man, Colt's father is of little help. He is preoccupied with the physical rather than the spiritual. Mr. O'Dell's attendance at church has waned as well as his prayer life, leaving his family vulnerable to the evil one's attack."

Prince Argos stroked his chin. "That is disconcerting. I had hoped after the matter of the White Witch, we had settled the matter of prayerfulness."

Nodding, Prince Leo's grim face reflected his leader's worry.

"Maybe if we remove a level of protection from around Mr. O'Dell ..."

"You know, to do so would put his life in grave danger," Prince Leo said.

"His times are in the Almighty's hands, no instrument of war fashioned against him will prosper unless He permits it."

Prince Leo straightened and gave his commander a crisp salute. Argo smiled, “My friend, why so formal.”

Leo relaxed his stance. “Because, as you said, we serve each other willingly and with deep respect, so it is I salute you.”

Prince Argos sharpened his stance and returned Leo’s salute. “Go in the strength of the Lord of Hosts, my friend.”

Chapter Four

After staying in the attic for over a year, it was a big relief for the wise men to finally rent their own place. The three bedroom house on the south end of town provided them with enough space to move about without getting on each other's nerves; not that it mattered to Gasper. He had a way of annoying his two compatriots with his constant complaints. First, it was the oppressive Georgia heat, then it was the unpredictable weather, but his favorite was the slow moving automobile in front of him whenever he took to the road. With each complaint, he got the same response. "Accept the things you cannot change and change the rest." Balthazar and Melchior would often say.

Ever since his first driving experience when he climbed behind the wheel of the church's Volkswagen bug, Gasper had become an avid motorist. With Jacob Myer's assistance and Ty Huntley's instruction, he passed the test and received his license to drive. That was the good part. The bad part was his tendency to ignore the speed limit; a condition which caused him to encounter Deputy Huntley on less than friendly terms, and on more than one occasion.

Sitting on the back porch, Balthazar enjoyed watching the winter weather surrender to the fairer days of spring and spring to summer. His only regret was hearing Gasper's constant complaints. *My allergies are acting up, it rains too much, I'm bored.* He chuckled. It reminded him of someone very dear to him, but his oath to never speak his name raked across the memory, burying it beneath layers of guilt and pain.

All at once, Balthazar's phone rang. The sudden jangling brought him fully alert from his afternoon nap. Tentatively, he lifted the phone and pushed the green button. "Hello?"

"Hello," a rather chipper voice said. "Is this Mr. Balthazar?"

"It is, how may I help you?" he inquired, scanning the quizzeled faces of his friends.

"My name is Sharon Welsh. I am the administrative assistant to the principal at North Hamilton High School. How are you today?"

"I'm fine for an old man. These hot summer days are a real drain on me. It seems I can't drink enough water, but I'm sure you didn't call just to see how a two -thous—I mean, how I'm doing."

Miss Welsh let out a light chuckle. "Well, no. Actually, I called to see if you and your colleagues would mind if I set an appointment for you to meet with Mr. Davis, the high school principal."

"You must be kidding. We're a bit too old to return to school."

Not missing a beat, Miss Welsh continued. "No, Mr. Balthazar, you don't understand. I'm not calling about attending school. Mr. Davis would like to speak with you about being adjunct teachers. We understand you have traveled quite a bit and we thought your experiences would be of interest to our student body."

"Hmm, I'll have to consult with my colleagues, but the idea of us sharing our wisdom is very interesting. When would you like to meet with us?"

Miss Welsh covered the phone while she conferred with someone, a moment later, she returned. "Could you come down today around four o'clock?"

Taken aback by her haste, Balthazar eyed the faces of his wondering friends. "We could, but why the hurry?"

After an extended pause, Miss Welsh spoke in a conspiratorial tone. "Well, it seems we have had a few openings develop in recent days. Actually, it started after the Christmas break. Some of our teachers simply didn't show up for class. No warning, no notice, they just vanished. We struggled to cover the classes all spring and now with summer nearing a close, well, we thought—" she let the sentence dangle.

Balthazar nodded into the phone. It came as no surprise that the school had missing teachers. The coven proved to be larger than anyone suspected and touched every level of society within North Hamilton Township. "Well, now that you put it that way, I think I can speak on behalf of my colleagues and say we would be happy to meet with your principal. We'll see you in a few hours."

For the next thirty minutes, the wise men discussed the possible ramifications of getting involved with the community. They still had the medallion to deal with, and then there was Randy Baker, the former sheriff. He'd sworn to get even with Colt and Balthazar could only assume he meant it literally.

***

Shortly after four o'clock, the three wise men found themselves gainfully employed as adjunct teachers. The principal, having set aside the obvious qualifications such as teacher certifications, agreed to hire them on a temporary basis giving them the latitude to use their years of experience. Balthazar, with his knowledge of ancient history, was given the History teacher position. Melchior found an opening in the Science department, and Gasper, with his skills in math and astrology, was assigned high school math classes.

Three weeks later, August rolled around marking Georgia's first day of school. Having been warned by Colt about Hamilton High School's reputation of chewing up and spitting out new teachers, it was not without a bit of trepidation that Balthazar and his friends entered their classrooms for the first time.

"Well, Melchior, it's just like old times," Balthazar said as he led his friends to the school entrance.

Melchior nodded. "Yeah, very old times."

"Hey, they're young people. How much could they have changed? Most of them have come to learn."

"And the rest?" Gasper inquired. He, unlike his compatriots, was still considered the junior member of the threesome and had never instructed anyone.

Balthazar scanned the columns of teens as they disembarked scores of yellow painted buses. "I'm sure there are those who will test you. It is at those times you become the learner."

"A learner?"

"Yes. You are learning patience, gentleness, meekness and how to speak a wise word under pressure."

Gasper was silent for a moment. "Sounds like the perfect place to grow in grace and knowledge."

"You know? I think you have just passed your first test." Balthazar said patting the younger man's shoulder.

After forming a tight circle the three bowed their heads for a brief prayer before parting in different directions.

Chapter Five

In the months following North Hamilton Bible Church's victorious prayer meeting and subsequent revival, many new converts and people came into its membership. Multiple services sprang up allowing the church to offer several worship times, one on Saturday evening, and two on Sunday.

As new attendees flocked in, so did Dr. Cecil Clavender and his second wife. Having recently relocated from Detroit, he came with high qualifications. His doctorate in theology made him stand out above many of the seekers who arrived Sunday after Sunday.

Knowing Clavender's history, however, Prince Selaphiel became deeply concerned when he saw Cecil and his wife step forward and present themselves for membership. During the usual three month intern period, in which all new members were required to attend an orientation class, Selaphiel tried to warn the pastor through godly advice provided by Miss Nash.

Miss Nash, an elderly woman in tune with the Word and the Spirit's promptings, was often kept at home due to her painful, arthritic condition. On good days, however, she would venture out to church. Her presence always caused a stir of enthusiasm among the Senior Saints and the younger children. Her overstuffed purse smelled of sugar-laden sweets which she readily distributed to all comers. It was during one such encounter, that Pastor Scott stuck his hand out in a boyish manner to receive a cellophane wrapped cinnamon candy.

Instead, she clasped his hand in an iron-firm grip.

"Preacher," her shaky voice carried little of the authoritative tone of yesteryear. "I'm a bit concerned about some things in the church." Her matter-of-fact approach caused Pastor Scott to bristle.

"Oh, and what might that be Miss Nash ... our direction?" His defensive tone didn't escape the elderly woman's keen spirit.

"I wouldn't say it's as much direction as it is who is on board with you."

In the excitement and revival atmosphere, he had readily accepted the Clavender's into their membership without completing the orientation class. Had he done a background check, he would have discovered Mr. Clavender's checkered past. His membership in four churches over a span of three years should have given them pause for concern. Instead, he was welcomed into the church family and, because of his academic prowess, installed as the Adult Sunday School Curriculum committee, a position left vacant with the passing of Todd Huntley.

Miss Nash's cryptic response left the pastor wondering where the conversation was going. "And who have we taken on board but a host of new converts. Isn't that what we are supposed to be doing?"

She continued to grip his hand, though he tried to free himself. "Yes, that is true, but I sense along with new believers you have inadvertently allowed a wolf in sheep's clothing to slip into our midst."

Taken aback, Pastor Scott eyed her wearily. "A wolf, you say," his tone carried a stream of doubt. "Can you point out this wolf? I certainly wouldn't want him snatching up one of these little ones." He grabbed a toddler who happened to walk by and tickled her.

The child's laughter broke the tense moment and Miss Nash released his hand. She narrowed her eyes and let out a tired sigh. "No Pastor, we wouldn't want that. We can't start pulling up the tares without uprooting the wheat too, but be warned. Not all who say Lord, Lord are really under his Lordship. Many in that day will say—"

The pastor waved her off. "Look, Miss Nash, I appreciate your concern. It's duly noted. Please excuse me, I've got a sermon to preach," he said, backing away without a hard candy.

***

With most of the elderly prayer warriors gone due to attrition, the responsibility of carrying the prayer torch was left with the next generation. However, most of them found their prayer life, like the seed which fell among the thorns, choked out by the cares of the world.

An exception to the status quo was Ty Huntley and Samantha Myers. Though not yet married, they often spent their date nights, like Ty's father, in the gazebo praying. Having taken special interest in their growing relationship, Prince Argos summoned one of his chiefest commanders. "Prince Selaphiel, I want you to place an extra hedge of protection around Ty and Miss Myers. Do not let the enemy anywhere near them. I feel they will play an important role in the lives of the wise men. Also, the Almighty has not yet revealed to me His plans, but it is my contention that this church and its pastor have another trial to face. They will need someone besides the wise men to stand in the gap."

Prince Selaphiel nodded thoughtfully. "Is there no other way for these people to avoid testing?"

After a pause, Prince Argos scanned the ethereal horizon. "I'm afraid not. It is only through testing, these believers learn to depend on their Savior, develop spiritual maturity, and have the dross removed. It has always been that way. Remember the trials the great saints of old suffered; Stephen, Peter, Paul, Andrew. These men were pillars and pioneers of the church age and yet they, too, needed the dross of fear, partiality, and the old nature burned away. It is all a part of the Master's grand scheme to make His children like His Son."

"And what of Ty and Samantha? Is there not a testing for them?"

Prince Argos adjusted his sword on his hip. "Yes, although Ty has been severely tested, he still has not reached his full potential. As for Miss Myers, she is a new believer. She has a long way to go before Christ is formed in her. It is for her good and God's glory that we allow such suffering to take place, but not to worry. Even God's Son learned patience by the things which He suffered. That's not to say He had any dross or sin in His life, but still, His humanity was sorely tested. The glory of it is this; He is a priest after the order of Melchizedek who can be touched with the feelings of their infirmities for He was tested in all things like unto them, yet without falling."

Prince Selaphiel bent a knee, lowered his chin and for a few soft moments, he knelt in silent wonder. After a while, he stood and swiped his hand across his face.

"My friend, is that a tear, I see?" Princes Argos asked, a wry smile wrinkling the lines around his eyes.

"What, you've never seen an angel cry?"

Argos let out a soft chuckle. "No, I have seen many angels weep, but none so tenderly as you."

Chapter Six

Being Jews, the wise men understood what the Law and Moses commanded concerning worship. But the concept of the church was totally foreign to them. *How could Jews and Gentiles worship together?* He mused. For centuries, the Jews were occupied with the sacrificial system. The church, however, proclaimed Jesus is Lord and worshipped the Father through Him. They went directly to the Father in prayer invoking the name of Yeshua as their mediator. While attending North Hampton Bible Church, the wise men spent hours studying the O'Dell's family Bible and quizzing the pastor about the doctrine of grace, the mystery of the church.

After doing an exhaustive study, they were convinced they were living in the age of grace and readily proclaimed Jesus is Lord both of the Jews and the Gentiles. After the wise men submitted to immersion, the church welcomed them with a fellowship meal after the evening service.

Standing in the welcoming line, Melchior, Balthazar, and Gasper shook hands with the church members as they passed by. "Good evening, Mrs. O'Dell," Melchior said. "Where is Glenn this evening?"

Karen tried to step away quickly without answering, but Melchior's hand held firm.

"Oh, I'm afraid he wasn't up to coming this evening. He'd had a lot on his mind recently. I'm sure he'll be back in the saddle next Sunday." Her eyes searched the floor.

Melchior nodded. “I see. Maybe I should stop by and encourage him in the Lord.”

Karen glanced at Colt, then at him. “That’s a good idea. Maybe you should. It might be better coming from a man rather than—” All at once, she clapped her hand over her mouth. “I think I’ve said too much, please excuse me.” Then she turned abruptly and disappeared in the crowd.

Giving Colt a quick wink, Melchior smiled at the boy’s overflowing bowl of banana pudding.

Colt gave him an apologetic shrug and headed back to the desert bar.

***

As Balthazar milled about, he stepped into a tight circle of men carrying on an animated discussion. Looking into their somber faces, he realized too late that he had walked into a serious conversation.

“I tell ya, I’ve heard some of his lines from another sermon. I think he’s getting his sermon material from other preachers. You would think, with all the time he has from Sunday to Sunday, he could come up with something original.” The conversation was led by Cecil Clavender one of the newer members. His position as Adult Sunday School Curriculum Director emboldened him to question the pastor’s veracity. “I’d say, you’d better watch this guy. He’s probably plagiarizing other preachers, trying to make himself look like a big shot. He’s probably using this church as a stepping stone to bigger and better things.” Cecil continued his assault, ignoring Balthazar’s obvious displeasure.

Heads nodded and it seemed to Balthazar, Cecil’s accusations were gaining a foothold. Although he knew little of the Internet, he knew enough about the nature of the tongue to know once one got loose, it was hard to stop. He cleared his throat and stepped deeper into the circle and gazed directly into Cecil’s eyes. “Sir, from what I’ve read in Ecclesiastes, the Preacher said, *there is nothing new under the sun.* And with so much being posted on Blogs, Facebook, and websites, it would be nearly impossible to not quote someone. I would say it is to Pastor Scott's credit that he has sought out men more astute than he and repeated them. Didn't even our Lord quote the Torah by saying, 'It hath been said'?"

Balthazar let his question linger for a moment before proceeding. "Quoting other men's words is the highest form of praise. That he doesn't give credit, if credit is needed, is a mere technicality. Why don't you bring this to the pastor's attention? Possibly it was an oversight." His eyes remained fixed on Cecil ... waiting.

The man licked his lips and took a step back. It was clear to Balthazar, he hadn't expected anyone to call his hand.

"Tell you what, Mr. Clavender, how about I give you a week to speak with the pastor directly. Then I'll check with him to see if you have. If you haven't, then it is my responsibility as a loyal member of this fellowship to bring your gossip to his attention along with the names of your friends." As he spoke, the small gathering began to scatter like sheep without a shepherd. Balthazar smiled to himself. *It was as I thought.*

***

Sitting atop the church steeple, Prince Argos peered into the Hamilton Bible Church's Family Life Center. From his vantage point, he had a perfect view of the exchange between Cecil Clavender and Balthazar. He smiled at the elderly man's boldness. Over the centuries, he'd learned one thing, all it took for evil to prevail was for good men to remain silent, yet his timing was all wrong. It was obvious Balthazar recognized the genesis of division ... a wagging tongue, but in this case, his boldness emanated from a heart filled with pride. It was Prince Argos' hope the matter would be settled within the week ... but he knew it wouldn't.

Giving Prince Selaphiel a nod, the mighty angel stepped forward. "Yes, my lord?"

Maintaining visual contact with Cecil, Prince Argos pointed to the elderly man walking away from him. "See that man? He is one of the wisest men on earth, yet he is filled with pride and self-confidence. He confronted a man in the church who the Almighty sent as a means of testing it. If Balthazar succeeds in interrupting the Almighty's plans, the church will miss a wonderful opportunity to grow, and Mr. Balthazar will go on trusting in his own wit and wiles."

His subordinate's face contorted into a confused expression. "I'm not quite following you, my lord. You want me to restrain a good man from standing in the way of evil? But why?"

If it weren't for the seriousness of the situation, Prince Argos would have had a good laugh. "Yes and no. You see, sometimes we must, by the Almighty's sovereign will, stand aside and allow evil to prevail ... for a season, I might add. I have observed over the centuries, our all-wise, all-knowing Creator has often used evil men to teach His children humility. As the ancient scripture says, *'surely the wrath of man shall praise him and the remainder he restrains.'*"

Prince Selaphiel held his position for a moment trying to grasp the complexity of his Creator's inscrutable plan, then shook his head in wonderment. "I'll never understand His ways, they are past finding out. But I'll follow your wishes. I will keep Balthazar preoccupied and allow Mr. Clavender to continue his divisive ways. I fear for the church, however. What if they turn on the pastor? What if they follow Mr. Clavender's pernicious ways? Won't that be a bad testimony in the community?"

"Yes, all the above. But the Good Shepherd will not allow His church to go through the trial long before He intervenes. Then woe be to the ones who touched His anointed."

With a quick nod, Prince Selaphiel extended his wings to their full width, rose silently skyward and disappeared into the velvety night.

***

Having overheard their conversation, Prince Leo slipped up next to his commander and whispered. "And what of Pastor Scott and Angela? Haven't they been through enough?"

"Yes, my friend, they have been through quite a bit, and they are the stronger for it. Since the ordeal with the child, Ashton, Pastor Scott's faith has grown and he has turned his attention fully to his wife. As to his sermons, well, he has been choosing selected passages from some renowned preachers of days gone by. For that, he should be commended, not condemned. I want you to place a hedge of protection around him and Angela. Strengthen them and keep the enemy at bay. They will weather the storm, but the church itself needs refining. Once they have passed the test, they too will be the stronger for of it. You mark my words."

Prince Leo always liked the confidence of his commander. After a quick nod, he ascended skyward followed by a legion of angelic beings.

Chapter Seven

In the months since his arrest for attempted murder, Sheriff Randy Baker's life had taken an unexpected turn. His excuse for drawing his weapon on two unarmed, and otherwise upstanding members of the community, fell on deaf ears in his arraignment. The judge was prepared to throw the book at him when his attorney pointed out the sheriff's stellar, twenty year, record. Blaming his actions on a misunderstanding between the accused and the Myers, he was able to get off with only a slap on the wrist; a suspension without pay, three years' probation, and a $10,000 fine for pain and suffering to be paid to the Myers, followed with community service. He was assigned a probation officer, who happened to be an old friend. Giving him a good ole' boy pat on the back, the probation officer let Baker go on the condition he keep his nose clean and his hands out of mischief. Baker left feeling better than he should have.

His only consolation was the stern warning Colt O'Dell received from the judge for shooting Baker in the back of the head with his sling-shot. The O'Dells were fined a thousand dollars for Colt's violating an obscure ordinance prohibiting the use of a sling-shot inside a building. The way Baker figured it; it would take Colt about as long for him to work off his fine as it would him to fulfill his community service. But he had no plans on doing that. As far as Colt was concerned, he had his own plans for him. *Revenge is best served cold,* he mused.

Finding himself an unemployed policeman, Baker had

few options. His run-in with the law made him something of a pariah in the small township of North Hampton. The first order of business was to find a means of supporting himself. After renting a run-down cabin on the outskirts of the Cohutta Wilderness, he turned his attention to setting up a still. It wasn't much, but the local bar paid well and it gave him a chance to keep his thumb on the pulse of the town. His network of runners, a motley crew of former residents in his jail, turned out to be quite resourceful ... and cheap. As long as he paid them in 'mountain water,' they were more than happy to do his bidding.

With his immediate financial needs settled, he turned his attention to other, more pressing matters. As one of the last living members of the White Coven, he made it his mission to carry on the work started by Mrs. White; to gain full use of the medallion's power.

The first order of business, however, was to locate it. The few survivors of the melee in the cave reported a fierce battle between three sword-wielding men and a boy with a slingshot; he assumed it was Colt O'Dell. But none of his fellow coven members saw Mrs. White wearing the medallion when she fell. He guessed she'd lost it in the battle. After questioning the other members of the coven extensively, he was certain none of them had it. It either perished when the cave collapsed, or one of the wise men had it. But which one? Or did the boy have it?

After tailing the wise men for weeks, he'd come to the realization that they were being shielded. Every time he got close to one of them, it was like a barrier formed between him and his query. He got the same feeling whenever he came close to Deputy Huntley. Once, Mrs. White complained that Huntley and his father posed a greater threat to her work than all the other church-goers in North Hampton combined.

Chapter Eight

"If our brethren could see us now," Gasper exulted; referring to the Magi they left behind over two thousand years ago. It was Friday night and he and his colleagues prepared to attend their first football game. To him and his friends, the idea of young men running, kicking and knocking each other down and not killing each other was a bit bizarre compared to the blood-sports they had seen in their day.

Balthazar handed his ticket to an elderly volunteer sitting inside a small booth. The woman's hair was stained with the school colors, and she wore a jersey proclaiming the year she'd graduated. It surprised him that she still functioned as well as she did. But then he had to question his own functionality. Turning to his friends, he said, "I'm sure the people of our day would not comprehend this game. I certainly don't. However, it does give me some insight as to why my students act the way they do in class."

"And why the young ladies idolized the players," Melchior added. "There are the hero's, they call, 'jocks,' and there are the losers which they call, 'nerds.'"

Gasper took his seat on the bleacher, having returned with a hot dog and soda.

Balthazar watched him gnaw into the steaming frankfurter, then continued. "And then there were the geeks."

Gasper bristled and attempted to say something, but a morsel of food lodged in the back of his throat. Grabbing his cup, he took a big gulp to wash it all down.

"I resemble that comment," he croaked.

"Present company excluded, my boy. I was referring to the

brainy ones with their minds absorbed with technology and gadgets. The verbal abuse leveled at them is enough to cause them to abandon their geeky ways, but no. It drives them into small cliques with their own language."

After regaining his composure, Gasper gazed at his friends. "And then there are the Christians. They are a tightly knit group who face ridicule with courage and poise. Have you noticed the group who meet each morning around the flagpole to sing and pray? I stood and watched one morning. It was a source of encouragement."

A cheer rose among the onlookers interrupting their conversation. Standing, Balthazar and his friends glanced around. He leaned over to the middle-aged lady next to him. "What happened?"

She paused to scan him like he had just arrived from Mars. "We just scored a touchdown in the last seconds of the first half. If you guys are going to come to the game, you need to be quiet and watch rather than dissecting the student population."

Taken aback, Balthazar took a hard swallow. "I'm sorry, we're just not into sports that much."

"Then why did you come?"

Balthazar considered her question. "You're right. We will do our best to show our support in the second half."

Satisfied, the woman retook her seat. "Well, actually, you're not too far off the mark in your assessment. My son is one of those Christians you were talking about. He would really appreciate it if you guys would attend the prayer and praise meeting around the flagpole one morning."

A smile spread across Balthazar's face. "Thank you. That is a wonderful idea."

***

"'Scuse moi. Mind if I squeezed by?" came a voice tinged with a European accent. Its owner, a young woman sporting a broad-brimmed hat, pushed passed them. Eyeing the only open space next to Gasper, she placed her colorfully decorated

Gucci purse between him and herself and took a seat. A moment later, she removed her hat and placed it in her large handbag, then began digging through it. Within seconds, she lifted a compact and applied a fresh layer of red lipstick.

With each additional movement, Gasper grew more agitated. Not wanting to be rude, he pinched his lips together and glanced at Balthazar, who watched their seat-mate with growing interest. "Kinda makes you feel like you're sitting next to a sack full of cats," he whispered.

"I heard that," the rutchie woman said. I'm a teacher and I hear everything ... *everything.*"

Her laugh was contagious. She smiled and revealed a set of perfectly aligned teeth outlined in red. A pair of hazel eyes invited his stare, but he blinked them away.

"Oh? And where do you teach?" thinking her to be a first grade teacher.

"I'm on loan from France. I'm doing an internship with the local high school. I thought I'd come to a football game to see if I could understand the great American pastime. My name is Felicia Beauchamp. What's yours?"

Not revealing his association with the school, Gasper cleared his throat. "My friends call me Gasper. It's kind of a family name." Heat crept up his neck and he hoped she didn't notice. "Do you understand the game?"

The young French teacher gazed wide-eyed at the action on the field and cocked her head. "It is nothing like the football in my country. Could you explain what's going on?"

Gasper glanced at the lady on the other side. "I'm really not from here either. Maybe this lady could explain it better than me."

Leaning back, he let the older woman give a thumbnail sketch of the basics. It was both instructive and gave him a chance to admire the younger woman's features.

A light breeze stirred the flags high on the poles and Felicia shivered. "Is it my imagination or is it getting colder?"

Shifting, she turned her attention to her overstuffed purse and pulled out a thin wrap. Tugging it around her shoulders, she brushed a layer of goose-bumps from her arms.

Her action made Gasper's eyebrows hike up a notch. It had been over two thousand years since he'd been this close to the fairer gender. Her cologne began wafting in his direction, sending his pulse into overdrive. With great effort, he turned his attention to the action on the field. The cheerleaders were just finishing their routine and the two teams retook the field.

"Enjoying the game?" she asked.

"Yes, even though after it was explained to me, I still don't understand the concept."

The woman on the other side leaned over. "If you think football is confusing, just wait for basketball or worse ... baseball. All those hand signs and nodding and spitting. I don't get it. But it's a good diversion, don't you think?"

Diversion, Gasper mused. The way Americans worship their sports heroes, it seemed to him, it was far more than a diversion. The sports world played a major role in the shaping of a nation; that, and the entertainment industry. Yes, in his day, they had their games and their theater. No Roman city was complete without its coliseum, amphitheater, and colonnade or shopping district, but entertainment was reserved for the rich and powerful. The common man worked hard all day and if a minstrel happened to pass through his village, the people would throw a festival. Then they would go back to work. It was a hard life ... not so much now.

Refocusing, Gasper continued, "Yes, I suppose it is, but I can't help but think the young people of today have too many *diversions*. That's my observation."

Suddenly, a whistle blew and the crowd stood to their feet screaming at the umpire. Gasper, not wanting to appear ignorant, joined them. "What happened?" he asked, looking confused.

Once again, the older woman came to their rescue. "One

of our boys got a little too rough with one of his opponents. The man in the striped shirt threw a yellow flag in the air and blew his whistle. I personally think he likes doing that. Anyway, he stopped the game while he conferred with the other men wearing striped shirts. I'm guessing his call was not so popular."

After the referee gave the explanation for the penalty, two young boys moved the chain back ten yards and the game resumed. As the final seconds on the scoreboard ticked down, Gasper stood. "I think that's our signal to leave," he said, giving Felicia a slight bow.

Melchior and Balthazar followed him to the end of the bleacher. All at once, he stopped, causing the others to bump into him. For a long moment, he gazed at the line of cheerleaders.

"Ah, hum." Balthazar's signal broke his stare.

"I was just—"

Melchior cocked an eyebrow. "You were just," his tone turning dubious.

Chapter Nine

Three days after Colt and his mother mailed a brown paper wrapped box containing the golden medallion, the doorbell rang. Karen, thinking it was her neighbor, Cindy Myers, swung the door open. Rather than it being Cindy, she was surprised to find the mailman.

"Can I help you?" It was not unusual for FedEx or UPS to deliver something, but a mailman was totally unexpected.

The mailman smiled and handed her a tattered package. Its brown paper was scarred and its corners rumpled, but the address recognizable. "How did you know where to deliver this?" Karen asked, fingering the box. "It doesn't even have our return address."

The mailman shrugged his shoulders. "The postmaster said he saw you drop it in the out box. Said he figured if it came back, to be sure you got it. But I need you to pay the postage."

An icy finger wormed through Karen's stomach. "Wait here. I need to get my purse."

She left the mailman standing outside while she made a quick phone call. "Glenn, you know that medallion you were supposed to have mailed."

After a long pause, he answered, "Oh yes, I totally forgot about it."

"I know, but don't worry. I took care of it. But here's the thing, I mailed it to some place in Alaska and it came back."

"Well, what did you think? If you mailed it to an empty warehouse, of course it would come back. You put your return address, silly." His demeaning additive "silly," made her cringe. Biting her lower lip, she stayed focused.

"That's just it ... I didn't put our *return address* on the box and I made sure no one saw me put it in the out box, *silly.* So why is the mailman standing on our front porch with a brown paper box in his hand?"

Her statement was met with silence.

"Are you there?" Karen asked after an impatient moment.

"I'm here, but as to why the package came back, I'm clueless."

You're clueless, all right. "Okay, I'll pay the postage, but when you get home, we need to talk about what we're going to do next."

She hung up before he had a chance to give his usual statement about being late for dinner. As the revival fires waned, so did Glenn's commitment. In the months following the New Year, he'd acquired two new properties and spent hours on the phone trying to fill them with renters. His other leases were coming due, and suddenly he found himself overwhelmed with work. The first to suffer was his church attendance. The second was his family. Torn between his satellite offices and his home office, he often missed dinner along with many other important events.

Karen tried to put her best face on the situation; making excuses for her absentee husband at church and explaining to Colt that it was only temporary. In her heart, however, she felt she'd lost her soul mate. *Was he seeing another woman? Was he planning on moving out?* The whispered doubts crept ever closer. If things didn't change soon, she'd be forced to take matters into her own hands. Divorce was out of the question, but maybe they needed a little space apart ... time to reassess ... to think.

***

The Saturday morning sun was greeted by birds and insects singing in a language known only to their creator. Sun rays, like golden ballerinas, skipped across the floor in O'Dell's kitchen. It was the first in a string of Saturdays in which Glenn didn't have to work and he sat, sipping a cup of coffee, reading the morning paper.

Across the table sat Colt and his mother. Their attempts at retrieving Glenn's attention were met with unintelligible grunts. Finally, Karen had had enough. "Glenn," her tone caught his attention, "what do you think we should do with the medallion?"

He shifted his gaze between Karen and Colt. "I don't know. I thought you took care of it."

"I did, remember? But it came back. And now all I want to do is get it out of our house. Ever since it came under our roof, Colt's been sick." Her voice broke and she choked back a sob. "And we've been at each other's throats."

"Okay, okay," Glenn held his hands in surrender. "Colt and I will go to the local pawnshop and see if he's interested in it."

Standing, Karen placed her hands on her hips. Giving him a frustrated huff, she said, "I was thinking more along the lines of smashing it to smithereens."

Colt, who had been watching the exchange, suddenly perked up. "That won't work. I tried that already."

Forehead wrinkling, Glenn peered over the rim of his mug. "You did? When?"

Smiling sheepishly, Colt shifted in his seat. "A few weeks ago. I know how particular you are about your tools, but I was desperate. I took your big hammer and put the medallion on the workbench and smashed it with all my might."

Studying the medallion, in Colt's hand, Glenn picked it up. Its golden surface sent a cool stream of energy up his arm. It beckoned to him. Wrapping his fingers around it, he squeezed it until it left an impression in the palm of his hand. Opening his fingers, he held it up to the light. "It doesn't look any worse for wear. Are you sure you didn't miss?"

Colt gave his dad an incredulous expression. "Dad, I may be a kid, but I know how to use a hammer. I smacked it right in the center."

Still examining it, Glenn turned it over. "What happened when you hit it?"

Colt's eyes went wide as he reflected on the memory. "Like I said, I hit it right on the numbers and sparks flew everywhere. It was like I'd cut an electric wire."

"It's electrical wire, Colt," his father corrected.

"Electrical schmectrical ... it threw sparks like crazy. It almost put a hole in my shirt."

Glenn ruffled his son's hair and pocketed the medallion. "Well, it's a good thing it didn't or you would have had the devil to pay."

At his statement, Colt's face turned pasty white. "Don't say that. Ever since we mailed the medallion, I've had the feeling like I'm being watched. It feels like the devil is watching my every move."

Karen reached out and tugged her son close. "Glenn, why don't you pray for us and ask that whatever is plaguing our home would leave us alone."

Glenn shifted uncomfortably. It had been a while since he'd gotten serious about prayer. He'd let his work schedule crowd out his quiet time. His excuse that, 'if any man does not provide for his family he is as good as an infidel,' carried little weight in the O'Dell household. He cleared his throat and began, "Lord, thank you for healing Colt and keeping him safe. Thank you for our home and your provision, but right now, we need you to help us get rid of this medallion thing. I ask that you would do whatever is necessary to remove the curse that's upon our home. In Jesus' name, amen."

***

Prince Leo guided Glenn's shallow prayer to the throne of grace. As he delivered the request, a soft thunder reverberated across the heavens.

Chapter Ten

Rather than increase the tension which already existed between him and his wife, Glenn canceled his tee time and changed into a pair of jeans and a tee-shirt. Wearing a pair of sandals, he left the bedroom and headed to the family sedan.

"You coming?" he asked Colt who was preoccupied with their new puppy. After having buried Harley in the same hole where he'd buried the medallion the first time, it had taken them only a few weeks to get another dog.

"Yes, Sir." Colt tossed the tennis ball across the yard and dashed through the gate before the dog realized he was gone. By the time he climbed into the back seat, Glenn had the engine running and sat, drumming his fingers on the steering wheel.

As the drove through town, Colt leaned forward. "Are you and mom getting a divorce?

His question nearly caused Glenn to swerve off the road. Looking in the rear view mirror, he tried to think of why Colt would ask such a question. "No! Why?"

Giving his dad a boyish shrug, Colt stared at his feet. "I don't know. You guys are always fighting. It's my fault, isn't it? If I had not found that medallion, all this wouldn't be happening."

Colt's assessment struck Glenn in the gut. His palms began to sweat and his throat felt like he'd swallowed a bucket of sand. "No, son, that's not true ... well, I mean. Yes, we have had our differences, and yes, ever since you found that medallion you've been sick. But think of this, I've been blessed with more work than I can handle." He hoped his answer didn't sound as shallow to Colt as it did to himself. "Look, once we get rid of that medallion and I get through this work crunch, what do you say about going on a father and son camp out? You know, just you and me?"

Colt's face brightened. "Can we take Bailey?"

Glenn pulled into a parking slot in front of the local pawnshop and shut off the engine. Glancing over his shoulder, his face reflected an inner joy. It was the first time in a while that he felt connected to his son. "Yeah, that's a good idea. We can make it a threesome." As they approached the door, Glenn leaned down. "Let me do all the talking. I know how to handle guys like this. I'm an experienced negotiator."

Colt took a hard swallow and followed his dad into the shabby building. The long-haired twenty-something college dropout held the floor down behind the counter. His bored expression was only partially hidden behind a pair of shaded glasses. Glancing up, he watched his two visitors with suspicion as they entered and began to browse.

"Can I hep ya?" His deep-south pronunciation of *help* amused Glenn. *He certainly wouldn't fit into our church,* Glenn mused as he stepped up to the counter with a swagger. After dropping the medallion on the velvet place mat he said, "I'm interested in getting an appraisal of this piece of jewelry." He waited while the scruffy bearded man peered at it.

"Hey Mike, come out here and get a look at this thing," he called to someone deeper in the building.

Mike, a tall, undernourished man in his mid-forties pushed through a curtain of beads. Giving Glenn a forced nod, he stepped up to the counter and began to inspect the gold disc. "Is this what you're talking about?"

Glenn nodded. "Yes, can you tell us what you think this is worth?"

The man named Mike muttered something under his breath and opened a drawer. It squeaked, but yielded to his tug and he lifted out a magnifying glass. "We'll know in a minute."

With fingers that had their nails gnawed to the quick, he turned it over and inspected the other side. Laying it down, he held the magnifying glass to his face and began studying the inscriptions.

Colt gripped his father's hand so tight, that Glenn had to pry their hands apart. His eyes grew big and he said, "Don't try to read those markings. It will give you bad dreams ... real bad dreams."

Mike straightened and peered at his customers through the looking glass. His eyeball looked like the All Seeing Eye from the *Lord of the Rings.* Colt sucked in a sharp breath and stepped back.

"Anyone ever tell ya not to disturb a genius while he's working?"

Colt took a hard swallow. "No, Sir. It's just that, you don't look much like a genius."

His outburst caused Glenn to bolt upright. "Colt, how dare you speak to an adult like that. Apologize."

Mike waved him off. "That's all right, kid. You and your dad don't look much like antique dealers. I'll give you ten bucks for it."

"Ten bucks," Colt blurted.

Pushing his son back, Glenn cleared his throat. "You'll have to excuse my son's exuberance. He's sorta grown attached to it. I think the gold itself is worth a lot more than that. Is that the best you can do? Just look at the intricate inscriptions on it."

Pawnshop man burped, then excused himself. "Let me make a phone call."

He disappeared behind the curtain and Glenn heard the pawnshop owner's muffled voice as he talked with someone on the phone. A few minutes later, he returned with a fifty dollar bill between his cigarette-stained fingers. “I am authorized to give you this,” laying the crisp bill on the counter.

“Fifty?” It was Glenn’s turn to blurt. “That thing is worth a lot more than that. It has cost me several hundred dollars in doctor bills. It also killed my son’s dog—” Glenn’s mouth snapped shut when he realized how absurd his last statement was. Snatching up the medallion, he dropped it in his pocket. “I think we’ll take our business elsewhere.” Turning on his heels, he said, “Come on, Colt.” Then he stomped from the pawn shop.

Looking over his shoulder, Glenn saw the shop owner lift the cell phone to his ear. Whoever he was talking to must have heard their heated exchange. He wanted to get rid of the medallion, but the problem was, to what extent was he willing to go to do so. Selling it for a measly fifty bucks was not an option.

Chapter Eleven

After a grueling first week, it was a relief for the wise men to have a little quiet day at home. In the old days, it was called Sabbath. Now it was called Saturday after the Roman god, Saturn. Even though they knew Sunday was the Lord's Day, they still felt the pull of tradition and treated the day with respect. As predicted, their students cut them no slack. Nevertheless, to the man, they met the challenges with grace and strength.

Having finished a simple breakfast, Melchior decided to take his morning walk through the nearby park. Halfway around the walking track, he was met by a large, friendly golden retriever. "Hey, buddy," he said, trying to hold back the dog's enthusiastic greeting. He extended the back of his hand allowing the dog to sniff it. Satisfied it was safe; he began to rub behind the dog's ears. Apparently it was his favorite spot. As he did so, he checked for a collar to identify the dog's owner. Nothing. For a stray, the dog appeared to have been cared for. His teeth were in great shape and even his toenails were manicured. His hair shimmered in the morning light and even gave off a soft fragrant aroma. *Whoever owned the animal was quite fond of him. I wonder why he was wandering loose.*

Glancing around, Melchior expected to see the dog's owner trot up and reclaim his or her pet, but the park at that time of the morning was deserted. Melchior eased down on the grassy carpet next to his new friend and began stroking his neck. He let his mind drift across the ages to a time long ago. His quest to find the Christ-child was only supposed to have lasted a year; follow the star, get to the Holy Land, find the child king, give Him their gifts and return home.

His heart ached at the thought of his wife and children growing up without him. Knowing her as he did, he knew Naomi, his wife of thirty-seven years, would hold a constant vigil, watching the horizon for his return. He often wondered what became of her, and his children. If only he had a picture, something to help him recall their faces. But all he had was a faded memory of five young sons. A silver tear formed in the corner of his eye and coursed down his rugged cheek.

All at once, the golden retriever laid his large head on Melchior's shoulder. It was as if the dog could sense his pain. The next thing he knew, he was laying on his back with a large, slick tongue licking his cheek. He jolted upright and leaned on one elbow. *I must have drifted off.* All around him, children played, couples dined on large blankets while elderly men played shuffle-board, and he suddenly felt old, and alone. *Yes, I could use a companion right about now.*

Giving the dog a fresh round of attention, Melchior took a dry swallow. His two closest friends, Balthazar and Gasper seemed to have made the adjustment into the twenty-first century quite well, but not him. He longed to go home, but that wasn't to be.

Standing, he waited for the blood to reach his brain before continuing his walk. By the time he'd finished, he wished he'd remembered to bring along a bottle of water. Fortunately, there was a water fountain nearby and he and his furry companion took a long time soaking up the cool liquid. When he'd finished he said, "Okay, buddy, it's time for us to part company." After giving him a gentle pat on the head, he started off in the direction of his home leaving the dog sitting, looking forlorn.

By the time he'd reached the front door, he again longed

for another long pull of water and thought about the dog he left behind. Trudging up the steps, he opened the front door, when something thundered behind him. It was the golden retriever. Before he could stop him, the dog bounded past him, knocking the door open in the process. Fortunately, Gasper wasn't in the living room or he would have bolted from the house. His experience with dogs had not been pleasant and he avoided them at all costs.

Taking a seat in Melchior's favorite chair, the dog glanced around, clearly at home in his new surroundings. Melchior lowered himself to look the animal in the eyes. "So, it looks like you and I have something in common. We both are quite out of place. You wandered from your owner, and I traveled across two millennium and ended up in the twenty-first century." He sighed heavily. "At least you have a chance to return home, but me?" he shook his head, "Not a chance. I'll never see my homeland again."

***

While Melchior was on his morning walk, Balthazar took a seat on the back porch overlooking a shaded lawn. After the Bible, reading the Encyclopedia Britannica had become a great pastime and sitting in an easy chair made it all the more pleasant. He found it very instructive to learn what had taken place over the centuries. The world had changed quite a bit since the days of Caesar. Rome had fallen, as predicted. In its place, other kingdoms had come and gone. Israel had been dispersed; the Roman Catholic Church marched on the Holy Land in a quest to possess it during the great crusades. Europe grew in size and world prominence. Then the one-hundred year war ripped it apart. Napoleon marched across the land unhindered. Great Britain expanded her reach around the globe. The United States of America was birthed with the vision of freedom and justice for all. It wasn't long before that lofty goal was tested and retested.

As he turned the pages, he learned that Germany became

greedy and began gobbling up country after country and the world was thrown into its first world war. It was the war to end all wars. But the citizens of earth discovered all too soon that evil didn't die so quickly. A few short years later, the world was once again drowning in the blood of another global conflict followed by yet another. Even Babylon, his homeland, had been renamed Iraq and his beloved Baghdad was reduced to nothing more than a pile of rubble. It, too, had been relegated to the trash heap of history until Saddam Hussein stirred up trouble and brought the entire world to his doorstep. He nodded and sighed deeply. How he longed to return and find a resting place among his father's tombs. But he knew that would never happen, not without a miracle.

By the time he'd caught up on his ancient history, Balthazar had drifted into a deep depression. He'd hoped with the coming of the child king, the Prince of Peace, the world would have become better, but instead, it became worse. What he failed to fully understand was the period of time between the Messiah's ascension to his father's right hand and his return. Looking back across the last two-thousand years, he realized the importance of Jesus' parting words when he assigned the task of world evangelism to a group of rag-tag disciples. But he and his friends missed all that. They were clay manikins, observers, but not participants. Now he and his friends were left in a world they didn't understand. Suddenly, he felt old, very old.

***

Having finished his workout at the gym, Gasper returned to the house and slipped passed Balthazar, unnoticed. After taking his shower, he emerged, his hair still wet. Towel drying it, he stepped into the living room and heard someone at the front door. Not wanting to disturb Balthazar, he hurried to answer it. To his surprise, it was his landlady and she came bearing gifts.

"Oh, Mr. Gasper, I'm so glad I caught you. I was so worried I'd missed you and I didn't want these to fall into the hands of the wrong person." The aroma of freshly baked chocolate chip cookies filled the air even before she lifted the cover from the plate. As she spoke, she peered over his shoulder.

With a bow, Gasper lifted the proffered plate and inhaled deeply. *If the way to a man's heart is through his stomach is true ... it's working.* "Well thank you, my good lady. I'm sure my friends and I will thoroughly enjoy them."

As he spoke, Balthazar strolled into the living room carrying a thick book he'd checked out from the school library. "Greetings, Mrs. Littleton." His nose moved in the direction of the plate of cookies. "Are these for us? You shouldn't have."

Joann bit her lip as his fingers inched closer.

Lifting the corner of the cover, Gasper followed his leader's example before placing it on the table. Turning, he noticed his landlady surveying the living room. *What is she looking for? Maybe she is making sure us bachelors are not living like slobs.*

With a shrug, he ushered her toward the door. "Thanks again for the cookies, Mrs. Littleton ... have a nice day." As soon as she was gone, he closed the door and leaned against it.

Eyes wide, Balthazar held his gaze. "What was that all about?"

Gasper swiped his hand across his face. "I don't know, but I think our landlady has taken an unnatural interest in me. Either that, or she came to see how three single men live. What should I do?"

Stifling a chuckle, Balthazar said, "From what I've heard, there are a few more than Mrs. Littleton vying for your attention." He took a large bite of cookie. "If this keeps up, we'll all gain ten pounds. Let's get some milk and talk about it," he said, leading the younger man into the kitchen.

After pouring two glasses of milk, Balthazar took a seat next to Gasper. A wry smile crinkled the lines around his eyes. "Maybe you shouldn't have been so hasty in rushing her out the door. We wouldn't want to offend her. These cookies are absolutely delightful."

For a moment, Gasper held his gaze, speechless.

All at once, the front door burst open followed by the scuffle of feet. Peering around the corner, Gasper saw Melchior kneeling beside a large golden retriever who had taken up residence in Melchior's favorite chair. The memory of seeing himself shimmying up a tree followed by a pack of barking dogs made chicken-flesh crawl up his arms and down his back.

"Wherever did you get that furry beast?" he asked, still keeping his distance.

Melchior straightened. "Don't worry, he's harmless as a kitten. Aren't you ole'' buddy?" he asked. As he spoke, Gasper began sneezing.

"I think I'm having an allergic reaction to him. Maybe another cookie will help." Turning, he retreated to the kitchen where he attacked the platter of cookies.

Chapter Twelve

From the road, the Oasis Bar and Grill carried all the charm of an old barge. Its sky blue shutters clung to the windows as if falling would condemn them to life in the underworld. The faded paintings of palm trees had long ago lost their color and stood like skeletons on either side of the door.

Inside wasn't much better, but its loyal patrons didn't come for the ambiance ... they came to drown their troubles. By mid-afternoon, a decent crowd had formed around chipped tables and the raised bar. A blue air hung over the heads of three men playing poker while an inane tune throbbed in the background. It was here, the former sheriff did his best thinking. Sitting at a cluttered desk in the back room, Randy Baker chewed on a half smoked stogy, and sipped a double-shot of 'mountain water' from a dirty glass. He called it "Quality Control." Others would call it, "getting drunk," but getting drunk was not the reason he was there. He was there to plan his next move.

The phone rang. Hoping it was Clyde telling him his next shipment of *mountain water,* was on its way, he answered it on the second ring. "Yeah?"

It was Mike, the local pawnshop owner.

"What's up?" Baker asked, his tone gruff.

"I've got a guy and his kid in here trying to fence a piece of jewelry. Thought you might be interested."

"I'm not into buying stolen goods, you fool. Why are you

calling me?"

Mike gave him a dry laugh. "I heard on the street you were looking for a certain four-inch disc. Said you'd pay someone nicely for information leading to its recovery."

Baker, who'd been sitting with his feet propped on the desk, dropped them to the floor and sat upright. "You don't say. And how much are they asking for this certain disc?"

"I offered them ten bucks, but they balked."

It was Baker's turn to laugh. "Well, what-did-ya think, you jerk? If that is the real deal, it's worth a lot more than a measly ten bucks."

"Oh, it's real, all right. I inspected. It's got cryptic engravings on one side, and a pentagram on the other side."

At the mention of a pentagram, Baker shifted his stogy from one side of his mouth to the other. "So you say, a pentagram, hmm. Offer him fifty bucks. If he takes it, I'll double it and take it off your hands."

"Triple it and it's yours," the pawnshop owner said.

A few minutes later, Mike returned with a huff.

"So? What'd he say? Did he take it?"

"No, he didn't take it. Said he's spent more than that in doctor bills ever since his kid found the thing."

Baker leaned in closer to the phone. "Mike, you didn't happen to get a name of that kid, did you?"

"It will cost ya."

"Don't jerk my chain, Mike. What's the kid's name!?"

"Okay, okay, don't get so huffy. I think he called him Colt."

Baker bit the stogy in half and spit it out. *So Colt O'Dell has the medallion ... and he's been sick. I wonder if Dr. Damian knows anything about this.*

After hanging up, Baker dialed a number he'd committed to memory.

***

With his hands shoved deep in the pockets of his white smock,

Dr. Damian went through his hospital rounds with dispassionate ease. His feigned concern was just that, fake, artificial. He was just biding his time, hoping his past wouldn't catch up to him. Having altered his employment records from the last hospital where he served, he tried to forget his mistakes. His patients were probably going to die anyway. The fact that he didn't try to give them a little more time was more humanitarian, not barbarian. In the end, he knew their organs would fail and would fetch a higher price by him waiting another month. It wasn't his fault he made a boatload more money in the deal.

And then there was the matter of Mrs. Ramirez. Her abusive husband left her badly injured outside a nightclub. If word got out that a City Councilman was under investigation for wife abuse it wouldn't set well with the public ... especially in an election year. Despite her insistence, it was her husband who beat her up; thanks to Dr. Damian, the hospital records painted a different picture and he was the richer for it, with the public being no wiser.

"Dr. Damian, you have a phone call," the nurse announced over the intercom.

Mid-stride, the doctor reversed his direction and headed to the Nurses Station. "Yes," not hiding his impatience.

Nurse Linda Whaley stood, leaving her chair empty for the doctor. "Line two," her tone flat.

The doctor's eyebrows knit. *I'd bet a million she was involved with Bill Koontz's disappearance.* Taking the seat she vacated, he gave her a curt nod. "Thanks."

Turning so no one could overhear his conversation, Dr. Damian spoke in a hushed tone. "Hello?"

"Hey doc—"

It was Randy Baker.

"I told you never to call me at the hospital."

"I have a question and it can't wait."

Sweat beaded on Damian's upper lip, and he glanced from

side to side. *Good, no one is listening.* "What is it?"

"Have you seen a patient by the name of Colt O'Dell?"

Damian rubbed his chin racking his brain. He'd seen scores of patients in the last six months. How was he supposed to remember one name? "Describe him."

"He's a kid, for crying out loud, short, blondish hair, freckles, I don't know. Said he'd been sick off and on for a while."

Again, Damian rifled through his memory banks. A face came to mind. "Okay, I think I remember. The kid came in with his mom a couple of times. I wasn't the attending physician, but I saw him. What's this about?"

"Can you pull his records?"

It grated against Dr. Damian like sandpaper over raw knuckles to answer to the sheriff, but what was he to say. Baker knew his background. As a part of showing solidarity to the coven, each member had to disclose their deepest secrets. He knew Baker's and Baker knew his, but there was one difference ... Damian still lived on the right side of the law and Baker had crossed the line. Now he was faced with a choice.

"Yeah, I can pull his records." As he spoke, his fingers tapped in the information needed to pull up Colt O'Dell's medical records. "What do you want to know?"

Baker chuckled. "Oh, the usual stuff. His address, what was wrong with him. That kind of stuff."

The doctor scrolled down a few lines. He hated to violate the HIPAA laws, not to mention patient/doctor confidentiality, but Baker forced his hand. After releasing a pent up breath, Damian filled Baker in with all the details he wanted to know.

"So you say, he's been sick with some unknown ailment since Christmas?"

"All I can tell ya is what's in the report. Look, I got rounds to make. Can we end this?"

Baker laughed, "Why so testy, doc?"

Damian, in a rare moment of personal disclosure, sighed

into the phone. "Sorry, I've had a lot on my mind."

Baker released a string of expletives. "I'm leading a shadowed life, and all you have to do is worry about what? Where to invest your fat salary? Give me a break."

Dr. Damian had had enough. "Look, nothing bad better happen to that boy, Baker. You hear me?"

"Or what? You gonna cancel my parking pass?"

"Baker, we're done. I'm through with you and your ilk. Don't call me again." He slammed the phone down with such force, it made the nurses jump. Feeling heat creep up his neck, he apologized and retreated to the doctor's lounge. He needed a stiff drink.

Chapter Thirteen

Despite the early start of school in Georgia, the dog days of summer dragged on like a 'B' rated movie. The sun glared down the crusted earth, punishing both students and teachers alike as the end of the second week of school mercifully came to a close. By now, football season was in full swing and pressure from the coaches for the teachers to keep their student players eligible mounted with every injury. It didn't take long before the wise men realized how difficult it was to hold the attention of high school students. Their insolence and lackadaisical attitudes caused the wise men to rethink the wisdom of their decision.

Riding home, Balthazar rehearsed his day in the classroom. "I just don't understand. From what I've studied, the lessons I was asked to teach don't reflect a true picture of history. I should know, I've only been around for the last two thousand years. Why the history books are missing vast portions of medieval times. They have rewritten the Crusades and have even changed the history of this nation. Major figures such as President George Washington and Abraham Lincoln have been relegated to a paragraph while extolling the virtues of men like Trotsky, Darwin, and Carl Marx." He shook his head in bewilderment. "When I tried to correct the record, I got odd looks from the students like they'd never heard such things. I'm beginning to wonder if the educators are intentionally trying to change the thinking of these students."

Melchior crossed his legs and adjusted the strap on his sandal. He and the others had never gotten used to wearing leather shoes, preferring rather, to go with what was most comfortable. It got them a few smirks from the other faculty, but high-fives from the students, thinking they too were doing it out of silent protest against school rules. "You wouldn't believe the confusion I'm facing in my class. Those poor souls actually think their great, great ancestors swung from trees. And before that, they crawled out of some primordial goo. I tried to tell them the creation story and they ridiculed me as if it were a ... a fairy tale. They said it wasn't scientific." He released a weary sigh. "It takes more faith to believe the theory of evolution than creation. That's all I've got to say. Ms. Stephanie Schweitzer informed me in no uncertain terms that it's a violation of state law to talk about religion, but the way I see it, evolution is a religion. It just goes by another name."

Balthazar nodded. "'A rose by any other name' ... you know how the saying goes."

Sighing deeply, Melchior continued. "Yes, but a snake is still a snake, and a wolf in sheep's clothing is still a wolf. We may be in the wrong profession. Have you ever considered that?"

Jasper eased up on the brake and pulled through the intersection. Out of the corner of his eye, he caught a flash of movement as a Hummer, driven by a high school student, slammed through the red light. Jasper stomped the brake pedal throwing his passengers forward. Their vehicle came to a stop inches away from where the giant vehicle had just been. He wiped the acclimated sweat from his upper lip and continued the drive home; albeit, more cautiously.

"I'm beginning to think you're right. Whenever I turn my back to draw diagrams or write on the white-board showing how I calculated the movement of the stars, some wise guy throws a wad of paper at me or some girl screams. By the time I turn around, the class is still as church mice. Then, when I ask them a question, I get blank stares. I believe these kids cannot think critically whatsoever."

Heads nodded in agreement.

Gasper continued. “It’s sad but true, the only stars these kids want to talk about are the ones on stage. If you ask me, those people are nothing but wandering stars, for whom the blackness of darkness is reserved. The only bright spot is the one student who actually listens. He’s a senior and wants to become an astrophysicist. He and I have had some very interesting discussions after class. He thinks my theorems of the time-space continuum are amazing. But then he starts quoting a guy named Nostradamus, says he was a time traveler. Humph, and what are we? Chopped liver?”

As they neared the house, a large golden retriever bounded from the porch. By the time Gasper got the car stopped, the dog had placed his front two paws on the driver’s side door. He stuck his large head through the open window and offered Gasper a slobbery tongue.

Pulling back, Gasper did his best to ward off the dog’s affection. “Yuck, don’t you know I don’t believe in kissing before marriage?”

Chuckling, Melchior came around the car and tugged the dog back. “Well, well, old buddy. It looks like you’ve found a new friend.”

Gasper wiped the slobber from his face. “Who are you talking to, me or him?”

Melchior stroked the dog’s head. “Don’t be such a Scrooge. You know you enjoy the attention.”

Standing, Gasper inched toward the house. “Yeah, about as much as I like being kissed by my camel.” After a moment’s reflection, he added. “I wonder what ever became of Habibi. Now that was a comfortable camel.”

Balthazar patted him on the shoulder. “Like mine, she probably found a new master or returned home. Something we will never do.” His tone bore the pain they all felt whenever the topic of home arose. Looking at the dog, he said, “I wonder why he hasn’t returned home.”

As Gasper eased up the steps, he turned to Melchior. "I don't know how you can let that beast anywhere near you. The animal smells and he probably has fleas," ignoring his friend's disapproving look.

"This animal, as you call him, is a highly sensitive creature. I read that a dog's nose has nearly three million olfactory receptors. That fact alone disproves evolution. And to think, the part of a dog's brain devoted to analyzing smells is about forty percent larger than ours."

Gasper's sneeze went unnoticed. "I'm just glad he's got the snout and not me."

Chapter Fourteen

The following afternoon, Balthazar, Melchior and Gasper sat in the waiting area reserved for unruly students. Having never been called on the carpet before, they didn't know what to expect. The tone of the note, however, left them wondering. The principal's door swung open and he stood, framed in the late September sun streaming through the window. "Come in men and take a seat." His tone sounded friendly, but his set jaw and icy expression betrayed him.

As the three men got comfortable, Gasper leaned over to Balthazar while Mr. Davis walked around his desk. "This kinda reminds me of the time when we stood before King Herod."

Balthazar glanced around the ornately decorated room. "Well, the decor has changed, but I have a feeling the same pompous attitude hasn't," he whispered.

After taking his seat, Davis crossed his arms and leaned his elbows on the desk. Looking like Larry King, the noted late night talk show host, he made it clear who was in charge. "Gentlemen," his face bore a dower expression, "I have received some disturbing news."

Gasper gave Balthazar a knowing look as the tension, in the already warm room, grew thick.

"It seems the teacher's union and the PTA have received numerous complaints against you."

The three men exchanged glances. "Oh? And who in particular brought the charges? I'd like to respond in person to whatever he or she said. I think that would be the right thing to do," Balthazar said adding, "you know, face my accusers."

Heads bobbed.

The principal shifted uncomfortably. "Well, I'm not at liberty to disclose that information, but suffice it to say, several people have taken exception at your presentation of history. They are saying you are emphasizing a Judeo-Christian world view as opposed to a more Globalist world view. And as for you, Mr. Melchior, several students have brought it to my attention that you are teaching creation as fact. That's such a radical view nowadays, it is confusing them, and, frankly, rather disturbing. Think of the consequences of such teaching. If we were created, then there is a creator. And if there is a creator, then we are accountable to him, to obey him, to worship him. But we know that can't be true. What we are trying to instill in our students is a sense of freedom from such archaic restraints. We want them to throw off the shackles of the dark-ages, to step into the age of enlightenment, to embrace it. How are we going to do that with you inserting your personal-religious views? You can understand that, now can't you?"

Melchior stood, laced his fingers behind his back, and began to pace. "Mr. Davis, you invited us here as adjunct teachers because of our wisdom. Such wisdom comes from God and we can't change that, nor would we deSire such change. Our knowledge of history, science and mathematics stems from applications of that wisdom. If we deny the truth, we would be found liars. Which would you rather, we obey God or man?"

Mr. Davis sat stone still. He'd never been given such a choice. As a career administrator, he'd bent whichever direction the politically wind blew. "Look fellas, I'm getting pressure from the students, parents, the teacher's union and the PTA, for crying out loud. Now I need you to get on board. This fixation with your Biblical views has got to stop." His gestures grew more animated. "Oh, it's okay to believe such things on Sunday, but on Monday, you've got to toe the party line."

Gasper, who'd never heard the term, 'toe the line,' flicked a glance at his sandaled feet. "Sir, this isn't about us wearing sandals, is it?"

An incredulous expression darkened the principal's face. "Mr. Gasper, this is no joking matter. We are talking about something far more serious than your sandals. We're talking about you teaching material which is contrary to the state sanctioned curriculum. Now, would you try and focus? Keep your personal beliefs to yourselves or I'll be forced to let you go." With that, he gave them a dismissive wave, signaling the meeting was over.

As they stepped back into the hall, Gasper peered around. "What did he mean, let us go? Go where?"

Melchior stifled a chuckle. "I think he meant he'd have to release us from our teaching responsibility."

"You mean, fire us? Why the nerve—" Gasper sputtered.

Cutting Gasper's outburst off with a wave of his hand, Balthazar intervened. "Hold your voice down. You wouldn't want impressionable ears to hear you, now would you? I, for one, wouldn't want to give the man the satisfaction of seeing me upset. Let's just keep a low profile, try not to upset to donkey cart and see what Jehovah wants us to do next."

***

As they made their way to the teacher parking lot, one of Melchior's students from his science class called to him. "Hey, Mr. Melchior,"

"Hey, Josh."

The lanky junior with broad shoulders and a quick smile broke into a run in his direction. "You're not going to let Mr. Davis bully you, are you?"

Slowing his pace, Melchior waited for the young man to catch his breath. "Whatever do you mean?"

Still breathing hard, Josh Mattingly continued. "The principal, Mr. Davis, he tried to shut you guys up, didn't he?"

"Now, how would you know that?" Melchior asked, rocking back on his heels.

Josh laughed. "Oh, that's not hard. Everyone's been talking about it. I just wanted you to know, we're pulling for you."

"Who is pulling what?" Gasper asked, a blank expression marked his face.

Balthazar took a step closer. "Uh, Gasper, I know you're new here, we all are, but you've gotta stop taking these cliché's so literally. What the young man means, is ... he and his friends are on our side. They want us to not give in to the administration's demands.

His face brightening, Gasper patted Josh on the back. "I knew that."

Melchior turned to Josh. "So much for impressionable ears hearing us. I wonder who made all those complaints."

Josh cut his button-brown eyes over his shoulder. "I think I've got a pretty good idea."

"Who?" Balthazar and Gasper asked in unison.

"I think this whole thing stems from one teacher who's got it in for you." Scuffing the ground, Josh jammed his hands in his pockets and continued, "It's the same person who complained about me and my friends gathering each morning around the flag pole to sing and pray. She's against anything Christian."

Glancing at his friends, Balthazar stroked his chin. "Maybe we should join your little prayer and praise gathering. It just might be the thing that turns the tide."

Josh's thick lips parted into a broad grin. "That'll be cool. Would y'all really do that?"

Returning his grin, Gasper reached out and high-fived him. "You bet we will. We'll be there tomorrow morning at seven sharp, with bells on the fringes of our garments."

Mouths gapping, Balthazar and Melchior exchanged incredulous looks. "I think the saying is; 'with bells on,' though I really don't quite grasp the statement's meaning," Balthazar admitted.

"Come to think of it, neither do I," Josh admitted, rubbing his chin.

Chapter Fifteen

Thursday morning broke crisp and clear giving the town's residents hope for a bumper apple crop. Predictions of an early peak leaf season promised crowded highways and bulging profits.

As the sun displaced the remaining shadows hiding behind the North Georgia Mountains, a small group of young students gathered around a stainless steel flagpole. The school day hadn't officially begun and the pole stood empty like a sentinel pointing heavenward.

Had it not been for the young people, Prince Argos, and his warriors would have overlooked the scene, but that was not the case. To him, this gathering was the key to unleashing God's mighty power. Though all hell sought to block these young people with worldly philosophy and peer-pressure, it was his responsibility to see that they were not distracted. Their zeal for spiritual things was birthed in trial, and bathed in prayer. The teen prayer warriors watched the explosive effects of North Hamilton Bible Church's prayer revival and yearned to experience that power for themselves.

Despite the principal's insistence that they relocate, the determined young people remained steadfast. It was to this group Prince Argos assigned his most trusted warrior, Prince Selaphiel.

"Guard them well. I sense a storm of persecution brewing and it has its eye centered on this group of young people."

The burly red-haired angel fisted his chest in a sharp salute. "You can count on me. I and my legion will stand constant vigil over them. These souls, though all hell should endeavor to shake, we will never, no never, no never forsake."

Prince Argos coursed his arms. "You're not fooling me. You got those lines from our friend Martin Luther."

"Yes, my lord. If you will remember, it was you who assigned me to guard the dear saint."

Argos nodded ruefully. "Yes, my friend. I did. And you fulfilled your duty spectacularly."

As his commander spoke, the memory of his past near-defeat wormed across his minds. It was only a few months ago that the believers needed an extra push to respond to his promptings. Had he not called for Prince Argo, the battle might have been lost. As it was, it took a young boy and a badly wounded elderly man to bring the church to its knees ... literally.

As his host of defenders took up their positions around the pole and began their youthful praise and prayer meeting, three stately men drew closer. Dressed in casual attire except for their sandals, the wise men looked like ordinary people rather than two-thousand year old Magi. Balthazar, followed by Melchior, and Gasper took a guarded step into the group. Not wanting to intimidate the nervous teens, he nodded and smiled. "I heard there was a praise and prayer meeting. May we join you?"

Smiling, Josh glanced at his friends then back to the three wise men. "Well, yeah," in typical fashion. Taking him by the elbow, Josh guided Balthazar into the center. "Hey guys, Mr. Balthazar and his friends want to join us. How 'bout we give them a big welcome." An enthusiastic cheer erupted, followed by several choruses. After a few minutes, the teens closed ranks and began to pray. Some lifted their hands, others bowed their knees, while some stood, arms extended, heads laid back in unabashed boldness before the throne of grace. Their prayers varied from praying for families in need, to lost friends, to the administrators of the school. Their simple petitions brought smiles to the wise men's faces, knowing every request was a flaming arrow shot into the heart of the darkness.

***

While the teens prayed, a distant warbling grew louder until it drowned out their voices. Prince Selaphiel nodded to his cohort who placed themselves between their young charges and the oncoming storm. Within minutes, a caravan of police cruisers and vans bearing the letters of news media outlets descended on the scene. Among the show of force, was Deputy Ty Huntley. Having been ordered to form a circle, the officers gathered around the wide-eyed teens.

Why is he there? Prince Selaphiel wondered.

The new sheriff, Bud Carlton, stepped through the circle of blue. "Who's in charge?" His commanding voice had its desired effect. Some of the younger teens shrank behind the older ones and began to cry. His jaw set, Josh stepped forward. "I am, Sir," his anger kept in check by Balthazar's restraining hand.

"Be respectful," he whispered.

Josh nodded, his shoulders rigid. "Is there a problem, Sheriff?"

Sheriff Carlton crossed his arms and waited for the press to get settled. It was obvious he wanted this to be a media circus with him as the Ring-Master. Once the cameras were in place, he dropped his arms and addressed the young man. "This is a violation of city ordinance 2011.56." His voice carried across the open field for all to hear.

"That's a crock and you know it." A voice shot from the back of the group. It was Jacob Myers. Having been tipped off by Ty, Jacob arrived as quickly as possible. Taking long strides, he pushed through the police barricade and joined the young man in the center of the storm.

Shielded behind dark sunglasses, Sheriff Carlton stood rock-solid while eager reporters and cameramen moved in closer like blood-thirsty sharks, not wanting to miss a thing.

"You know perfectly well that ordinance applies to large parties, not innocent teens praying around a flagpole. Your intrusion is a violation of First Amendment Rights of Free Speech."

His protest went unheeded as the sheriff's men began to herd some of the teens toward the waiting vans. "That's for the courts to decide. I'm just doing my job."

"Your job? When did you start working for Richard Davis, the principal of the high school?" Jacob made sure his question was clearly heard by the nearest reporter. "I have an anonymous source that says this whole thing was staged by you and the principal just to intimidate these young people."

All at once, a reporter shoved a microphone in Jacob's face and demanded, "Who's your source? Can you be more specific?"

Another reporter pressed in closer. "How did you know to be here this morning? Who are you working for? Have these young people hired you as their attorney?"

Jacob waved them off. "Sheriff, is your department prepared to face an unlawful arrest suit? Because if you or your men touch one of these young people, I'll have you up on charges so fast, you'd think you were in the Light Brigade."

In the background, cameras clicked and reporters jostled for a better position. Like two linemen squaring off between the Georgia Bulldogs and Alabama's Crimson Tide, the two men stared each other down.

"Uh, Sir?" Josh's voice broke the tense moment. "I have written permission from the Secretary of Education allowing us to meet here." With trembling fingers, he pulled a crumpled envelope from his back pocket and handed it to the sheriff.

Glaring at the boy, Carlton snatched it from his hand and ripped it open. For a moment, time held its breath while he read its contents. Then, with a huff, he nodded to his fellow officers. "Okay men, looks like we've bothered these folks long enough. But if I find out you violated the terms of this," he waved the single sheet of paper in the air, "I'll be back and next time you won't be so lucky. I'll haul your butts to jail quicker than you can say, 'amen.' You got that?"

Josh lifted his chest and eyed the sheriff, unblinking. "Yes, Sir, loud and clear, but until then you can—"

Balthazar's hand gave his shoulder a gentle squeeze.

A cheer went up when the last of the officers left. Only Deputy Huntley remained and he stood, hands in his pockets. Looking at Balthazar and the others, he spoke in a low tone. "I'm sorry you guys had to see that. Your being here was not expected. I was ordered to be here, but not before making my position clear."

Balthazar stepped closer to Jacob and Deputy Huntley. "That's all right. I had a feeling something like this might happen. There is definitely an anti-Christian sentiment growing around here ever since we dispensed with the White Witch and her coven. You would think the people of North Hampton County would be grateful. On the other hand, I think Satan is mad at us."

Heads nodded as the meeting broke up.

***

From his perch, high above the valley, a dark figure clawed the ground. Over the last six thousand years he'd gone by many names: the spirit of jealousy, the spirit of envy, the spirit of greed, but to those who knew him, he went by the name Leviathan, and he was angry. His counterpart, Dantalion, had met his match in the Witch's Cave and was condemned to an early residency in the pits of Hades. It was a fate he knew awaited him, but he was not going down without a fight and not without taking as many souls with him as he could.

Through the centuries, he'd earned the reputation as a cunning hunter. Now, having his jurisdiction expanded to include the North Hamilton Township, he had a fresh supply of victims. He wondered who would be next.

Chapter Sixteen

Sitting behind a meticulously clean desk, Richard Davis scanned the list of names taken by the sheriff earlier that morning. To his surprise, the names of three of his teachers appeared at the bottom. Even though it was on their time, it drove him to madness that after warning them, Mr.'s Balthazar, Melchior, and Gasper continued to flaunt their religious views. Joining the 'prayer band,' as he called it was just another smack in the face.

The phone rang making him nearly spill the mug of coffee sitting next to his elbow. Still fuming at the report, he snatched the phone from the receiver. "What is it?" he barked.

"Sir, there's a call for you."

"Is it a reporter?"

"No, Sir. She said it was a private matter ... that it is urgent she speak with you."

"Did the caller give you a name?"

"No, Sir. Her voice was a bit muffled."

After a curt *thank you,* he pushed the door to his office closed and returned to his seat before punching the flashing button.

"Hello!?"

"Richard, it's me ... Olivia."

Richard's heart skipped a beat upon hearing the Fine Arts teacher's voice. He'd used his position and power to coerce the first-year teacher to yield to his demands. His little escapade across his marital boundaries was a closely guarded secret.

"Olivia, what a pleasant surprise, but why the cloak and dagger? My secretary didn't recognize your voice. How can I help you?"

"Richard, I'm sick."

"Oh? I'm sorry ... is the flu? I've heard it's going—"

"No! It's not the flu or any other bug."

His voice softening, he said, "I'm sorry to hear that. How long do you need off?"

"Oh, about seven months."

Bolting upright with the realization of her request, he blurted, "Seven months, but, but,"

"Richard ... I'm pregnant."

The word caught in his throat like an over-chewed piece of meat. "Pregnant?" He wanted to ask the obvious question but knew better. If she was pregnant, he was the father, and he had a big problem. "Look Olivia—"

"Don't even say it, scum-bag. First, you used your position to force me to do something against my will. You're not going to do it again. I'm having this baby and you're going to pay for it ... all of it or else—"

"Don't threaten me, Olivia. What we had was good. I can work things out, just give me some time."

"Time?" she spat. "You've got the same amount of time as me, about seven months."

"You'll ruin me if you go public. You know that, don't you?"

"I know. That's why I called you not the newspaper. Now, I'm going to take a leave of absence. I want fifty thousand dollars deposited in my bank account by the end of the week or you'll get a call from someone in the news business. Is that clear?"

Despite the air-conditioning, Richard mopped his soaked brow. "Yes, anything, just don't go shooting off your mouth."

"Or what? Or you'll make a few phone calls and ruin my career?" Her tone carried a defiant edge to it.

Richard knew she had him. He'd disclosed his connection with the former sheriff after having a few too many drinks and now he was paying for it. "Or nothing. I'll have the money transferred to you by Friday. Give me your account number and I'll take care of it." As he jotted down the numbers, large sweat rings marked his crisply steamed shirt and his mouth felt like gravel.

After Olivia finished, the line went dead.

Davis rubbed his temples. He couldn't afford to have his reputation ruined by this woman's accusations. After all, in today's environment, anyone could say anything on the Internet and get away with it. Fifty thousand dollars would be a small price to pay to keep his secret out of the public's attention. But paying it to Olivia wouldn't guarantee that. There was only one way to guarantee her silence. His fingers still shaking, he pulled out his cell phone and dialed a number.

After offering two former students a fraction of Olivia's demands, he finished his call by saying, "Make it look like an accident; quick and painless as possible. You got that?"

A gravelly chuckle echoed through the connection. "You really liked her. Didn't you?"

"Shut up and get the job done." He cursed as he slammed the phone shut.

Still shaking with rage, Davis buzzed his secretary.

"Yes, Sir?"

"Mrs. Welsh, call Mr. Gasper and set up an appointment with him for tomorrow morning."

***

When the phone rang a second time, Gasper stared at it like it was possessed. "Should I get it? It might be another reporter." Ever since the incident at the flag pole, the phone hadn't stopped ringing.

Balthazar glanced at the younger man. "You might as well. If not, they'll just keep calling."

Giving him a worried look, he lifted the phone to his ear.

"Hello, this is Mr. Gasper."

The others waited and listened to the one sided conversation. "Okay, I'll be there bright and early."

Balthazar and Melchior waited until Gasper set the phone back down. "Well?" They asked in tandem.

"Mr. Davis wants to meet with me tomorrow. Something about filling an open slot in the Drama Department."

"The Drama Department," Melchior echoed. "You don't know anything about theatrics."

Gasper's mouth dropped open, then snapped shut.

Balthazar tried but failed to keep the smirk from crinkling his face. "I'm sorry, Melchior, but if my memory serves me, I'd say his performance in the Live Nativity was quite good."

Nodding, Melchior had to agree. "Yes, especially at storytelling."

At hearing their comments, Gasper assumed a theatrical pose. "Now that you mention it, I do think I have a knack for acting. Maybe I should think about a career change." He stood gazing into a mirror trying to determine which was his better side.

***

The following morning, Mr. Davis' musings about his former Fine Arts teacher were interrupted by a knock on his door. "Yes?"

Mrs. Welsh stuck her head around the door. "Sir, Mr. Gasper is in the waiting area, do you want to see him now?"

Having forgotten about his appointment, Davis shuffled a stack of papers and shoved them into an empty drawer. "Yes, send him in."

A moment later, Gasper entered … a questioning expression on his face. "Sir, did you want to see me?"

Giving him a practiced smile, Davis stood and extended his hand. "Yes, thank you for coming. Take a seat. I have an offer for you."

Once settled, Gasper crossed his legs at the ankles and

waited.

"From what I've heard, I understand you did a little acting."

The memories still fresh from his role in the Live Nativity, Gasper nodded slowly. "Yes, Sir, but it was just a small—"

"—I have an opening in the Drama Department and thought you could fill it."

"An opening, but I thought—"

Again, the principal cut him off. "That's right. Miss Olivia McKinney was our Fine Arts teacher, but she has had to take a leave of absence. When I heard of the opening, your name immediately came to mind. I'd like to assign you to take over in her place."

Gasper felt his face heat. "I hope it's nothing serious. When do you expect her to return?"

Davis shifted his eyes to the side, then back to Gasper. "It's an indefinite leave of absence. You'll have to handle things through the rest of the year."

Gasper's mouth fell open. "But, Sir, I don't know anything about—"

"Doesn't matter. The kids pretty much know what to do. You just need to keep them from killing each other." Standing, Davis indicated the meeting was over.

Gasper pushed himself up on wobbly legs. "By the way, what play are the students working on?"

"Fiddler on the Roof."

Chapter Seventeen

As Gasper emerged from the principal's office, Balthazar and Melchior met him with broad smiles, clearly enjoying the moment. "Well? What did he say?" Balthazar asked.

Gasper pushed past them and stood in the hall, shaking his head. "I'm beginning to hate getting called to the principal's office. It's worse than standing before King Herod. All he could do was chop off our heads. This guy feeds me to the lions."

After breaking the news to his friends, he concluded by saying, "I'm counting on you guys to back me up on this. You know, all for one and one for all."

Slapping him on the back, Melchior smiled. "You can depend on us. We're behind you all the way ... way behind you."

Gasper sniffed at his attempt at humoring him. "I mean it, guys. I'm over my chin with this," once again, mixing up his cliché's. As he turned and stepped into the throng of students moving in the opposite direction, the crowd parted and a familiar figure emerged.

"Mr. Gasper."

Surprised to hear his name, he glanced up. It was Felicia Beauchamp.

"Mr. Gasper, what are you doing here?"

"I, I," Stuttering, Gasper gaped first at Felicia, then at his friends who stood in the midst of a torrent of students like to

Fly-fishermen. "I, we, are teachers—"

"Correction," Melchior interjected, "adjunct teachers. We are because of our vast years of experience traveling the world."

"And not the world wide web," Gasper added, trying to regain Felicia's attention.

Her eyes shifted from Melchior and Balthazar back to him.

"I'm sorry I didn't mention it, but I got caught up in the drama of the football game."

Ignoring his lame excuse, Felicia stepped closer so as to not get washed away in the floor of students rushing by. "Speaking of drama, did I hear you say you are taking Miss McKinney's place in the Drama Department?" Her French accent stood out like a Connecticut Yankee in King Arthur's Court.

Nodding, Gasper pushed out a nervous smile. "Yes, I was just informed, because of my vast experience and all."

He shot a glance at Melchior. *"Vast experience my derriere."*

Felicia's forehead wrinkled with interest, she continued, "Why? Where did Miss McKinney go?"

His palms extended, Gasper shrugged. "All Mr. Davis said was she had to take an early leave of absence."

Felicia gave a knowing nod. "I see. Well, if you need help, I have some experience in theater. In my provincial town of Piana, I used to act in the annual pageant. I've played leading roles in *Beauty and the Beast* and *Les Miserables*."

Impressed, Gasper released a pent up breath. "Would you? I mean ... not that I'll need that much help and all."

Balthazar's eyes narrowed. "Do you think that's a good idea?"

For a moment, Gasper held his gaze. He knew nothing about acting but was too despite, and proud to admit it. Sliding his hands in his pockets, he rocked back on his heels. "Yes, I do. It always looks good if there is a director and assistant director on the marquee." Turning to Felicia, he gave her a dramatic bow. "I would be delighted to have your assistance, madam."

Felicia giggled and returned the gesture. Straightening, she said, "Oui, I mean, yes. I would love to."

Relieved, Gasper added, "There is just one condition."

Her large brown eyes rounded. "Only one?" Her French inflection painted the two words in a rainbow color.

"Well, maybe two."

"And they are?"

"That we are never seen alone."

"And the other?"

"That you never invade my personal space."

Giving him a smug expression, Felicia huffed. "You think a little too much of yourself, Mr. Gasper, but I agree. I'll see you on stage." Smiling, she pranced down the hall in the direction of the auditorium.

***

Inside the auditorium, a raggedy group of teens gathered near the stage. Some lounged in the seats while others stomped around on the stage acting like rock stars. Seeing Miss Beauchamp, a few offered her the usual cat-calls, which she ignored. It was obvious the main topic of discussion was their missing drama teacher. Whispered rumors of Olivia McKinney's dalliance with the principal were only that, rumors, innuendos, but with her sudden replacement striding down the aisle, it gave the theory credence. The door to the auditorium closed behind Gasper just as he heard Felicia's silky voice make the announcement.

"Mr. Gasper and I have been asked to fill the void left behind by Miss McKinney's early leave of absence."

A general moan spread across the open space as Gasper took his place next to Felicia Beauchamp's diminutive figure. Then, striding to center stage, he locked his thumbs in his belt and squared his shoulders. Motioning her to join him, he waited, then began.

"That's correct, your principal, Mr. Davis wanted to act quickly and decisively in choosing the best possible replacements for your beloved teacher. Now we know no one could fill the void Miss McKinney left in your hearts. But with Miss Beauchamp's and my combined experience, we hope to guide you through this most difficult time in your young lives." Gasper paused and whispered, "How am I doing?"

"From what you've told me about your theatrical experience, I'd say you're laying it on a bit thick. You might try to lower their expectations rather than them finding out later your only experience was standing as a manikin in the local department store." Felicia's tepid warning didn't dampen Gasper's spirit.

Like a coach trying to rally his beleaguered team after losing to a hometown favorite, Gasper gathered the young people in a tight circle. "This reminds me of the legend of Pagoda Springs."

"Isn't that Powder Springs?" The interruption came from a tall, muscular senior wearing jeans and a flannel shirt with his sleeves rolled up.

Unfazed, Gasper continued. "Legend has it, in 1867, two tribes, the Utes and Navajos claimed ownership to an important spring. They believed the hot springs could bring healing to their sick and demanded the other tribe allow them access to it. Skirmishes broke out until they decided to settle the dispute once and for all. Each tribe chose a man to represent them in a to-the-death battle."

"Mano-a-Mano," a round, non-athletic type teen announced. "This ought a be good."

Felicia nodded. "Please, do continue, you have our undivided attention."

Emboldened, Gasper inhaled a steadying breath. "Well, the Navajos picked their biggest, meanest, fighter and sent him into the ring. The Utes chose Col. Albert Pfeiffer; a smaller, white man and friend of the tribe to represent them. Armed with Bowie knives, the two men faced off."

By now, he held everyone's imagination in the palm of his hand. Even the two teens who demonstrated an inordinate attraction for each other had interrupted their ardent conversation and turned their cow-eyed expressions to center stage.

"What happened next, Mr. Gasper?" Madi, a girl with fawn colored hair, and large brown eyes asked with growing interest.

Wiping his upper lip, Gasper pressed ahead. "Stripped to the waist, the two men snarled and cursed in an attempt to intimidate the other. 'Bring it on,' said the one to the other. 'Give me your best shot,' the other replied. One would lunge and the other would dance inches out of reach of the twelve-inch blade. The fight continued into the night as neither man yielded to the other. Finally, Pfeiffer, the quicker of the two out-maneuvered his larger opponent and plunged the knife in his chest."

"Yuck," a squeamish girl cried."

Smiling at his overly dramatized rendition, Gasper concluded, "The point of my story is this, no matter how big our opponent or opportunity is, the bigger the reward. On Colonel Albert Pfeiffer's tombstone it is written, 'Soldier and Scout with Kit Carson, Indian Agent adopted by the Ute Indians.'"

"Cool story, Mr. Gasper," the tall senior said, looking at his phone, "but doesn't Pagosa Springs mean 'smelly water?"

Chagrined, Gasper lowered his voice. "Yes, but the point is—"

"—The point is, young people, we have a job to do and sitting around moping isn't going to get it done. Now I want everyone to take their places and let's begin from the top." With that, Miss Beauchamp clapped her hands and the teens leaped on stage, smirking.

Ninety minutes later, the exhausted actors and stage hands emerged from the auditorium and scattered … some to their homework, still others to the local drive-in hamburger joint.

Closing the door to the auditorium behind them, Gasper walked Felicia to her car. "I thought that went rather well, don't you?"

Felicia adjusted her handbag on her shoulder. "Yes. The kids showed real talent, but I think a motivational speech involving a Native American getting killed by a white man isn't politically correct. I can hear the globalist-parents now. 'Teachers at North Hampton High endorsing genocide.' Where'd you come up with that story, anyway?"

Gasper gave her a defeated shrug. "I've moved around a lot over the years and heard many such stories."

"It sounded a bit like, 'David and Goliath' if you ask me." Felicia's observation stopped Gasper mid-stride.

"You know, now that you mention it, the two stories are quite similar. It's kinda like the Ark stories recorded by ancient civilizations all around the world. Why, even in my country of India. We had tales of a big boat carrying lots of animals." He sighed and gazed upwards. Above them spread a blanket of velvet salted with glistening specks of light.

Following his example, Felicia looked up. "And to think, men used to use those stars to guide them on their journey."

Not wanting to get into a lengthy discussion with someone he'd just met, Gasper wisely chose to change the subject. "Are you going to the next football game?"

Felicia held her gaze. "I was thinking about it. Are you?"

"Though I don't understand it, I do think it's a good way to show school spirit, so yes. I'm going. Want to meet and sit where we did last Friday?"

Nodding, Felicia turned her face toward his. Her smile sent his heart rate through the star-spangled sky. "That would be fun. See you tomorrow. Oh, and, be sure to familiarize yourself with each of the parts. You'll need to know them if someone is sick the night of."

It had never occurred to him that he might actually have to step in and fill a part. It was a sobering thought; one that drove him to long hours spent studying the script.

Chapter Eighteen

It had been another sleepless night for Olivia McKinney. Since her phone call with Richard Davis, she'd had nothing but fear as her companion. After wrestling with the sheets for hours, she gave up and fixed herself a cup of tea. For her, there were only two things that could get her out of the funk she found herself in; ice cream or a new outfit. But with her growing belly and the early hour, neither were viable options. Pulling on an old jogging suit, she laced up her running shoes and decided to go for an early morning run.

Stepping from her condo, she took several deep breaths to clear her mind before going through her stretching routine. Then she took off in a slow jog, increasing her speed as her muscles warmed. By the time she'd reached the street corner, she was at full speed and ran along the empty sidewalk with the wind whistling in her ears.

The light tapping of her shoes on the concrete reminded her that time was ticking by. If she was going to make a change in her life, she needed to do it soon. Being in her first trimester, running was still an option, but she knew it would only be a matter of time before her condition warranted the first of many changes. Later, she would have to settle for walking and breathing deeply. She hoped with the infusion of funds provided by Richard Davis, she would be able to start a new life. One that didn't depend on men for happiness.

Having recently finished the R.A.D program, better known as the Rape Aggression Defense program, she hoped to become a trainer. She'd already completed the three days of intense physical and educational training and received her certification. Now all she needed was to pass the two day, 20 hour Advanced Self-Defense course which covered more strategies, multiple person encounters and even low and diffused light situation exercises. With her military background, she felt confident she could provide her clients with the best preparation money could buy. But first, she had to get past what the doctor called a complicated pregnancy.

As she rounded the last corner and ran over a bridge which spanned a railroad track, two hooded men stepped from the shadows. The first man's hulking frame filled the sidewalk limiting her options. She either had to leap over the railing ... not an option, run into the street where early morning traffic sped by or face down her foe. Immediately, her training kicked in. Taking a calming breath, she assumed a defensive posture and waited. The man lunged forward and she deftly sidestepped him. The move exposed his right side and she took full advantage of his mistake. A quick pivot and her foot came up with full strength. It landed hard, knocking the man off his feet. Sucking air, the brute cursed and came at her a second time. As he lumbered forward, he extended his right hand, the stun gun ready to do its evil work if it found its mark.

Again, she swirled and landed another solid kick. The man groaned and fell. The gun clattered to the concrete and was immediately picked up by the second man. His thin form stood in stark opposition to her former opponent. He was light on his feet and danced around like he was a puppet on a stick; all the while chattering the words from a Rap song about a trashy white girl. His lips pealed back revealing a set of yellowed teeth. His wild eyes showed no fear.

For an instant, Olivia considered if there were others. She hoped not. The blast of a train as it passed under the bridge sent an icy chill through her veins. It was quite possible one of them would end up on the tracks or worse, getting crushed under the unforgiving wheels of the locomotive. She didn't intend it to be her.

Feeling a fresh surge of adrenaline, Olivia let the force of energy spread to her legs and arms. She knew what she had to do. It was him or her. Retaking her defensive posture, she lowered herself and prepared for the attack. Just as her new assailant advanced, the big man on the concrete grabbed her foot, throwing off her balance. Olivia found herself unable to use her best defense. In an instant, the other man was upon her. His fist came down hard. Lightening flashed across her sight as the man's knuckles jacked her jaw. Searing pain shot down her neck as her head snapped back, then darkness.

Clinging to the last shred of consciousness, Olivia knew this was the end. She would never start a R.A.D. program, she would never deliver her baby, she would never even see the light of another day. Regret stabbed her. All those lost opportunities. Fear gripped her heart and squeezed. *Where will I go when I die?* All those nihilistic theories she'd been taught in college evaporated as the realization of facing an eternity without God came into focus. *Oh God, help me!*

She felt her body being lifted. Rough hands held her by the shoulders and feet. She wanted to fight, but there was no fight left in her. She knew she was going to die within seconds. The men lay her on the cold, hard concrete guard wall. Beneath her, the train rumbled passed.

"Davis said to make it look like an accident," the larger man growled.

"Then this is good as any," the other man laughed. "Let's do it."

The next thing Olivia felt was a rush of air whistling in her ears, then a bone crushing jolt, then nothingness.

***

As the two men leaned over the wall, all they saw was the blur of railroad cars whizzing beneath them, disappearing under the bridge. The train's deafening rumble drowned out the footsteps behind them. Before they could act, the man slipped up and tased them. Their bodies slumped to the concrete unable to offer any resistance. It only took a few seconds to lift the two men up and roll them over the top of the railing. As the last boxcar disappeared into the shadows of the bridge, two bodies tumbled to the barren iron tracks below. When wheels of the next train passed they would easily slice the bodies into pieces, leaving little to offer the vultures.

***

As the train rolled along the tracks, Prince Uriel stood over Olivia's broken body. He had warded off the attack of the grim reaper, but there were others who claimed ownership of the woman's body. She had given in to lust and promiscuity. Now she was paying the price. Fortunately, the price had been paid on Calvary. Once he was sure her life was in no more danger, he moved to the front of the long string of cars until he reached the engineer's compartment. He slipped in unnoticed and as silent as a morning breeze, whispered something in the engineer's ear. Staring straight ahead, the man's hands moved at Uriel's will.

Hours later, as the sun poured its rays down upon flowers, trees, and manmade surfaces, Olivia's eyes fluttered open. Stinging pain pricked her skin and she realized she had landed on the top of a boxcar loaded with insulation. The soft material had broken her fall, offering her another chance at life. Life for her, life for her baby. *Maybe God heard my plea.* The thought pleased her and she determined to find the first church that offered her sanctuary and promised she would mend her ways.

Locating a ladder at the end of the boxcar, Olivia climbed down and gazed around. For reasons known only to the conductor, the train had come to a stop. The ticking sound of hot metal offered no clue, but the blast of an approaching train, did. Carefully, she stepped over the parallel set of iron ribbons, and clambered down the bank and crossed a field. In the distance, she noticed what looked to be an abandoned town. The closer she came, the clearer it became. This was no town or city she'd ever seen. It was a mock village. Old shops and cattle stalls stood in various stages of decay, but the wooden structures were held together with modern nails. The wooden sign which hung at the entrance, creaked in the breeze saying, 'Welcome to Bethlehem.'

A narrow dirt path wound through an overgrown field to a series of modern buildings and Olivia began to follow it. With every step, fire raced through her joints and screamed at her. Willing herself forward, she realized she was nearing civilization. But it wasn't the modern buildings that pushed her forward; it was the sight of a cross located high on a steeple.

The blast from the train behind her stole her attention and the last words, "Davis said to make it look like an accident," raced across her mind. "It was no accident that I survived, and it was no accident I found this church," she muttered. "I'll deal with Mr. Davis later, but first, I have a promise to keep."

As she limped to the front of the sanctuary, a wispy figure stepped from the door into the bright sunlight.

"Help!" Olivia called, then collapsed. Her desperate call brought the woman to her side.

In an instant, gentle arms engulfed her. Warm, tender eyes bore down upon her. Sinking into unconsciousness, Olivia relaxed and let herself drift.

Having accomplished his mission, Prince Uriel spread his ethereal wings like a great monarch butterfly and silently rose heavenward.

***

The following day, Olivia awoke to the sound of soft music playing somewhere deeper in the house. Daylight streamed through sheer curtains and she smiled. Beneath her, silky sheets enfolded her in a soft grip. A snuggly comforter lay across her body like a fresh layer of snow. The fragrance of shampoo from her hair tickled her nose and she felt clean. Despite her throbbing head, and searing pain from every joint, she knew she was alive. This was no dream. Movement in the room caught her attention and a face appeared.

"You gave us quite a scare, young lady." It was Angela Wyatt. Her warm smile melted the icy fist surrounding her heart. "Do you remember anything?"

Olivia tried to sit up, but her body rebelled. Flopping back on the pillow, and began. Starting with her name, she told all, including her illicit affair with Richard Davis and his deadly instructions to the goons who jumped her …

Chapter Nineteen

After observing the wise men's movements for several weeks, Baker noted a pattern. Monday through Thursday they would stay late and work with the Drama team. They seldom got home before eight o'clock which gave him an idea. Picking up the phone, he called an old friend.

"It's me."

Joann Littleton recognized Baker's voice. They needed no introductions. "What do you want?"

"Information."

"What kind of information?" her voice carried no warmth.

"Incriminating information."

"Oh? About anyone I know?"

"Yeah, you've got three guys living in one of your rental homes."

"I know them. They're teachers out at the high school."

"The one and the same. They are also responsible for breaking up our little coven, if you'll remember."

"I wasn't there, but I heard about it. I was just waiting for you to call. I knew you wouldn't let it alone. Whatcha need?"

Without missing a beat, Baker peeled off a list of items he was sure he'd need.

"Okay, but if I get caught—"

"Now, now, Joann, you're a rather shapely woman, use it to your advantage. They'll never suspect a thing."

"Why sheriff, I didn't think you'd noticed."

He let a wicked chuckle percolate in his chest. "Just get it done. We can celebrate later."

***

After a trying day in the classroom, the wise men returned home. It was their routine to relax around the dinner table before separating, each to their little corner of the house. As Gasper entered the house, he was greeted with the aroma of freshly baked cookies. The still warm plate occupied the center of the table along with a jug of milk.

"I wonder who brought these," he asked as the others gathered around him. The floor creaked and he looked up at the stairs.

"Mrs. Littleton, what are you doing here?" Balthazar asked.

With a wave of her hand, she brushed past him. "I came to bring you another plate of cookies," eyeing the half-eaten stack on the plate.

"Upstairs?" he pressed.

"Oh, that, well, my husband, the louse, is too lazy to replace the batteries in your smoke detectors so I had to do it. I hope you don't mind."

Gasper sniffed the air. "I don't smell any smoke, and we don't use wood to cook with; at least not anymore. So why do we need a smoke detector?"

"It's part of the fire code." Her answerer didn't satisfy him.

"Code, like a code of silence?" His forehead wrinkled as he glanced from side to side.

"No, that's just another way of saying, it's the law." She sounded frustrated.

Still not satisfied, Gasper pressed on. "So you're saying, these detectors are supposed to sniff the air for smoke, even when we don't cook or heat the house with fire."

"Yes, but if there is a fire, they will sound an alarm so you can get out of the house in time."

Gasper's face brightened. "Okay, I get it. So if, for an

example, on a cold night we start a fire in the fireplace, it will tell us we need to go outside in the cold. Somehow that doesn't make much sense."

Balthazar patted his young scholar on the shoulder. "Don't worry, Mrs. Littleton, I don't think you have much to worry about. We don't plan on starting a fire anytime soon."

She smiled. "That's comforting, enjoy the cookies." Making a hasty exit, she left the door standing open.

"That was odd," Melchior said. "I wonder why she couldn't have asked us to do that rather than entering our house, uninvited. And, where is Gideon?" Heavy panting announced the dog's arrival as he pranced through the open door. A broken rope dangled from his neck causing the men to exchange worried glances.

Balthazar stroked his chin. "It isn't our house, if you will remember. We are renting it from her, so I guess she has the right to enter it anytime she pleases."

While they watched their landlady disappear, Gasper climbed the stairs and inspected the smoke alarm. It's LED light glowed red. Being too short to test it, he entered his room in search of his staff. Noticing the open window, he wondered. *I don't remember opening it.* Not giving it another thought, he continued his search. "Hey guys, have your seen my staff?"

***

Back in her own home, Joann pulled her cell phone from her pocket and dialed a number she'd committed to memory. "I got what you want, but I almost got caught. Those three stooges walked in on me right as I was finishing up. I even had to toss one of those walking sticks through the window," she said, peering through the blinds.

"What'd ya tell them?"

Joann let out a nervous laugh. "I told them I was replacing the batteries in their smoke detectors."

"Did ya?"

"Nope, I lied. If the house catches on fire, I hope they burn to death. It serves them right for what they did to our little coven."

"Don't worry, Joann. They'll get what's coming to them, but first I need everything brought to the Oasis, tonight."

"Tonight? Why the hurry?"

"Just do it. I've got plans and it can't wait. When I get through, those three musketeers will wish they never came to our little town."

Chapter Twenty

A lone sixty-watt bulb hung over a rickety table in the center of Baker's shack. Half of the building housed a large brass pot with copper tubes curling out of it like snakes on Medusa's head. The other half served as a residence for the former law enforcement officer. He had always played it close to the edge when it came to the law. Now he had crossed over. If caught, his illicit activities would land him behind bars for a long time, but he had no intention of letting that happen. If his plan worked, he'd be the one calling the shots, not Sheriff Carlson.

Huddling with his men, Baker mapped out his plan. "Okay, here's how this is going down. Mike, get us three maintenance uniforms from the school, Archie, you go to the hardware shop and get everything on this list." His cigar-stained finger punched the list as he spoke, emphasizing every word.

The straggly man gazed at the list, his head bobbing with the action of Baker's finger.

Handing him a wad of bills, Baker continued, "Here's enough money to cover your expenses. Bring the change back, and don't stop at the local watering hole. You hear me?" The scruffy man with hair that hung loosely in front of his eyes, nodded.

"Once we have everything we'll make a visit to the high school."

The two guys exchanged dull expressions and gave each

other a high five. "Hey, I told you I'd make it to high school." Mike's crooked smile revealed an uneven set of teeth that would make any dentist run for the hills.

It took only a day for Baker's two goons to round up the needed items. Meanwhile, Baker did some checking around and learned that the O'Dell family usually attended church on Wednesdays. A quick glance at the calendar confirmed the date ... *Perfect timing.*

***

Later that evening, Baker and his crew dressed as maintenance men, slipped through an unlocked door in the back of the auditorium and made their way to the electrical panel. On stage, several young people stood reciting their lines without much feeling. For a moment, Archie stood, gazing at the pair. It was obvious, he'd never been on stage, let alone walked across one in a graduation ceremony.

It took only a few minutes to jury-rig the device. With any luck, it would blow the electrical panel leaving the auditorium in total darkness. If Baker played his cards right, the damage would be minimal and they would have the lights back on in forty-five minutes tops. While the repairs were underway, the wise men's whereabouts would be in question.

With that completed, he led his men back outside. "All right, now for the fun. Follow me."

"Where we going, boss," Archie asked, his jaw hanging half open.

Giving him an exasperated look, Baker huffed. "Where'd ya think, to the O'Dell's house. We have a lost item that needs to be found."

Archie gave his partner a confused expression, then followed without speaking. He'd learned from the past not to ask too many dumb questions.

By the time they arrived at the O'Dell's subdivision, it was almost seven-thirty. Baker pulled the corner of his shirt sleeve back. *The device should have gone off. We only needed fifteen minutes. By seven-forty-five, we'll be gone.*

Using an unguarded gate near the swimming pool, he and his men made their way to the O'Dell's house. Having been there recently, he knew most of the homes in the O'Dell's subdivision had the latest security systems. Fortunately, he'd taken note of the type of system the O'Dell's had when he was there to investigate the kidnapping. He was quite familiar with it and knew how to disable it and its backup. With that done, he jimmied the lock on the back door and slipped in.

"Mike, you stand by the back door and keep watch."

"What do ya want me to do?" Archie asked. Baker knew he'd do more damage than good and wondered why he even brought him along. "Sit in the car and keep the engine running. And don't draw any attention to yourself."

Archie snickered. "Like playing the radio too loud?"

"Yeah, like, don't play the radio at all. You stooge."

Once inside, Baker began to place pieces of evidence Mrs. Littleton had stolen, in key locations where they would be discovered by the detectives ... a thumbprint on a light switch, a footprint in the carpet.

Guessing where to find his query, Baker climbed the stairs to the second floor and began to rifle through Colt's dresser. "Got it," he muttered. After placing a fiber from Gasper's robe in Colt's bedroom floor, he backed out of the room, being sure not to leave any of his shoe prints behind.

As he descended the stairs, movement in the den arrested his steps. *Were the O'Dell's home?* He'd failed to check the garage for cars and assumed the house was empty. *Apparently it was not.*

All at once, the door to the study opened and Glenn appeared in the hall. It was obvious he'd heard something, but had not seen Baker. It would only be a matter of time before he did. With cat-like movements, Baker leaped over the railing and pounded on the unsuspecting man before he had a chance to react. One swift blow from the butt of his gun and Glenn crumpled to the floor like a deflated Air Dancer.

Five minutes after they broke in, Baker closed and locked the door making sure he left one of the wise men's footprints in the soft dirt. "There, that ought-a do it. Now let's disappear." Turning, he and Mike stalked across the yard in the direction of his car.

***

Hovering over Glenn's crumpled body, Prince Leo stood, his bow stretched to its limit, its diamond tip pointed at a dark figure. In a breath, the figure plunged his scythe at the heart of the unconscious man. Leo let his arrow fly striking the shadowy figure in the chest, throwing him off balance. The scythe whizzed past Glenn's upper torso barely missing him. Wounded, but not destroyed, the grim reaper lunged again. This time his icy grip found Glenn's throat, and he began to squeeze. Seeing his charger's death struggle, Prince Leo reloaded and fired two more times. His arrows found their mark and the death angel's fingers weakened, but by then Glenn's color had paled to an ashen gray. If Leo didn't act fact, he'd lose him. Desperate to save the man's flickering life, he materialized into human form ... a rare act that he'd performed only once before. It was when he and Prince Selaphiel accompanied Theophany to warn Abraham of Sodom and Gomorrah's impending doom.

Lifting Glenn in his arms, he leaned over and whispered, "Lord God of the spirits of just men made perfect. It is not this man's time. I know that because you have revealed to me this man's usefulness to the kingdom. I implore you; breathe the breath of life into this man as you did the day of Adam."

Still holding Glenn, Prince Leo waited. As sudden as lightening, a sliver of golden light cut across the heavens, through the walls of the O'Dell's house and down to where the stricken man lay. With the gentleness of a mother, it touched him, revived him, sent life surging energy through him. Glenn jolted upright, then slumped back down. He was alive, but not out of danger. God, in His sovereignty, had not chosen to bring complete healing. But like the man whose eyes needed a second touch, so also Glenn needed a second touch, but none came.

Chapter Twenty-One

As Karen and her church family finished the Prayer Meeting, she suddenly felt overwhelmed with emotion. Fighting back tears, she tried to steady herself. Her breathing shallowed, her skin turned clammy and she doubled over.

"What is it?" Angela, the pastor's wife, asked as she helped her to a pew.

Hand to her forehead, Karen tried to breathe. "I don't know. I just had this deep sense of loss. Like some part of me had been ripped away."

Angela, sensing a spiritual battle raged over the life of someone dear to her, called for the prayer group to huddle around. "Ladies, let's lift up Karen and her family right now!"

Without hesitation, the women formed a circle and began to plead the blood of Christ for their sister and her family.

Unseen by mortals, Prince Selaphiel fanned the flames of prayer until they glowed with fervent heat. Around them, myriads of angelic beings guarded the ascendant prayers, funneling them upward, protecting them from the enemy. Finally, when the women had exhausted their resources, they fell in silence and allowed their tears to speak on their behalf.

At seeing the spectacle, Prince Selaphiel summoned his commander. "My lord, have you ever seen such display of love where the saints of God joined into the suffering of one of their own? They have moved heaven with their tears?"

Prince Argos lowered himself to one knee, lifted a hand

and silenced the whispers of the heavenly hosts behind him. "Listen. Can you hear it?" He paused, then tipped his head. "There, the soft drumming of falling tears." Like a gentle rain on a tin roof, the broken-hearted tears fell, then began to grow in intensity. Within minutes the heavens shook with the rhythmic beat. And then they stopped. In its place, a rich silence stretched across the void. They had their answer.

Taking a halting breath, Karen stood with the help of her friend. "Thank you ladies, I feel a great burden has been lifted. Now I must find Colt and go home. My husband is waiting for me."

***

As Karen and Colt rode home in silence, a host of angels formed an impenetrable barrier around her car. Leading the troupe, Prince Argos, his glistening sword held high, cut a swath through the blackness. He knew what awaited her and her son and it grieved him, yet he knew his Master was in control.

Karen pressed the remote control and the garage door rose silently. By the time she shut off the engine, Colt had already released his seatbelt and jumped from the backseat. "Mom, can I have a glass of milk and some cookies?"

As he disappeared through the door, she knew she'd agree. It was a routine they'd established for as long as Colt could even walk. Suddenly, his scream sent a jolt of adrenaline surging through her veins like ice crystals.

In a near panic, Karen slammed the car door and ran to her son's side. He knelt over his dad, shaking him, calling his name.

"Call 911, Colt." Her response was instinctive.

Colt snatched the cell phone from his mother's purse, punched in the numbers.

"Glenn, what happened?" Karen pleaded.

Nothing!

"Mom, the lady on the phone wants to talk with you."

Colt handed the phone to his mother and waited as she began answering questions and giving information. Within minutes, an ambulance arrived and a team of medics stormed into the house.

As Karen fielded a bevy of questions, Colt dashed upstairs. A moment later, he ran back down. "Mom, Mom, my medallion ... it's gone!"

The news caused Karen's stomach to knot. Gasping for air, she asked, "Gone? Gone where?"

"It's totally gone. Someone tore up my bedroom looking for it and left it a mess. Come and see for yourself."

Not wanting to leave her husband, yet concerned with the disturbing news, she pushed herself up on shaky legs and followed Colt. One look and she knew what had happened. Someone broke into their house, ransacked his bedroom, and stole the medallion. Glenn must have discovered the break-up, tried to stop it and suffered a blow to the head. Now his life hung by a thread. Once again, the urge to pray overtook her and she slumped to the bed. "Colt, let's pray. Pray with all your might for your dad."

While they held hands and prayed, a gentle knock interrupted them. "Ma'am, we are taking your husband to the hospital. Do you want to ride along? Is there someone you want to call?"

The Myers name came to mind. "Colt, I need to call the Myers. You stay here with them until I get back. When the police arrive, ask Deputy Huntley to take a look around. Maybe he can figure out who did this."

***

Within minutes of the call, three police cruisers rolled to a stop in front of the O'Dell's house. Their flashing lights brought wondering looks from the neighbors. A small group of onlookers gathered in a nearby yard to observe. Meanwhile, Deputy Huntley and his partner, Mark Rigby got out of their cruiser and began collecting information. Knowing it wasn't his job to do a complete investigation, he called in the Criminal Investigation Unit who began their meticulous work of dusting for prints and collecting hair fibers. Before long, a grim picture began to emerge. There was a distinct shoe print on the carpet and one in the flower bed. The lead detective also found a fingerprint on the light switch. Using a handheld scanner, he ran the print.

Is there a problem?" Ty asked.

The detective thrust a sheet of paper in his direction and walked away. Ty scanned the sheet, but found no usable information. "Apparently, the fingerprint didn't match anyone in the national database," he said to anyone who would listen. A rustle of movement caught his attention as the team of investigators huddled around a familiar object.

"Where did you find that?" Ty asked, eyeing a familiar staff more closely.

"In the bushes," one of the investigators said. "You got any idea whose it might be?"

Ty did, but couldn't believe his eyes. *Why would the wise men break into the O'Dell's house? They are friends, for crying out loud. And why would they attack Glenn? It just didn't make sense.*

Deputy Rigby stepped into the circle. "Isn't that one of the wise men's?"

The hair stood up on Ty's neck. His suspicions were voiced by his partner, but he wanted to check it out before it became official. It was too late now. If someone wanted to frame the wise men, they just put the first nail in their coffin.

Sheriff Carlton, having just arrived, poked his head around the corner. "Got anything guys?"

Ty felt sweat run down his back. Speaking first, he tried to defuse the situation. "Yeah, Sheriff. We got an unmatchable fingerprint, some shoe prints and this." He held up the staff. "But I gotta tell ya, I know for certain it couldn't have been the wise men."

"And how would you know that? I saw them at the flag pole the other day. Maybe they've become religious nuts. They may be old, but even old men lose it. They could be turning senile ... or worse."

Sheriff Carlson called his dispatcher. "I want an APB and an arrest warrant for our three *wise men,"* his mocking tone made chicken-flesh crawl up his arms."

Ty knew it was useless to pursue it any further. *Follow the evidence and let the truth defend itself.* That was his motto. "You want me to interview them?"

"No, I'll let the lead investigator handle it. He's got the most experience."

Ty's heart hit rock bottom. There was enough circumstantial evidence to at least hold his friends, maybe even convict them and the one man who could exonerate them lay unconscious in the hospital.

***

While Sheriff Carlton and his team of investigators conferred, the Myers slipped in unnoticed. Having been called to watch Colt, they'd arrived amid the chaotic scene. Seeing Colt's tear-stained face, Cindy immediately wrapped her arms around him and tried to console him, while Jacob kept a guarded ear pointed in the direction of the sheriff.

He had his doubts that it was Balthazar or his friends who'd broken in and attacked Glenn. But proving it would be another thing. He'd already decided he would represent them and listening would help his defense.

After hearing all he could, Jacob leaned closer to his wife. "Look, Cindy, I need to leave you guys for a while. I have a feeling I'm needed down at the police station and I want to get ready."

Cindy eyed her husband with admiration. "You just can't stay out of the courtroom, can you?"

A sheepish grin spread across his face. "It's in my blood, plus, there are three innocent men about to be railroaded. I can't stand by and let that happen."

Cindy leaned forward and kissed him on the forehead. "And I love you all the more for it, but you are not leaving us here. C'mon, Colt."

Chapter Twenty-Two

The drama team assembled in their usual places awaiting Felicia's instructions. She had taken over the rehearsals with the skill of a seasoned play director. By seven-o-five the players began their lines.

Gasper sat, perched on a four-legged stool enjoying the actors recite their lines. To him, it was an opportunity to see some of his students in a different light. Those who gave him the most trouble were transformed into new and interesting characters and he wondered how far they would go in the theatrical world.

Since being assigned the task, he and Felicia threw themselves into the task with total focus. He'd read and re-read the manuscript till he could nearly fill any role, but the singing part had him worried. Over the years, he'd never been able to master the art of carrying a tune, thus, when it came time for him to demonstrate the proper vocal technique, he surrendered the stage to Felicia, much to his delight. Sitting back, he allowed his mind to be carried away on the silvery wings of her voice.

"Okay you guys," she said after several attempts at corralling the unruly actors, "Let's take it from where Hodel and Chava sing."

Sheepishly, the two young people took center stage and began. Madi, the girl singing Hodel's part, began. "For Papa, make him a scholar!" followed by Kristi singing Chava's part, "For Mama, make him rich as a king!" then together, they sang, "For me, well, I wouldn't holler if he were as handsome as anything! ... Matchmaker, matchmaker, make me a match! Find me a find, catch me a catch! Night after night in the dark I'm alone, so find me a match of my own!"

Suddenly, a loud pop sounded somewhere back of the stage and the lights went out.

"Okay, which one of you wise guys threw the breaker," Gasper hollered over the sounds of the girl's screams.

"It wasn't me," said one male voice, followed by a chorus of others.

Felicia grabbed Gasper by the shoulder to steady herself. "What should we do?" Her voice was so close her breath tickled his ear. A gaggle of goose-bumps fluttered down his back.

"Maybe the maintenance man will be here in a minute."

As he spoke, a door opened and closed.

Click!

The beam of a flashlight illuminated a narrow swath and jostled back and forth was heavy boots neared where Gasper and Felicia sat.

"Looks like we blew a breaker, you two sit tight while I check it out." The voice was owned by Wally, the school maintenance man. He was an aging relic, but he knew the infrastructure of the school like the back of his hand. "And it better not be one of your drama queens messing with *my* electrical panel."

"We didn't do it Mr. *Wally,*" a chorus of male voices said in harmony.

For the next forty minutes, Gasper and Felicia listened to boys telling ghost stories and girl's occasional giggles. Then, as quickly as they went out, the lights came back on. Wally emerged from behind the curtain, a satisfied expression on his face.

"It was the main buss. Looks like someone," he cut his eyes in the direction of the boys, "rigged a remote device to the breaker. It took me a while to figure out how to reset it without blowing the whole electrical panel, and then my cell phone blinked out leaving me in total darkness. Anyway, they're on and you still have time to finish your rehearsal. I'll start locking up in about fifteen minutes."

Felicia stood and clapped her hands. "Okay, then let's go over the part between Tevye and Mendel."

Gasper enjoyed her enthusiasm and soon found himself looking forward to being with Felicia as much as he did rehearsing with the drama team.

Clayton, a tall lanky young man slinked on stage followed by a shorter boy playing Mendel.

"As Abraham said," Clayton began, "I'm a st—"

"Stop, that's not how it goes," Felicia interrupted. "Do it again." Her French accent kept the young people from getting too upset with her repeated demands for perfection. It gave the rehearsal an air of European elegance.

Retaking his stance, the young man began again. "As Abraham said, 'I am a stranger in the land ..."

"Moses said that," quipped Mendel, the Rabbi's son.

"Ah, well, as King David said, 'I am slow to speech, and slow of tongue.'"

Right on cue, Mendel corrected him. "That was also Moses."

Gasper's lips moved in sync with the players on stage.

"For a man who was slow of speech he talked a lot," he mouthed the words. A slight chuckle caught in his throat.

Standing, Felicia moved to center stage. "Okay, that's a wrap. It's late, let's call it an evening. See you tomorrow, and work on your lines, young people. We only have three weeks before opening night."

A collective groan rippled across the room and Gasper winked at Felicia. "You're doing great, for an assistant. I feel like I'm just here for the ride."

Felicia toed the carpet. It was obvious to Gasper, she had

feelings for him. Every time he looked at her, her face reddened and she refused to make eye contact. *This is craziness. Here I am, a two-thousand year old Jew from India. One of the famous Magi. And I end up half a world away only to find myself developing feelings for a woman from France.*

All at once, the door in the back of the auditorium swung open and Balthazar and Melchior entered, laughing.

"And what's so funny," Gasper asked, feeling like he was the brunt of an inside joke.

"Oh, nothing, we were just commenting on how quickly things have changed. It wasn't that long ago we stood outside in the cold pretending to be part of the Nativity Scene and look at us. We're fully integrated into society like real people." Balthazar adjusted a new golf shirt he'd recently purchased.

"Pretending?" I thought we were pretty real, especially in the Live Nativity."

Melchior rubbed his chin. "That reminds me, are we going to pull double duty at the O'Dell's and this year's Live Nativity?"

Gasper slumped into a seat. "Oh brother, not the cold again. If we do it, I want to be the Innkeeper." As soon as he said that, he stood and began to mimic the grand gestures of the ancient innkeeper from Bethlehem.

***

The building shook with the force of the auditorium door being yanked open. Colt rushed in gasping for air, followed by the Myers. One look and Balthazar knew something was very wrong.

"What's the matter?" he asked as Colt flung his arms around him.

"Oh Mr. Balthazar, someone broke into our house and attacked my dad. They've taken him to the hospital, he won't wake up." His uncharged voice squeaked out the words.

Balthazar exchanged concerned looks with the Myers.

Melchior stepped closer to the Myers. "What do you know

about this?"

Jacob nodded grimly. "There's more."

"Oh?"

"Colt said something about a medallion missing and the police found one of your staves near the back door. They're on their way here as we speak."

Gasper stared at the others. "And you were saying how quickly things can change. I think we're about to see them change again ... real fast."

Just then, Sheriff Carlson entered the auditorium and locked his thumbs in his belt.

Chapter Twenty-Three

Having overheard some of the detectives talking, Jacob knew he had to act fast. With his wife and Colt in tow, he headed to his new Lexus SUV, a recent acquisition since the return home of Samantha and grandson, Ashton. The entire scenario made his blood boil. *And to think, issuing an arrest warrant for three innocent men on such thin evidence*. Racing to the jail, he felt like a cheap personal injury attorney chasing an ambulance, but this was no neck injury. This was a frame-job if ever there was one.

By the time he stopped by his old office, collected some papers, and arrived at the police station, the wise men had been processed in. He stepped to the counter where a bored deputy sat, staring at a screen. "I am Jacob Myers and I am here to see my clients," his tone resolute.

The officer, a white-haired, portly man who appeared nearing retirement, looked up. "And who are your clients?"

"Don't play dumb with me. You know perfectly well, you are holding three men charged with breaking and entering."

The aging deputy huffed. "Okay, okay, you made your point. They just got their new uniforms and are being taken back to the interview rooms."

Knowing the strategy was to separate the three men and get conflicting stories which they would use to get a confession; Jacob decided to take the frontal approach.

"Not without my presence. Now would you kindly open the door and allow me to confer with my clients before the interviews begin?"

Slowly, the officer pushed himself up and walked to an iron door. Its aging paint was the same as when Jacob had his practice. *Nothing had changed.* The officer punched in a series of numbers followed by a soft click. The door popped open and he swung it wider.

Giving Cindy and Colt a wry smile, Jacob stepped through the opening. The door slammed shut with a loud clang which shook the building. Following the familiar corridor, He made his way to the holding cells, where another officer sat behind a desk. His annoyed expression was all the welcome he received. "I'd like to see my clients before you interview them."

"Sheriff figured you'd show up. The way he sees it, you have a better chance of getting Hannibal Lector out than you do those guys."

So much for being considered innocent in the eyes of the law. Jacob swatted the jab aside.

Seemingly frustrated that Jacob didn't take the bait, the guard stood. "Mind if I inspect your briefcase?"

Jacob complied and laid it on the desk knocking a half-empty cup of coffee on its side. "Sorry, I hope it doesn't mess up the carpet," Jacob said, eyeing the yellowing linoleum.

The officer muttered a few choice words opened the briefcase. After nudging aside its few contents, he slammed it shut. "Don't loan your pen to the inmates," he warned. Jacob knew the procedure but didn't comment. He needed to stay focused not get into a hissing contest with a no-named, desk-pushing, flat-bottomed police officer with a wad of keys.

He lifted the phone and ordered the wise men be brought to the interview room. After a short wait, the phone buzzed and he lifted it to his ear. "Okay, I'll send him in." Inserting the key into the lock, he pulled the door open. "Knock yourself out, councilor." Then he slammed the door shut behind him.

Jacob stepped inside and surveyed his surroundings. The gray paint had not changed, neither had the table and three chairs, but he didn't expect that to have happened. It suddenly dawned on him, they were one chair short. He turned and tapped on the window. An officer opened the door. "What's the matter? Lost your nerve?"

"I need an additional chair," Jacob demanded.

Taken aback, the officer grabbed the one from behind his desk and handed it to him. "I'll be right outside the door if you need me."

Taking his seat, Jacob waited until another door opened and three rather harried men, wearing orange jumpsuits shuffled in; their flip-flops smacking their heels with every controlled step the chains allowed.

After the officer connected each man to a chair, he backed away and took his place in the corner. "Could we have a few minutes ... alone?"

The man huffed and disappeared through the door.

"Gentlemen, fortunately in our country, you are considered innocent until proven guilty beyond a reasonable doubt in a court of law by a jury of your peers. Plus, you have the right to remain silent and not say anything which the prosecution could use against you, and you have the right to an attorney. Which, in this case, is me. Have they read you your Miranda Rights?"

The wise men exchanged glances. "I suppose that's what you call them," Balthazar answered for the others.

"Do you have any questions?"

Balthazar shifted uncomfortably in his metal chair. "Yes, we have lots of questions. But first, let me speak on behalf of the three of us. Whatever evidence they have, has been fabricated or placed there by someone who wanted to make it look like we were the perpetrators, but I can assure you, we are innocent of these charges."

Jacob's face relaxed into a weak smile. Tapping his notes, he said, "Gentlemen, I have heard that comment so many times I've actually come to believe it, but sadly, the jury is not always so quick to come to the same conclusion. My job is to not allow it to go that far. I have hired a friend of mine to do some snooping around. If there is a conspiracy to frame you guys for a crime you didn't commit, we'll get to the bottom of it. For the time being, don't speak to anyone about this case; not your cellmates, the guys in lock-up, the officers, not even the Chaplain. You got that?"

Heads nodded.

"I have a question," Gasper interjected.

"What is it?"

Gasper faced his lawyer. "Where are they going to find a jury of our peers? The last time I checked, they aren't making anymore Magi."

"Good point. I might have to use that argument if it gets that far. In the meantime, let's focus on the positive."

"And what of Mr. O'Dell? Has he regained consciousness?" Balthazar asked.

Jacob shook his head, "I'm afraid not. Seems he's slipped into a coma. If he recovers, he may not even remember the events of this evening. We need to prepare for the worst and hope for the best."

"And what is the worst?" Melchior pressed.

Jacob shoved his hand in his pocket. "Worst case scenario is, Glenn dies, and you guys are charged with murder, but let's not focus on that. Let's pray and work for a positive outcome. What we need is fresh evidence which is irrefutable. Now is there anything else you can remember about this evening, something you might have missed. Did anyone see you?"

Balthazar's face brightened. "We were at the school. Gasper was working with about a dozen students on a musical titled, *Fiddler on the Roof,* and we were helping the stage hands with the backdrops and props.

"And how long were you there?" Jacob asked.

Balthazar rubbed his goatee. "School let out at four and we worked with the students from about five in the evening to eight-thirty."

"And you say, there were about a dozen students who can vouch that all three of you were there the whole time?"

Balthazar glanced at his friends who exchanged nods. "Yes, we were all there. Even Felicia can give testimony of our presence. She was at Gasper's side the whole evening."

Looking at Gasper, he asked, "Can you explain how one of your staves was found at the O'Dell's house?"

"No," Gasper answered. "It has been missing for several days."

"Any idea who may have taken it?"

"None."

"How do you explain your thumbprint on the light switch in Colt's bedroom and on the doorknob of the back door?"

Gasper leaned back in his chair. "I have been to the O'Dell's a number of times. As a matter of fact, we actually stayed in Glenn's attic for several months while we sought for your daughter and grandson."

The memory of those trying days creased Jacob's forehead. "Yes, I remember, and I owe you a great debt of gratitude, both for your efforts and your word of testimony. I feel this is the least that I can do to represent you pro-bono."

"My Latin is a bit weak, but doesn't pro bono public mean you're doing this at no charge?" Gasper asked.

Nodding, Jacob's face brightened. "Yes, that's right."

The wise men exchanged confusion glances. "Well, how much do you generally charge if it weren't?" Balthazar inquired.

Not wanting to divulge his $1000.00 a day fee for defending a client in a criminal case, Jacob searched the floor while he considered his options. "Let's just say, it's a lot more than you guys are making as teachers ... combined."

Gasper took a dry swallow. "If we get out of this, maybe I should consider becoming a consultant. You know, 'Wise man for hire,'" his fingers formed air quotes.

Melchior reached to pat his young friend on the back, but

his hand suddenly snapped back as the chain restrained his movements. "What do you mean, *if*? Surely Jacob can clear up this mess. Anyone in their right mind knows we wouldn't attack Mr. O'Dell ... right?" his voice wavered.

"Don't be so sure of yourself. There are forces at work who would like nothing better than to see God's holy men brought to shame and disgrace. Now, is there anything else you remember that I could use in your defense?" Jacob asked.

As Balthazar scuffed the floor with his sandal, it made a tight squeak and he shook his head. "No, nothing."

"Actually, there is one thing." All eyes turned to Gasper. "Something blew the main breaker and we were in the dark for about forty-five minutes."

"Any idea how it happened?"

"No Jacob. The maintenance man, Mr. Wally said it looked like someone had fooled around with the main bus. Not that I understood a word he said."

Jacob nodded and made a few notes on his legal pad. "Anything else?"

"No, Sir."

"Good. I would appreciate it if you didn't mention that to the sheriff until I talk with Mr. Wally, understood?"

Heads bobbed.

As he spoke, Sheriff Carlton stepped into the room. "Are you ready?"

Jacob stood. "Yes, but I insist you interview my clients together."

Shaking his head, the sheriff huffed. "Nope, no can do. We do it by the book or not at all."

Turning, he watched three officers enter and begin to usher Balthazar, Melchior, and Gasper from the room. "Then I insist I be present when each of them is interviewed."

Carlton lowered his forehead and peered directly into Jacob's eyes. "Look councilor, I know it looks bad for your clients, but I want to get to the truth just as badly as you do. So let me do my job, you do yours and let's see who comes out on top."

His comments didn't leave Jacob with a good feeling. He'd seen what evidence could do. What he needed was new evidence, convincing evidence. Better yet, he needed Glenn's testimony.

Chapter Twenty-Four

Three hours after they entered the interrogation rooms, Balthazar, Melchior, and Gasper emerged feeling rather shaken, but confident they'd told the truth. Glancing at Jacob, Balthazar greeted him a weary smile. "Well, what's next?"

Jacob led the men into an empty room and looked directly at them. "I have arranged bond for you, so you can go home. Just don't leave the country while I'm gone."

"Where are you going?" Gasper asked on cue.

"Chicago, it's in America," Jacob said, not knowing why Gasper showed such interest.

Gasper stepped up and spoke theatrically, "Chicago, America? We are going to New York, America. We'll be neighbors," quoting Lazar Wolf's lines flawlessly.

Jacob couldn't help chuckling as he patted him on the shoulder. "Great timing, but seriously, don't leave town. It's just a formality, but the detectives might want to question you further. If so, don't hesitate to call me. And don't talk to anyone from the press, no matter how nice they seem. Remember, your words can and will be used against you in a court of law without my presence to shield you."

Melchior relaxed his stance. "I read just this morning in Psalms Ninety-one, verse four. 'He shall cover you with his feathers, and under his wings, you shall trust: his truth shall be our shield and buckler.'"

***

By the time Balthazar and the others returned home, they found Felicia sitting on the porch, in a deck chair. Her hands held a bucket with the familiar red and white letters, KFC, printed on its exterior.

"How long have you been waiting for us?" Gasper inquired, taking the bucket from her hands.

"I got a call from Mrs. Myers about twenty minutes ago. She said you were on your way and would probably be famished."

"It reminds me of the good old days up in Colt's attic," Gasper said, a whimsical smile tugging at the corners of his mouth.

Felicia blinked at his statement, her rounded eyes begging for more information.

"I believe you need to explain yourself. It seems your friend looks rather confused." Balthazar's comment caused Gasper's face to redden. They had not shared their little secret on how they arrived in the twenty-first century with anyone outside a close-knit circle. Telling Felicia had its risks and he hoped Gasper would guard his words. Fortunately, Gideon came to the rescue.

Melchior protested loudly and held the bucket over his head.

Sniffing the aroma of freshly baked biscuits and fried chicken, Gasper rubbed his midsection. "My stomach says it thinks my throat has been cut."

"Mine too," Balthazar added, following his friends into the house. "Care to join us?"

Felicia shook her head. "No, it's late and I have tons of stuff to do to get ready for tomorrow." As she spoke, she backed down the driveway.

Gasper took a step in her direction, then stopped. Maybe it was better this way. He didn't need the distraction of having someone in his life right now. Or maybe he did? Confused, he stepped back into the house.

While they ate, Melchior brought up the question that was on all their minds. "Who knew of the medallion's existence? That's what's got me baffled."

Balthazar dropped a meatless chicken bone into the empty bucket, wiped his lips with a napkin and peered at his friends. "I don't know, but whoever broke into the O'Dell's wanted us implicated."

"There can't be that many other suspects. We killed most, if not all the members, of the White Coven."

"Not all, Melchior. Samantha told Ty there were no less than eighteen members. We took out four or five the first time and probably a dozen including the witch in the cave. That leaves two. We know one is the former sheriff."

Gasper collected the remaining containers and shoved them into the trash can. "Maybe you should call her in the morning."

"Good idea," Balthazar answered, but as he did, the phone rang. After three rings, Gasper asked, "Are you going to answer it?"

"Let it go to the answering machine," he said.

A moment later, a click announced the beginning of the recording. Since none of the wise men knew how to set the recorder up, Colt did the honor. His cambric voice could have landed him in the Vienna Boys Choir, but for now, it served as a reminder of how quickly things change. In the short time since making the recording, his formerly crystal clear tone had deteriorated into a throaty squawk which turned his cheeks rosy red and sent him scurrying.

After the pre-recorded message ended, Ty Huntley began speaking. "Uh, guys, if you're there, pick up. Samantha and I are worried about you."

Before the message ended, Balthazar snatched up the phone. "Hello, Deputy Huntley." A pause held everyone's attention.

"Yes, I know you're off duty."

Listening,

"Yes, I know. I shouldn't be so formal. I guess it's my upbringing."

He caught his breath as Ty continued.

"All right, in the future, I'll call you Ty. But I'm sure you didn't call to get me to be less formal."

Gasper and Melchior exchanged whimsical smiles as Balthazar bantered back and forth. Finally, he got down to business.

"I appreciate your concern. Jacob Myers is representing us. We'll be fine."

A pause.

"No, we don't need anything, just your prayers. Oh, and one thing. Could you ask Miss Myers if she recalls the names of any of the members of the White Coven?"

A frustrating pause filled the connection as Ty held his hand over the phone. Finally, Balthazar's wait was rewarded.

"Yes, I have a pencil and script." Nodding, he jotted down the names of the former coven.

After he hung up, Gasper and Melchior peered over their leader's stooped shoulders. From the on-line obituary, they were able to cross off all but three names. One they knew ... Randy Baker. The others sent a chill throughout the room. Dr. Damian and Mrs. Joann Littleton ...

Chapter Twenty-Five

Gathered around the wobbly table in Baker's shack, three men popped the lids off bottles of ice-cold beer. It wasn't long before their drunken laughter spilled outside disturbing the solace of the forest surrounding the decrepit building.

Leaning back in his chair on two legs, Baker reminisced. "You should have seen him. Man—he looked like a deer in the headlights just before I whacked him. His skull cracked like an egg and his knees buckled. For a moment, I thought I offed him, but I checked. He was still breathing. I think he wet himself, too." Another round of laughter broke out as the three men tapped the tops of their beer bottles together in a mock salute.

Having successfully broken into the O'Dell's house and made off with the witch's medallion, Randy, and his men celebrated late into the evening. Unseen by Baker and his men were scores of red eyes glowering at them from the shadows. The creature's talons lashed out with blood-lust at their drunken hosts. If it were possible, they would have already sunk their teeth into each man and sucked their life right out of them, but they waited.

Fingering the medallion, Randy turned it over several times and wondered what the inscriptions meant. Obviously Mrs. White knew and drew upon the power it commanded. *If I could only read it, I would have power beyond my wildest imagination ... but how?* The more he focused his attention on the cryptic letters, the more it pulled him in. He began to see things, dark images, claws, scales. “Do you see them?”

Archie leaned forward, his bleary eyes peered under sagging eyelids. “What’d ya say?” he slurred.

Baker glared at him. “I said, do you see them ... they’re all around us,” waving his arm in a wide circle.

Archie glanced around the room. Not seeing anything, he wobbled his head. “Man, you’re drunker than me and I’m pretty drunk.” He doubled over, laughing uncontrollably. “There ain’t nothing in this here room but us thieves.”

As he spoke, a buzzing sound started on the other side of the room and grew in intensity. All at once, Archie swatted at something. Missing, he swatted at it again. “What is that?” he demanded. Stumbling to his feet, he gripped the edge of the table to keep from tumbling over. His eyes grew wild with anger as his invisible nemesis circled his head. He lifted his hand and swung.

Crack!

“What did you do that for, you fool?” Randy raged, rubbing the welt on the back of his head.

Archie continued to flail as the source of the buzzing zinged past his ear. He swung again striking himself and losing his balance. “Some insect is attacking me.” His red eyes scanning the room wildly. Not seeing what it was, he stomped across the room and pulled his 45. Caliber revolver from his holster.

“Put that thing away, Archie,” Mike, the other co-conspirator, said, ducking behind his chair.

Archie waved his weapon around trying to get a bead on his attacker.

Bang!

The room shook from the gun blast. Pieces of ceiling tile and wood showered down upon the three men.

Angered by his miss, Archie swung around. His two hands gripped the handle. A black spot appeared on Pete’s cheek and

Archie took aim.

Bang, bang!

Archie stumbled backward, a shocked expression on his face. Clutching his chest, he slumped to the floor. "I see them." Lifting his weapon, he tried to aim again.

Two more shots exploded from Baker's weapon, ending Archie's miserable life. As his last breath eked from his throat, a pair of claws gripped the man's soul. And, like pulling a butterfly from its chrysalis before its time, dragged him kicking and screaming into outer darkness.

***

As the deafening concussion from Baker's weapon subsided, the flutter of leathery wings filled the room. Glancing around, Mike backed into a corner, the whites of his eyes stabbing through the growing darkness. All at once, his body rose until his feet dangled in the air. Kicking wildly, he hung, suspended between the floor and ceiling. Then, like a rag doll he was slammed against the wall. Slumping down, he began to choke. Eyes bulging, his fingers clawed at his throat as an unseen hand closed around his windpipe. His face turned a deep purple, while Baker stood helplessly by watching his partner's death-struggle. Not knowing what to do, Baker lifted the medallion and held it at arm's length.

"I command you to release him," he yelled, his voice barely loud enough to be heard over the beat of the wings.

A moment later, Mike's head jerked to the left, snapping his neck. His body shuttered one last time and fell limp. Another victim was silently dragged from his body and cast into the flames.

Still holding the medallion as a shield, Baker took a step back. Whatever was in the room had a thirst for blood. He just hoped it wasn't his blood it sought next. Stumbling over Archie's body, Baker hit the floor and rolled. He felt the creature's icy breath on the back of his neck and fought to keep from screaming. He knew enough about the spirit world not to beg for his life. What they wanted, what they always wanted was surrender ... submission. Whether he believed in God or not was irrelevant. He did, however, believe in Satan, and he felt his presence.

Taking a halting breath, Baker forced himself up on shaky legs and extended his hand, still holding the medallion. "Teach me how to read the inscriptions."

The dark presence withdrew enough to leer at him through two slitted eyes.

Baker stared into them, his breath frozen in his throat. If he attempted to run, he knew his life would end suddenly and violently. Then he heard it. At first it was a whisper, then, like a morning breeze through the tops of the pines. "Read the Book of Incantations."

Baker felt his breath leave his lungs. "The Book of Incantations? Where can I find it?"

The rustle of wings told him the creature wasn't finished. "The White Witch's house," emphasizing the s's.

The air scintillated with demonic energy and Baker found it hard to swallow. "Yes, I will do it ... Master."

Suddenly, the light whisper deepened into a guttural ... "Good."

And then it was alone.

***

Hours later, great muddy drops of sweat ran down Baker's face, and he pulled an old rag from his pocket. Still huffing from exertion, he stared into the black hole he'd dug for his two former associates. After shooting Archie and seeing Mike strangled to death by an unseen hand, he was in no condition to report their deaths, and burying them in the woods was his only option. Plus, with the investigation still open, he couldn't trust his replacement, Sheriff Carlson, not to take an interest in his profession. He leaned heavily on the shovel trying to catch his breath. Finally, when he thought he'd dug halfway to China, he rolled the two plastic entombed bodies into the hole and covered them with a heavy layer of Georgia clay. When he'd finished, he dragged several tree limbs over the domed earth to conceal it from unwanted eyes.

"Maybe I should dig one more grave while I'm at it ... for Mr. Glenn O'Dell." He said between exerted breaths. He knew if Glenn regained consciousness he could blow the whole operation. He had to act fast and he needed to get that Book of Incantations even faster. But with the police watching the wise men around the clock, he couldn't afford stirring up a hornet's nest with another break-in.

Knowing Dr. Damian would never agree to killing Glenn O'Dell, he was on his own. *Somehow I need to eliminate Mr. O'Dell and get that Book of Incantations without drawing attention.*

Fingering the medallion, he felt a dark presence beckoning him into his hide-out. Sitting bolt straight, Baker held his breath. Had the spirit returned for more blood? Should he run? He couldn't sit by and let that thing strangle him like he did Mike. On the other hand, why hadn't it killed him already? *No, I'll sit perfectly still. Maybe it has a message for me. Instructions. Yes, I'll wait.*

Feeling the hair on his neck bristle, Baker remained motionless while the presence, like an angry beast, hovered nearby.

Ty Huntley is getting too close. He suspects us. The dark presence whispered, its icy breath tickle his neck. Shiver-flesh crept down his back until he nearly lost control of his loins.

"What do you want me to do?"

The spirits of anger and fear forced its talons deeper into Baker's psyche. "Maybe you should have dug three more graves. Your thinking was too small. I likes graves. Do you ... like graves?"

Baker couldn't determine if he was thinking these thoughts or if it was the spirit of darkness. Either way, the notion of him digging his own grave sent a wave of panic all over him.

Fearing whichever way he answered could be fatal, Baker forced air through his parched throat. "Yes, I like graves."

The spirit released a deep, throaty laugh. "Yes, good and soon you will join me, but first I have a job for you. I need you to dig three more graves. One for each of the wise men. Then go and find the book. I will tell you what to do next."

"But why must I kill the wise men? Why can't I just go and break into Mrs. White's old house, take the Book of Incantations and leave?"

"No," the voice boomed, "because I am thirsty for blood ... their blood. Plus, if Mr. O'Dell recovers, he will tell who attacked him and it will be your blood I drink."

"But why must the wise men die?"

"They have powers which they know not and must never discover. If that bungling fool, the Witch of Endor, had destroyed them like she was supposed to, we wouldn't be having this conversation. As it is, they have not remembered that they are far more than mere wise men. They are wizards of the first order, like that of Moses, Elijah, and Elisha.

***

Prince Argos held his position just above the shack where Baker and his host communed. Having overheard their plans, he nodded to his most trusted warriors, Prince Leo and Prince Uriel. "My friends, I fear the forces of wickedness are already at work. A new and dangerous presence has emerged and his power is greater than that of Dandalion's. If Baker gets his hands on the Book of Incantations, this new enemy will use Randy Baker to gain access to the door to the abyss. This we cannot allow."

Prince Leo shifted his bow from one shoulder to the other. "But my lord, what would happen should he do this thing?"

Argos peered at the two figures in the shack; one human, the other a dark shadow with it clawed feet deeply planted in Baker's skull. "If he gains access to the door of the abyss, he could release all the demons of hell."

"My lord, would the Almighty allow such a thing?" Prince Leo asked.

"The door to the abyss will indeed be opened and yes, all the dark forces of evil will one day flood this world. This may very well be part of the Almighty's plan, but from what I understand, it is not to be until late in Daniel's week of Trouble."

His two compatriots remained silent. They had never been told the mystery of the ages and how the consummation of days would end. And if they had, they would not have been able to comprehend their meaning. This glimpse into the future, which their mighty prince just revealed, boggled their minds.

Finally, Prince Leo spoke although he knew he would probably not understand the answer. "What should we do? Should we even try?"

Prince Argos held his shoulders firm. "Yes, we must try. Remember, the battle is not ours. Satan is a defeated foe. Our first priority is to protect Mr. O'Dell and our three friends at all costs. As to the dark force controlling Mr. Baker, leave him to me."

Chapter Twenty-Six

The dark circles around Colt's eyes spoke of long, sleepless nights. His sullen expression made Karen's heart ache. Up until recently, he had been a good soldier. But as the hours stretched, his resolve seemed to flag. Seeing his little hands clenched into tight balls, she could only guess the battle which raged in his mind. Jutting his chin, he asked, "Mom, why did God let this happen?"

Karen stood and faced the hospital window. Outside, several floors below, cars entered and departed the parking lot with no knowledge of the pain she was feeling or the pain she knew Colt was feeling. It was like they were disconnected from the rest of the world.

Pastor Scott and Angela along with the church care group had come and gone. Each took their turn praying for Glenn's complete recovery, that God's will would be done, that all things would work for the good of those who love God. Yet Karen felt a deep sense of loneliness. *Has God abandoned me? Has He abandoned Colt?* She wrapped her arms around her waist and sighed deeply. "I don't know, Honey. Sometimes God does things we will never understand." Her answer neither satisfied her nor Colt.

"It's my fault." His tone was flat, colorless.

"Colt, why would you say such a thing?"

"Because it's true. If I didn't take that medallion thing, those guys wouldn't have broke into our house and—" his words morphed into sobs.

"Colt, Honey, if your dad was in prayer meeting like he

said he would, he wouldn't have been home. wouldn't have stumbled upon him, and all they v done was steal the medallion. So really, it's his fau were going to blame anyone."

"So you're saying dad is to blame?"

His logic was unarguable. Glenn had become so preoccupied with work that he'd shut out his family ... including his church family. It cost him his deacon's position and it might cost him his life.

The more Karen thought about it, the madder she became. Her mind screamed, *Glenn, why didn't you listen. I tried to tell you, the pastor warned you, church friends counseled you against putting things in front of God, but no. You wouldn't listen. Now look at you.*

Tears scalded Karen's cheeks as she considered life without her husband. Being married to a workaholic was no better than being married to an alcoholic. It was a constant roller coaster. First, there were the promises to do better, then the dashed hope, the disappointments followed by moments of recovery. It all blurred into a menagerie of shattered dreams. Slumping in a chair next to the bed, she pulled a corner of the sheet which covered her husband's sleeping form and dabbed her eyes. Looking into her son's innocent face, she prayed, *If the best thing to come out of this marriage was Colt, I'd do it all over again, but he needs his daddy. Lord, would you reach out and touch my husband?*

***

Hearing voices in the distance, Glenn listened, tried to comprehend them, but his mind refused to cooperate. The sharp pain stabbed the back of his head with every pulse. It was like sitting in the center of Big Ben at noon, the pounding relentless. Cold fingers pressed against his arm followed by a sharp prick. A moment later, warmth crept up his arm, and he felt himself drifting.

How long he floated was not measured in seconds, or

minutes or even hours. It was measured in breaths, in heartbeats ...

Movement.

I'm being carried.

Sounds ...voices ... someone whispering in my ear.

Ouch, that hurt, he thought as one of the paramedics flashed a light in his eyes.

I'm so tired, but I want to wake up?

Like climbing a mountain of sand, Glenn forced his legs and arms to claw upward, only to lose his footing and tumble to the bottom.

In the silence, Glenn sensed a presence drawing near him. Unsure of whether it was real or imagined, he welcomed it, hoping it was his wife or son.

Where have you been, son? The presence asked. He spoke with such tenderness that Glenn yearned to hear more, but instead ... silence.

Finally, Glenn sensed it was his turn to speak. Struggling, he tried to form a cogent thought, but the best he could do was ... *I've been busy.* He knew it was an excuse. He'd repeated it so many times he'd begun to believe it himself.

Busy, hmm. I remember a woman named, Martha. She was busy, too.

Glenn knew where this conversation was going. His pastor mentioned it in a sermon a few weeks ago or was it several months. *Had it been that long?*

Yes, it had been that long. The presence whispered.

It suddenly occurred to him that this presence knew his every thought.

And how about your devotional life? How's that been going?

Glenn tried to remember the last time he'd cracked open his Bible or led his family in prayer. *Good point.*

Yes, now what am I going to have to do to bring you back into a growing relationship with me?

Relationship? I'm your child, what more do you want? Again, Glenn knew the answer, but he refused to acknowledge it.

What do I need to take from you before you make me Lord of your life? Your business? Your wife? ... your son? ... your health?

The questions cut through deep into Glenn's heart. His priorities were skewed and he knew it. For as long as he could remember, it was work, hobbies, family, and church, trailing a distant fourth. His spiritual relationship fell somewhere between going to the doctor for a physical and having his teeth cleaned.

I get it, Lord. I've been so focused on being successful, that I've failed at being your child or being a husband and father.

The presence drew closer. *That's a start. Now, what are you going to do about it?"*

Repent?

Define repent. The presence said.

Turn from the direction I'm going and go the opposite direction?

A bit simplistic, but it will do. Can you be more specific?

Glenn took a dry swallow. *Well, I repent of being a workaholic. I relinquish my right to manage my businesses to your Lordship. I'll even cancel my membership at the golf club.*

And? The presence prompted.

Focus Glenn, focus, what more does he want? And put you first in my family, reestablish a personal devotional life and commit to faithful attendance and participation at church.

Do you mean it? The question resonated deeply in Glenn's psyche. He was so used to negotiating, and making deals, that it seemed natural to throw God a few disposables, but these were not items on a checklist. This was tearing up the list and starting all over. *What am I going to get out of this deal?*

Your life! His tone darkened.

Glenn had his answer. *Yes, Lord. I mean it. With all my heart, I mean it.*

Good ...

Glenn held still, waiting, listening. *Was that it? Had the presence of the Lord departed? Was He checking my motives? Will I suddenly wake-up and find it was all a dream?*

Like a gentle embrace, the presence of the Lord drew near, nearer than he'd been since the earliest days of his spiritual journey. As he waited, warmth invaded his body melting away the coldness which gripped his heart and illuminating his clouded mind.

When am I going to wake-up?

Soon, my son. I have a work to do in Karen's and Colt's hearts, too. For now, rest. When I have accomplished my work, I will call for you.

Chapter Twenty-Seven

It had been a fitful night for Ty Huntley. Visions of a great angelic battle played over and over in his mind like a video game. Though in his spirit, he knew it was not a game, it was deadly serious. Since sleep refused to come, he scooped up his tattered Bible and headed to the one place where he felt safe ... connected. It was the prayer gazebo located near his church. It was there his father had fought and won many-a spiritual battle.

Getting out of his car, he scanned the diamond-spangled sky. A heavy sigh escaped his lungs and he wished he had Samantha by his side. Caught in between his duties as a police officer and his loyalty to his fellow believers, Ty felt his chest compress. His instincts, keen eye for detail and knowledge of spiritual warfare kept him searching for the truth. Several things didn't add up. How did the wise men get across town and back in only forty minutes? Why would they be so sloppy as to leave incriminating evidence? And why did they have to steal the medallion when Colt would have gladly given it to them if they asked for it?

After spending an hour in the gazebo, it became clear to him what he had to do. He returned to the scene of the crime ... O'Dell's house. By then, the moon had come out from behind a veil of clouds and illuminated the area in a soft golden glow. As he retraced his steps, Ty couldn't shake the feeling he'd overlooked a detail. His inspection of the rooms revealed nothing. The house held its secrets, refusing to relinquish them to just anyone. He stepped through the back door and inhaled the cool night air. *What am I missing, Lord?* Seeing an impression in the flowerbed, Ty knelt down and took a closer look. It was a shoe print in the soft soil. Using his camera, he took several pictures. *I wonder who made this?* With his new evidence, he reentered the house and began to try to get a match. Finding none, he was fairly certain it didn't belong to anyone on the CSI unit. *I think I'll just keep this to myself, in the event things turn against Gasper, since it was his staff the investigators found.*

***

Later that day, Ty went to the high school. By then, news of the wise men's troubles had spread like the plague leaving the student body in a dark mood. The few teachers who agreed to talk had been instructed to repeat the mantra, "I've no comment."

Frustrated, Ty retreated to his cruiser. As he crossed the parking lot, he heard his name. Turning, he saw a young woman approaching him rather breathlessly. Her warm eyes communicated interest, but he also saw fear. Her quick glances over her shoulder confirmed his suspicion. As she neared, he noticed her hands were shaking.

"Officer, my name is Felicia Beauchamp. I am an exchange teacher from France." As she spoke, she took another glance over her shoulder. It was obvious she was not comfortable talking with a police officer. Or was there something else?

"Uh, could we talk somewhere less conspicuous?"

Ty followed her gaze from the principal's office window back to her. "Sure, would you like to go to the police depart—"

"No!"

Her response was as quick as it was determined.

"There is a bookstore not far from here. I know the owners, they're good people. Meet me there in five minutes."

Ty nodded and continued toward his vehicle, but just as his hand reached the door, he heard his name, again.

"Officer Huntley."

This time, it was the principal and he wasn't happy.

"I understand you were bothering some of my teachers." His eyes darkened as he spoke.

Squaring his shoulders, Ty took a step in Davis' direction. "That's right, is there a problem?"

The principal crossed his arms. "Yes, as a matter of fact, there is. I just got off the phone with Sheriff Carlson and he's as upset at your being here as I am. You have no authority to be here harassing my teachers. You're not officially on the case involving the wise men and you've crossed the line. If you return, I'll have you up on charges. Is that clear?"

Ty knew he was right, but he had to try. Relaxing his posture, Ty softened his tone. "You're right, I'm not here officially, but these are my friends. I had a few questions that kept bugging me. You understand, don't you?"

The principal remained stoic.

"Okay, so you don't understand, but that's all right. I won't bother your precious teachers anymore." Turning on his heels, he stifled a chuckle. *Maybe I can get what I need to know from Miss Beauchamp.*

***

By the time Ty found the bookstore, he was ten minutes late. Fearing he'd missed Miss Beauchamp, he stepped inside and was immediately greeted by the owner, a well-maintained sixtyish woman with a bright smile. "Hi, can I help you?"

Ty paused long enough to scan the area, wishing he had the time to just sit and read. "No Ma'am, I was looking for someone."

"Oh, okay. Well, if you're looking for Miss Beauchamp, she's in the back. She'll be out in a minute. As she spoke, a young lady emerged from around a bookshelf. Her large brown eyes flung questions in his direction.

Extending her hand, she smiled and waited. Ty took the proffered hand and returned her smile. "Relax, I'm not here on official business. I just have a few questions."

Felicia rolled her shoulders in an attempt to relax. "Could we sit? I feel so, so conspicuous."

Seeing a couple of wing-backed chairs, he led her to a private corner and took a seat. The aroma of freshly brewed coffee wafted from a coffee maker. "Coffee?" he offered.

Nodding, Felicia's face relaxed into a soft smile. "I'd love a cup."

Ty filled two mugs with the store's logo on the side and handed one to Felicia.

She wrapped her fingers around the sturdy mug and inhaled deeply. "Ah, Kirk's coffee. I love the Dominion blend."

Taking a sip, Ty let the rich flavor tantalize his taste buds. It was nice just to sit and not be constantly on the move. It was quite a change of pace since becoming a police officer. And maintaining a growing relationship with Samantha, Ashton, and her parents only added to his crazy life.

After a moment, he placed his mug on a coffee stand made of stacked books, pulled his notebook from his back pocket, and flipped to the page with blank space.

By then, Felicia had gotten comfortable and faced him expectantly.

"How well do you know the wise men?"

After a moment's reflection, Felecia's face darkened. "Not very well ... except for Mr. Gasper. He's nice."

"Nice, meaning—"

"If you're thinking he was involved in the break-in and the attack on Mr. O'Dell, no. He couldn't have done it."

"You're sure."

"Oui ... I mean, yes. We were rehearsing with the drama team from five to eight-thirty."

"And you were together the whole evening."

"Oui, sorry, yes," she let her voice fade.

"What is it? Do you remember something?"

She nodded. "Right in the middle of rehearsal, a loud pop sounded and the lights went out. We sat in total darkness for about forty minutes."

Ty felt a cold snake squiggle in his stomach. "Did you find out why the lights went out?"

Felicia licked her lips. "No, the maintenance man, Mr. Wally, said something about a remote device. We just thought one of the students did it as a practical joke."

A practical joke, hmm. Right at the time a crime was being committed. I'll bet whoever did the break-up didn't expect Miss Beauchamp to be sitting next to the main suspect.

"Miss Beauchamp, have the detectives questioned you about this?"

Shaking her head, she answered succinctly. "No, I don't think they even know I'm helping with the musical."

Ty handed her his business card with his name, and phone number. "Miss. Beauchamp, your testimony is really important. I'm going to ask one of my colleagues from the police department to stop by and take your testimony. Would you be willing to answer their questions?"

Felicia fumbled with the card. "I, I don't know, if it will help Mr. Gasper, I suppose so."

As Ty left, he couldn't shake the feeling that someone was watching them.

Chapter Twenty-Eight

The late Thursday afternoon sun peered down on the hospital's west side causing glimmers of razor sharp light to attack anyone who dared cross its path. Life within the air-conditioned halls of the hospital continued at a harried pace. Ignoring its hustle and bustle, Dr. Damian lurked outside the O'Dell's hospital room. The clock reminded him that he was nearing the end of his shift, but he wanted to stop by and see how the boy was doing. Since he overheard Colt asking his mother that heart-wrenching question, why did God let this happen?' he'd been looking for an opportunity to enter.

After losing his mother to cancer as a young boy, and seeing his father drink himself into an early grave, Dr. Damian asked himself that same question. Seeking an answer, he chased every kind of vice and device the world had to offer. His involvement in the coven was just one in a series of short-term commitments. At first, it was in a gang, then a fraternity, later, the united socialist's society, only to be replaced by his involvement in the dark arts. His marital life was a mirrored image of his abysmal social life. After three failed marriages, he'd given up on love. His only lasting commitment now was to his dog, a large golden retriever, and even that ended when he ran away. He didn't blame him, however, but he did miss him.

Over the years, Dr. Damian learned to co-exist in a world of pain, hope and devastating loss ... with him caught somewhere in the middle. There was one thing, however, that always ate at his gut ... it was when a child faced him with rounded eyes and asked, "Why?"

The notion of turning to religion for answers seemed simplistic. As a doctor, he'd learned to deal in facts, not faith. Yet even then, with all his medical expertise, his training, and his skill, was it not faith in the healing arts that made him get up and go to work every morning? He knew the answer, but it didn't satisfy him. His record of success was marred with enough failures to keep any man humble ... and searching. All he could do was his best and hope things turned out.

Hope.

The word lodged in his thoughts like a chicken bone in the throat. *I don't want a vague hope in some relic like a rabbit's foot or that ridiculous medallion. What I want, what I really need is confidence ... assurance that what I believe is not only worth living for, but worth dying for, and that's what Mrs. O'Dell has.*

***

Having placed a guard around the O'Dell's, Prince Argos was surprised to see Dr. Damian getting so close to the Glenn's room. Knowing the man's past association with the former sheriff concerned him. *Could the doctor have an ulterior motive in being there?* Nodding to Prince Uriel, he watched his fiery subordinate take up a shielding stance between Dr. Damian and the O'Dell's.

"Make certain he does nothing to touch God's anointed," Prince Argos said in a low tone.

Uriel's fingers gripped the spear tighter. "Yes, my lord. My spear will pierce his heart before he gets within ten feet of the O'Dells."

Satisfied he'd established a perimeter around all the saints in the North Hampton community, Prince Argo retook his position high above the township and watched the horizon. They were out there ... the dark forces of the enemy, that he knew, but their next move was a mystery and he had to be ready. He didn't have to wait long ...

***

By the time Sunday rolled around, Balthazar, Melchior, and Gasper were more than ready for a spiritual feast. Upon their arrival, they found the parking lot full and another packed house. They even had to split up just to find a seat.

From his vantage point, Balthazar could hear Mr. Clavender conferring with a couple of the deacons just before the main worship service began. "Look, guys, have your phones ready. Every time Scott says something or quotes somebody, do a quick fact check, then send it to me. I have already caught him plagiarizing Spurgeon, and Moody in Sunday School."

Balthazar felt hot blood coursing through his veins. He didn't like the disrespectful way Mr. Clavender referred to his pastor. Whatever happened to 'giving double honor, to the man of God?' He'd warned Cecil about causing division and even reported what he was doing to the pastor, but for reasons known only to the pastor, he chose not to act. In his sermon notes, he did reference his source material, but no one would know that if they didn't get the notes at the beginning of class. But he had the distinct impression that Mr. Clavender was out for blood.

The musical portion of the service began, interrupting Balthazar's musings. He did his best to learn the choruses, but some of them left him wondering about their spiritual depth. The occasional hymn greatly warmed Balthazar's heart and he longed for more. Even Gasper participated in the singing, and to his surprise, Balthazar didn't hear any off tunes coming from the other end of that pew.

An air of anticipation settled over the auditorium as the service moved along. After the last special, Balthazar leaned forward as the pastor took to the podium. Its crystalline surface glistened under the glaring lights making a sharp contrast between it and the darkened platform. All at once, the large screen television flickered to life and the title of Pastor Wyatt's message appeared. With ease, he moved from point to point citing scripture and making the application personal. Exactly forty-three minutes later, Pastor Scott stepped to the well of the auditorium and began an impassioned plea for sinners to turn their hearts to the Lord. Balthazar joined many others in prayer for a true moving of God in that place.

By the time the pastor had finished, Clavender was on his feet moving to where Pastor Wyatt stood.

"Scott," Cecil said, followed by a gaggle of deacons. "May we have a word with you?"

Pastor Wyatt, paused in the middle of greeting a new convert to face the group. "Yes, what is this all about?"

As he waited, the deacons formed a tight circle around them, keeping Balthazar and the others from interfering. "In your sermon, five times, you quoted other men and didn't give them credit. You are guilty of plagiarizing."

Before Balthazar could enter the fray, Bro. Burris broke through the barrier and stood next to his pastor. "Pastor, is it true you quoted famous men of the past?"

Scott scanned the faces of the men accusing him. He took a calming breath before speaking. "No, not directly. I will admit to using their thoughts for ideas, but I've been very careful not to quote them directly."

Burris' face beamed and he slapped his pastor on the back. "That's what I thought. I do the same thing in my business. For example, you said, and I quote, 'no one can show me a greater kindness than to pray for me,' but Mr. Spurgeon said it like this, and again, I quote, 'No man can do me a truer kindness in this world than to pray for me.'"

Humbled, Balthazar stood, his jaw hanging down. He'd assumed the pastor was alone in the fight only to discover there were many who stood with the pastor. He felt the pinch of guilt when he realized the battle was not his but the Lord's. His instantaneous repentance brought him back in fellowship with the one who bought and paid for his soul. "Thank you,

Lord."

A woman's voice behind him called their attention. "I remember Pastor Scott saying, 'Satan doesn't care how many churches there are, as long as they are filled with lukewarm people and preachers.'"

Pastor Wyatt couldn't contain his amusement. "Yes, I said that, but to put it in Charles Spurgeon's words, it goes like this, and I quote, 'I do not think the devil cares how many churches you build, if only you have lukewarm preachers and people in them.' So, Mr. Clavender, if you and your team of researchers don't mind, this meeting is adjourned. I expect your resignation and that of your friends on my desk by this evening service. In addition, you need to start looking for another fellowship to join because you and your divisive spirit are not welcome here."

Balthazar stepped next to his pastor in a show of solidarity. Within minutes, he was joined by the remaining deacons, their wives, and the remaining church members who'd lingered behind to pray for their pastor.

Turning on his heels, Cecil huffed. "This isn't over. When I'm finished with you, there won't be a North Hampton Bible Church in this town." Then he marched up the aisle followed by his defeated entourage.

"Did you expect this confrontation, Pastor?" Balthazar asked as he watched the last of the men leave the auditorium.

"Yes, thanks to you, and one other person, who tipped me off to their little scheme. After our meeting, I had someone do a full background check on Mr. Clavender. Seems he has a reputation for causing trouble wherever he goes. The last church he was in didn't survive. First, they kicked out the pastor, then they fired the rest of the staff leaving the church without leadership. He stepped in and tried to introduce false doctrine and that's when everything exploded. I feel bad for that community and worse for the testimony it left."

Heads moved in agreement.

Bro. Burris patted his pastor on the shoulder. "Don't worry, Pastor, you were never in danger. We all knew what Clavender was up to from the start."

Chapter Twenty-Nine

Rays of sun peeked around the curtains and stung Karen's eyes. She roused and looked at Glenn. He looked so peaceful, like he was taking a nap, but she knew better. The coma which held her husband in its tight grip had not relented no matter how gently the physicians tried to bring him out of it. It had been four days since the attack and yet her husband showed no signs of recovering and her faith wavered. Colt's simple prayers warmed her spirit, but still, the icy fingers of doubt had squeezed most of her confidence in God's power to heal from her heart. *Maybe it was God's will for him to remain in a constant state of vegetation. If that was the case, maybe I should pray that he would simply stop breathing.*

No sooner had the thought crossed her mind, than she chided herself. *No, I refuse to accept that. Surely you wouldn't take my husband and Colt's father from us ... would you, God?*

The crushing silence left her feeling alone, forsaken, questioning. Turning to the only source of comfort, she opened the Bible she'd found in the drawer next to the bed. The tattered book opened naturally to Psalms Twenty-Two and she fingered the first verse. It perfectly described her feelings. "My God, my God, why have you forsaken me? Why are you so far from helping me, and from the words of my roaring?"

The words screamed at her. They were her words, and yet she knew they were the same ones her Lord cried during those blackened moments before He dismissed His spirit.

Is this what You want? You want me to relinquish my right

to have a husband? To turn over my security, my dependence upon him to You? So far, all I've seen You do is bring me heartache. First Colt gets sick with some unknown illness, then You let my husband get beat into a coma. Is this how You treat Your children? If that's the case—"

Her mind stopped short before she thought blasphemously.

Fumbling for answers, she thumbed through the scriptures looking for anything that would give her hope. Her trembling fingers stopped in Jeremiah 29. Underlined in red ink were the words that lightened her burden. "For I know the thoughts which I think toward you, says the Lord. Thoughts of peace, and not evil, to bring you to an expected end."

"An expected end," she breathed the words. Letting them wash over her like a spring rain. She inhaled the fresh scent of renewed hope. "I expect my husband to wake up, Lord. But if that's not Your will, then I expect You to provide something better ... for him ... for me ... for Colt."

Biting her lip, she folded herself over and hugged the Bible. Silently, so as not to allow Colt to overhear her most private confession, she prayed. *Lord, I can't go on living like I have. Yes, my husband is a workaholic, and despite my complaints, I have to confess, I loved the lifestyle his income provided; the big house, new cars, latest clothes. I've become so accustomed to living the good life that I've forgotten how to live a holy life ... a life dependent upon You. I repent. If it means renting an apartment and getting a part time job in order to walk by faith, then, that's all right by me.*

As she prayed, a small hand slipped into hers. She cracked open her tear stained eyes and stared down at her son.

"Mom, why are you crying?"

"Oh, it's just that, I've been doing some soul searching. One day you'll underst—"

Movement caught her attention as Glenn reached down and lifted her chin. Their eyes met and she was in his arms in an instant. "Oh Glenn, you're back."

The respirator gave off a piercing beep as he yanked it from his face and let her lips find his.

Still weak, he tugged her close and whispered, "I'm back all right. You have your husband and Colt's father back."

"Daddy," Colt's boyish voice squeaked as he climbed on the bed. "We thought you'd never wake up."

Looking down, Glenn wiped the tears from his cheeks. "I tried to wake up, but God told me he had a work to do in your mother's heart, that he would call for me when he was ready."

Karen found it hard to swallow. "Are you telling me, if I'd surrendered my selfish pride sooner, you would have come out of your coma sooner?"

Glenn's face clouded, then broke into a weak smile. "Well, let's just say, God had a work to do in both our hearts."

"Me too," Colt added, his face stained with tears of joy. "I've been mad at God ever since the attack. I blamed him for letting something bad happen to you."

Karen tugged him close. "Me too. Are you still mad?"

Colt lifted his face to hers. "No, Ma'am. I read in Romans 8:32, where it said, "He who did not spare his own son, but sacrificed him for us, how shall he not with him, also freely give us all things?"

Glenn tried to sit up, but by then a team of nurses and doctors had rushed into the room and began to check his vitals. "I feel fine, really I do," he assured the medical team.

Someone cleared his throat and the nurses parted.

Dr. Damian stepped through the opening. "Well, I don't put much stock on miracles, but I've been standing outside listening to you and have to confess, you are a living, breathing miracle. I heard your prayers Mrs. O'Dell, and yours little man," looking at Colt. "I have to say, your God certainly is full of surprises."

***

"Can I quote you on that?" Pastor Wyatt's question interrupted the sacred moment. He and Angela entered the hospital room behind a bevy of nurses, their faces beaming. It was Sunday afternoon and they wanted to check on their wayward church member. Scott glanced at the doctor. The signs of his membership in the White Coven still showed on the back of his hand. "Dr. Damian, may I ask you a question?"

"Sure, how can I help you?"

Taking the doctor by the elbow, Pastor Wyatt guided him to the hall. "It's not a matter of you helping me. I'd like to talk to you about the God of surprises.

Dr. Damian's eyebrows hiked up. "Oh really? I'm listening."

As the door closed behind them, Glenn exchanged questioning looks with his wife.

Chapter Thirty

Taking a seat in the small chapel, Dr. Damian took in his surroundings. "You know, as long as I've worked in this hospital, this is the one room I've never visited."

Not surprised, Scott followed his gaze. As far as chapels go, it was quite small; not more than three pews on each side and a small cross-shaped podium in front. Icons of many religions hung from golden chains or stood in small niches. An emaciated form depicting the crucified Savior occupied the center of the stained glass window. *It is no wonder why so many people rejected the gospel. If Jesus had not left the cross and the tomb, we are of all men, most miserable.*

Dr. Damian cleared his throat. "You wanted to speak with me?"

Glancing at the doctor's hand, he asked, "What are those markings?"

Damian tugged his sleeve over the tattoo. "Oh, those. I'm embarrassed to say, I'm a member of a coven ... former coven, that is."

Scott felt the blood drain from his face. He'd never dealt with anyone involved with the black arts. Taking a steadying breath, he pushed ahead. "Have you opened yourself up to satanic influences?"

The doctor huffed. "Of course I have. I've been deeply involved with séances, midnight sacrifices. I'd say I've been to your cemetery more times than you."

Images of bloody headstones and cryptic signs skittered

across Scott's mind. Gripping his Bible, Scott asked, "Are you ready to turn your back on that life? Do you want to be free, really free?"

For a long moment, Dr. Damian stared at Scott. It was as if a battle raged behind the man's eyes. Slowly, Damian's head began to move up and down. Speaking in a near whisper, he said, "I think I am. I've been carrying a ton of pain for so long, that I've come to believe it was normal."

"It's not, normal that is. Jesus came to set us free of our guilt, and pain. He offers us life. Not just physical life free from our past sins, but eternal life. Once we have trusted Him, He cleanses us of all sin, past, present and future."

It took a moment for the words to register in Dr. Damian's mind. "Preacher, I'm not a man of faith. I deal in facts, not theory."

"It's not theory," Scott cut in. "And as far as faith is concerned, you rely on faith a lot more than you think. You have faith that your cure will work. Sometimes it does. Sometimes it doesn't. You see, you aren't really in control when it comes to matters of life and death. That's God's department. He has chosen to use doctors such as you to offer help, but he is the Great Physician. In Numbers 21, the children of Israel had sinned and God sent venomous snakes into their midst. They cried out to Moses to pray for them and God answered. He told Moses to make a bronze snake and set it on top of a pole. Then he instructed the people who were bitten to look at the pole. In so doing, they were healed. Today, that pole with the twisted snake is the symbol of healing in the medical profession. But in reality, it represents Christ upon the cross." His focus drifted to the poor rendition of the crucifixion in the stained glass window. My question for you, Dr. Damian, is, are you willing to look and live, to give your life to the one who gives life?"

Damian pulled back the sleeve of his smock and lc
the tattoo. It represented a lot more than just a fancy

meant he belonged to the dark lord. "How can I? I've done so much—" his throat closed, but not with emotion.

Scott watched in horror as Dr. Damian clutched at his neck, his eyes bulging.

"Doctor, what's happening?"

Gasping.

By now, the doctor's face had turned a deep purple. He flailed his hands wildly at an invisible hand that held him in a death-grip. In an effort to communicate, Damian ripped his sleeve back and pointed at the demonic insignia burned into his wrist. "Help!" he sputtered.

Guessing this was a spiritual attack, Scott stood and raised his Bible over his head. "I command you in the name of Jehovah Rophe, the one who heals, to release this man."

The grip faltered but did not release its prey.

"In Jesus Christ's name and through the blood of the eternal covenant, I command you to tell me your name."

His eyes straining, Dr. Damian eked out a guttural sound unlike any Scott had ever heard before. "My name is Marbas, the one that causes and heals diseases."

Scott felt the wind leave his lungs. *Was this creature sucking the very life from me?* Feeling faint, Scott grasped the end of the pew and righted himself. "Marbas, I command you in the name of Jesus Christ, your creator to leave this man. Come out of him and never return."

Dr. Damian's body shuttered violently and heaved in a contorted position. A loud shriek ripped through the thick air and he fell to the floor; froth forming, writhing.

"Leave, and never return," Scott demanded. Placing the Bible on Damian's forehead, he began praying in a loud voice.

Suddenly, the doctor's body convulsed one last time, then relaxed. Sitting up, he gazed around the room. Sweat rolled down his face and he swiped it aside. Pushing himself up, he tried to stand, but his legs refused to cooperate. "What happened?"

Shaken, Scott took a ragged breath and let it out. “Let’s just say, Satan has desired you that he might sift you like sand, but I have prayed for you. Now, if you are ready, let me show you the way to true freedom and happiness.”

While Scott opened the scripture and showed him God’s plan of salvation, Angela, Karen, and Colt remained in the hospital room as Glenn pled the blood of Christ on behalf of Dr. Damian and Pastor Wyatt.

***

Above the hospital, two mighty armies clashed. Prince Argos led his forces in hand to hand combat against the remaining dark hosts left behind after the destruction of Dantalion. The unseen upheaval spilled over into the physical realm. Angry youths took to the streets smashing windows and causing mayhem. In their wake lay a smoking strip mall and a number of desecrated church buildings. As police and fire units descended on the scenes, the teens scattered with the police close on their heels. By midnight, the riot was quelled and North Hampton Township returned to an uneasy lull.

In the moonlight, the few demonic spirits that stood their ground fell prey to the blistering light of Prince Argos’ forces’ swords and arrows. The conquering army took up a cheer and Prince Leo smiled at his commander. The battle for Dr. Damian’s soul had been fought and won.

Chapter Thirty-One

Relieved one crisis had been averted, Balthazar joined his friends in the parking lot. "You guys missed all the excitement." His description of the morning's confrontation was interrupted by Gasper's announcement. "I'm famished, but y'all don't have to wait on me."

"Y'all? When did you learn a new language?" Melchior asked.

Gasper grinned like he'd swallowed the canary. "My students have been helping me ... y'all."

Balthazar elbowed Melchior. "Humph, the next thing you know, he'll have us eating grits and biscuits smothered in sawmill gravy every morning."

Rubbing his stomach, Gasper smiled. "You read my mind. Now, if you would excuse me, I've got dinner plans."

The two men gaped at him. "You do? With whom?" Melchior asked after finding his voice.

A smug expression creased Gasper's face. "With Felicia." As he spoke, a recent model sedan rolled to a stop in front of them. "That's my ride," he quipped. Gasper gave his friends a sideways glance and strode toward the car, humming, 'Match maker, match maker, make me a match, catch me a catch—' his humming faded as he closed the door.

"Gasper, wait," Balthazar called, just before Felicia drove off.

Leaning into the open window, he asked. "When did you learn to sing on pitch, I mean?"

An impish twinkle danced in his eyes. "Oh, that, well,

Miss Felicia has been working with me." He hummed a few more bars. "And, I'm actually thinking about taking up a second language."

"A second language? I wonder which one." Melchior inquired, his eyebrow hiking up a notch.

Gasper offered his best smile. "I considered French for starters."

Leaning over, Felicia chuckled. "Oui, Mr. Gasper, he is quite a fast learner."

"I'm sure he is, Miss Beauchamp, I'm sure he is." Balthazar winked at his old friend.

Felicia put the car in gear and pulled away with Gasper still singing. His exuberant tones fading in the distance.

"I'm so ready for this musical to be over," muttered Melchior as he and Balthazar turned to walk home.

Balthazar rubbed his chin. "I tend to agree with you, but at least he's happy, and I'm happy for him." His voice lightened.

Shifting to look his old friend in the face, Melchior asked, "Not that I'm envious, but why would you say you're happy for him in such a whimsical tone?

"You and I aren't getting any younger. We have no hope of ever getting married again, at least Gasper does. And if so, a wife, children ... a home just might be God's will for him."

Melchior released a weary sigh. "Oh, how I long to go home."

"Home? We are home, or at least you will be if you don't mind walking."

As he spoke, a van rolled to a stop and someone yelled, "Need a ride?"

It was Jacob Myers. He and his family were leaving and offered the two men a ride.

"Yes, thank you," Balthazar said, stepping into the van and sliding over.

As they left the parking lot, Melchior leaned forward and asked, "Mr. Myers, any word on our case?"

Jacob shifted so he could watch the road and speak to his clients. "Nothing new, but all the evidence is circumstantial. What we need is for Glenn to remember."

***

After they'd arrived home, Melchior began to set the table while Balthazar stirred a pot of stew. Lifting the lid, he inhaled deeply as the warm aroma of roast beef, potatoes, and carrots with a sundry of spices filled the kitchen. It was their own concoction, but it rivaled any restaurant in the county ... at least according to the chef, Balthazar. By the time the biscuits were finished, the two men were more than ready to eat.

"May I do the honors?" Melchior asked, referring to offering the dinner prayer. Balthazar always enjoyed listening to his old friend pray. His rich heritage and knowledge of God's word guided his every phrase.

With the prayer completed, their conversation revolved around Balthazar's confrontation with Cecil Clavender."

Melchior listened intently. His mind wasn't on the verbal exchange between Clavender and the pastor; it was on Balthazar's words.

Looking at Melchior, Balthazar stopped mid-sentence. "My friend, you look miles away. Is there something bothering you?"

Unable to hide his thoughts, Melchior stood, placed his bowl in the sink, and retired to the living room. Taking his seat, he continued. "Yes, yes there is. Out in the parking lot, you said something that got me thinking."

"Oh? And what was that?"

"You said we are home, but this isn't really home. This is our residence." As he spoke, he waved his arm to encompass their living quarters. "For me, home is Persia, for you, it's Baghdad. That's where our families lived ... and died." His throat constricted and a single tear followed a deep crevice down his leathery cheek.

Balthazar eased into his favorite chair after nudging

Gideon out. Leaning back, he buried his chin in his chest and sighed. “You know, you’re right. But it is what it is. We are here and we might as well make the best of it.” He waited to be corrected ... nothing. Casting a sideways glance, he caught a glimpse of his old friend. He’d drifted off to sleep. Being careful not to wake him, he rose and padded to the back porch.

Chapter Thirty-Two

Fifteen minutes later, as Balthazar reclined on the porch, a memory flashed across his mind. He saw himself standing, his arms outstretched as if holding back a torrent. *Was it water, or something else? The* memory evaporated like the desert dew and he too drifted into a fitful sleep.

His mind carried across the void to a time lost to the history books. Darkness, like a tattered blanket, swaddled the city while overhead, a myriad of stars held their breath in silent vigil. In the distance, crickets sang their nightly lullaby. It was not a sound he'd grown up hearing, but he liked it.

Baghdad, on the other side of the world, had its own unique sights and sounds and he longed to hear them again. *For once I'd like to remember what life was like before we encountered the witch.* Since that day when he and his friends crossed paths with the Witch of Endor, his memory hadn't been what it used to be. He, like the others, only remembered sketches of their past lives. What they knew were pieced together, but specific instances danced out of reach in the foggy past.

All at once, a picture emerged. He was in the middle of a great battle. It was Babylon and the Meads and Persians were at the door. They had diverted the Euphrates River which flowed through the city and emerged from under its massive double walls. Up the muddy banks they came to flood the streets. The cries of his countrymen still rang in his ears as soldiers from both sides of the conflict clashed. Their leader,

King Belshazzar, had already fallen along with most of the nobility. His great, great grandfather, Daniel, whose name had been changed to Belteshazzar, stood among the captives. He raised his hand and tossed Balthazar his rod. He caught it in midair and immediately felt a surge of energy. "Run, Balthazar, run for your life," he hollered.

Gasping for air, Balthazar sat upright ... his heart pounding and his palms slick with sweat. *Was it a dream, or was it ... his memory?*_Confused, Balthazar staggered into the living room where his staff stood in the corner. Gideon lay sleeping on the couch, but rather than shove him off, he patted his head, grabbed his staff and returned to the porch.

Fingering the ancient rod made smooth by years of handling, he tried to remember how it felt the first time he touched it. Scattered memories of his grandfather holding it, swirled like a flock of sparrows. He focused, seeing only the staff in his hand. All at once a surge of energy jolted from the staff and his hand opened, and the staff clattered to the floor. Hoping it didn't wake either his friend or Gideon, he snatched it up. As his pulse returned to its normal rate, he held his breath, listening. The only sounds were the gentle snoring of the two in the other room.

Focus Balthazar, focus. The words were not his. They were his great, great grandfather's. He remembered Belteshazzar teaching him. *What was it?* His mind refused to work like it used to. *Focus.*

He closed his eyes, took a deep breath and gripped the staff with both hands. As he stood, he began to feel warmth creep up his arms. It was coming from the staff. Like Aaron's rod which budded, the staff came to life. He pointed the clawed end at a ball which Gideon left in the middle of the yard.

Rise. To his amazement, the ball followed the movements of his staff. Wherever he pointed it, the ball followed. *Release it.* The ball fell and bounced.

I remember.

***

By five o'clock Sunday afternoon, Balthazar held Melchior's gaze. "Shouldn't Gasper and Miss Beauchamp have returned by now?"

Melchior instinctively looked at his watch, a recent addition to his twenty-first century attire. "Yes, I'm sure they had plenty of time to eat. But it is a lovely day. Maybe they went for a drive, or headed to the lake."

"I can't imagine him doing that without informing us. I'm worried."

Melchior's forehead wrinkled. "Maybe you should call him."

Picking up Gasper's cell, he shook his head. "As much as Gasper likes his toy, he refuses to take it to church. And I don't know Miss Beauchamp's number."

His answer didn't satisfy him, but in their present situation, waiting was their only course. "We'd better get ready, Mr. Myers said he'd come by around five-thirty to pick us up for church."

Standing in the doorway to his bedroom, Melchior paused. "Maybe you should go. I'll stay back and wait for our young charge. He should be more careful, especially with this false accusation hanging over our heads."

Balthazar thought for a moment. "Yes, I think that's a good idea. You stay, I'll go. Maybe Felicia dropped him off for choir practice. The way he's taken to singing, I'm sure the choir director would welcome the addition."

Melchior smirked. "Believe me, the choir director doesn't need someone singing 'Match maker, match maker.'" The two men shared a laugh before Balthazar headed to his room to freshen up.

***

While Melchior waited, he had the sudden urge to hold his staff. It had been his companion for as long as he could remember. When he'd come of age, his father gathered the elders of his family together and led him through the traditional rites to become one of the Magi. It was a time-honored position. One reserved for the first born. From that day, his training took him from one master to another, from one wise man to another. Each one shared their knowledge, their skill. Over time, he'd developed his own ability. His was that of healing. His touch alone could draw out the source of pain and bring complete restoration. Then, with great skill and prudence, he could unleash that pain into the one inflicting it. It was a tool not to be used lightly.

As he held his staff, the memories flooded back. "I am a healer," he muttered. For the first time since meeting the Witch of Endor, he knew his calling. *I need to get to the hospital. Glenn needs me.*

Movement arrested his steps as Balthazar bolted through the door. "Any word from Gasper or Miss Felicia?" he asked breathlessly.

"No, I had hoped you would have news. It is obvious, he wasn't at church."

Shaking his head grimly, Balthazar, faced his old friend. "No one has heard from them. This is getting serious. If he doesn't return, the sheriff may issue a warrant for his arrest."

Slumping onto the couch where Gideon had just vacated, Balthazar fingered his staff. "You know, with all the hub-bub about Gasper, I failed to tell you about my afternoon."

Taking a seat, Melchior cocked his head. "Oh? Say on."

Balthazar held out his staff. "This afternoon, I had a dream. I was a boy no older than Colt. My great-great grandfather was caught in a throng of people being herded to their deaths. Moments before he fell, he tossed his staff to me ... this staff and—" the memories were as fresh as the day they were formed. "A surge of energy radiated up my arm. As those images flashed before my sight, I remembered."

The whites of Melchior's knuckles glowed through his

thinning flesh. “Yes, I too remember. It came to me as you said, this evening, while I waited. I am a healer and I must get to the hospital, to restore Mr. O’Dell’s memory.”

Balthazar remained motionless. “I wonder if Gasper is feeling it too.”

“How can we know without quizzing him, and until he returns—” The lines on Melchior’s face deepened. “There must be a good reason why he hasn’t come home.”

Standing, Balthazar patted Melchior’s shoulder. “Now you’re sounding like a doting parent. Maybe we should hike to the hospital and do what we can. By the way, have you heard the news about Officer Huntley and Dr. Damian?”

Melchior did a sharp intake. “No, tell me.”

By the time he’d finished, it was too late to take the two-mile hike to the hospital. And without knowing how to drive, they were stranded until morning.

Chapter Thirty-Three

It couldn't have been a more delightful day for a drive through the country and Felicia took her car through its paces; gearing up on the straightaways and gearing down on the curves. Gasper watched in amazement at her dexterity. Shifting gears, her feet dancing between brake, gas pedal and clutch while her left hand gently guided the vehicle around the bends in the road. Never taking her eyes off the black asphalt lined with yellow stripes, she didn't stop talking until a large truck cut in front of her. Even then, she spoke, but in a language he didn't understand.

Knowing North Hampton had little by way of dining choices; Gasper suggested driving the short distance to Blue Ridge. "I've heard Southern Charm on Main Street is a delightful place to eat," he added as he scanned a copy of the *Georgia on My Mind* brochure.

Felicia quickly did a Google search and brought up the directions. "This looks wonderful and my phone will give me turn by turn guidance."

Gasper leaned closer to get a better look. Her freshly applied cologne wafted in his direction and he inhaled deeply. "What is the name of the cologne you're wearing?"

She smiled, "Oh, it's just a little something I picked up the last time I was in New York. Actually, it was the only time I was in New York. It's called, *Euphoria* by Calvin Klein. You like it?"

He inhaled a second time. "Yes, very much. It reminds me

of a special blend of oils my mother made and wore on high holy days."

Felicia's forehead wrinkled into a question. "Oh, that's interesting. Did your family have money? I mean, were you rich people?" The more she tried to rephrase the question, the redder her cheeks became.

"You might say so. You see, my father was a sort of a guru. People came from all around to hear his words of wisdom, and they paid him nicely. Then one day, my mother died and my father became despondent. He let his hair grow long. His beard trailed him like a wandering bush. People thought he was crazy and stopped coming. That's when he sent me to Master Balthazar. I don't know how he knew he'd take me in, but he did. Balthazar is like an uncle to me. He's one of the few remaining wise men in the world. His order was called the Magi. Folks came from all over the world to hear him and Master Melchior's wisdom and to consult them. And when they came, they did not come empty-handed. They brought them gold, silver, bolts of cloth, oils of all kinds. The Magi dressed in the finest garments money could buy."

"You really believe your own story about being a wise man, don't you?"

Bristling, Gasper kept his voice level. "Of course I believe it … because it's true."

"You mean all that stuff about being manikins and arriving in America, the witch and all ... you're saying all that is real?"

Nodding, Gasper smiled at her frankness. "Yes, as real as I am."

Felicia downshifted to speed around a slow motorist. "When did you decide to become a wise man?"

Her question brought a chuckle to Gasper's throat. "Actually, I didn't decide. It was decided for me. When I came of age, I was inducted into the Order of the Magi. It was then I began my tutelage under Master Balthazar and Lord Melchior."

The city limit sign appeared and Felicia slowed her speed as they fell into the traffic flow. Within a few blocks, Southern Charm appeared, its rustic porch and high varnished wood exterior invited them to come inside. After a short wait, the waitress guided them to a polished wooden table overlooking the busy street.

With it being the peak of apple season, the sidewalks and streets bustled with shoppers looking for that perfect gift to take home. It was in that press of humanity, a lone figure stood watching the young couple park their car and walk hand in hand up the steps and disappear in the restaurant.

Once seated, Gasper and Felicia continued chatting about family, friends and their favorite topic ... *Fiddler on the Roof.* Gasper listened and smiled at all the right times.

Laughing till her sides hurt, Felicia wiped the tears from her eyes as Gasper recited line after line, much to the delight of the folks sitting nearby.

Finally, Gasper took a breath between chuckles and glanced at his watch. “Well, I guess we’d better be getting back before Balthazar starts to worry.”

As they entered Felicia’s sedan and left the parking lot, the conversation continued without interruption. “Does he try to maintain strict control over you?”

Gasper’s shoulders rose and fell. “No, actually, there’s not much need for wise men nowadays. But he does give me quite a bit of latitude. Much of my teaching comes in the form of me saying something and Balthazar or Melchior pointing out the error of my way.”

“That doesn’t sound very fun. Couldn’t they just teach you the wisdom of the ages before you stick your foot in your mouth?”

Gasper peeked at his feet and shook her head. “Nope, they encourage me to learn by doing. Most of the time it works, but occasionally, I mess up big time. That’s when Melchior gets a bit testy.”

Her eyes twinkled with interest. “Give me an example.”

“Well, it was when we were crossing the Nebo Mountain range. I had completed my mathematical calculations correctly, but it meant going straight up the face of a cliff. I suggested we take an alternative route.” Gasper’s face contoured with a pained expression.

“Go on,” Felicia said.

“Unfortunately, the excursion cost us several days of wandering in the wilderness. I felt like an Israelite there for a while. Melchior accused me of trying to find Moses’ bones, which I might have, had I been looking.”

Felicia’s chuckles came to an abrupt halt. Her eyes widened in the rear-view mirror.

“What’s wrong?” Gasper asked, glancing over his shoulder.

“There’s a car following us. It’s been doing so ever since we left the restaurant.”

Gasper craned his neck. “Maybe they’re just going the same way we are. This is a two lane road, you know.”

All at once the car following them lunged ahead, crossed the solid yellow line, and cut them off. Felicia spun the wheel and jammed on the brake. “I don’t think so,” she said over screeching tires and rising dust.

As soon as their vehicle came to a stop, the other driver jumped from his car and ran back. Before she could react, he yanked her door open and loomed over her. “Out of the car,” the large man demanded.

Clenching his teeth, Gasper jumped from the car and came around. “Hey, what’s the idea—”

In a move which caught him off guard, the big man swung, catching Gasper on the jaw. His legs crumpled and he fell like an empty potato sack.

Felicia’s scream was stifled as Baker grabbed her and stuffed a handkerchief over her face. The last thing Gasper saw was Felicia slumping over the man’s hulking shoulder.

Chapter Thirty-Four

Having a gun pointed at his head was a new experience for Gasper. When he'd come to, he found himself propped against the wall of a wooden shack, with his hands tightly bound behind his back. His jaw and head throbbed, the result of Baker's meaty fist, and his fingers tingled from the fast-ties binding his wrists. By the time his head cleared, he realized he was not alone. Felicia leaned heavily on his shoulder. She too was bound.

"Well, well well, if it's not Mr. And Mrs. Gasper, one of the renowned wise guys and his bride." Baker's mocking tone grated against Gasper's nerves, but he held his tongue.

"She's not my wife and I'm not her husband." Not that the idea hadn't crossed Gasper's mind, but now was not the time to discuss the merits of holy matrimony.

Baker nudged the scrawny man sitting at the table. "RJ, keep an eye on these two love-birds. I have a few loose ends to tie up and I need to be gone for a while."

Scrawny man, whose entire name was comprised of two letters, let a toothless grin part his lips. "Sure thing boss. You got anything in that 'refrigerator worth eating ... or drinking?"

Baker glowered at the remaining member of his little club. "There's pizza left over from last night and cola in the refrigerator, but stay away from the booze, you hear me?"

The scrawny man's grin faded. "Okay, okay, I'z just asking. No need to get all huffy. You go on about your loose ends while I get better acquainted with Mrs. Gasper." His grin returned.

"And keep your hands to yourself. There'll be plenty of time for that once I get back." Baker snapped, then faded from sight.

Gasper felt his blood pressure skyrocket. Biting his lip, he tried to restrain his anger. *He better not touch Felicia, or I might forget I'm a wise man.*

Rather than lash out, Gasper ground his teeth. *This man might be one of the members of the White Coven, and probably demon possessed. He could very well shoot me and Felicia and say we tried to get away.* "Better to comply than risk upsetting the man," he muttered.

Despite the coolness of the cabin, sweat beaded on Gasper's face and dripped into his eyes as he watched scrawny man munch on day-old pizza.

"Want some?" Scrawny man asked as he finished the last slice and tossed the crust to a snarling dog chained in the corner.

Gasper started to answer when the man interrupted him. "Oops, I'm sorry, I must have ate the last piece." His cackling laughter was interrupted with a phlegm induced coughing spell.

***

In Baker's absence, Gasper and Felicia were left alone to watch the skinny man take apart, clean and reassemble his weapon and listen to him talk to his dog.

Squirming, Felicia's eyes widened.

"Ah, Mr. RJ? I think my friend wants to say something," Gasper said, noticing the way she was pinching her knees together.

Scrawny man stood up, knocking his chair over. He stepped closer and ripped the tape from Felicia's mouth with a jerk.

Her eyes teared. "Ouch! Do you have to be so rough?"

"What do ya expect? A mother's gentle touch?"

Felicia ignored his crude statement. “Sir, could I use the lady’s room?”

“Lady’s room?! There ain’t no lady’s room here, just a pot-n-squat.” Jerking his head in the direction of a corner separated by a tattered curtain.

“That will do. Could you release my hands?”

RJ looked at his dog. “What do ya think? Should I let her go?”

“If you don’t, your boss might get pretty upset,” Gasper said through clenched teeth.

“I wasn’t talking to you, so keep your trap shut or I’ll—”

His next vulgarity was cut off as a car roared to a stop and a door slammed. Hope percolated in Gasper’s heart, only to be dashed on the rocks of despair. A pair of heavy boots pounded up the shaky wooden steps leading to the porch, and Baker reappeared.

“Any change in our guest’s condition?” he demanded.

Scrawny man shook his head. A few oily strands of hair, which escaped the bandana encircling his brow, fell loosely across his eyes. “Nope, but the lady wants to use our bathroom facility.”

Baker scratched the back of his neck. His face darkened. “She does, does she? Well, we can’t have her messing up the place, this being the pristine living quarters that it is. Release her and let her go. But be careful. I’d bet if you gave her a chance, she’d rip your throat out.” As he spoke he nudged Felicia in the ribs with his boot.

The action made Gasper’s blood boil and he strained against his restraints.

“What is this place, anyway?” Gasper asked, “It smells like a brewery.

“That’s because it is,” Baker growled. “You see, I’m an independent contractor. I provide an important service to the community.”

“Yeah,” scrawny man smirked. “White Lightning.”

Baker gave him a sideways glance. "I needed an income since your young friend thwacked me in the head with his slingshot. I'm still going to get even with him for doing that. He cost me my job."

"Serves you right," Gasper muttered a bit too loudly.

Gasper's jaw set as Baker stepped in front of Felicia and pulled his gun from his belt. "You have caused me a boatload of grief and I'm going to send you back to the world you came from. Now shut-up or I'll have to add a new hole in your head."

Felicia glared at him as he released her restraints. While she used their bathroom facility, Gasper realized how late it was. The sun had set and he knew his friends would be worried. He had no way of communicating with them and knew they'd expect him home at any minute. *Maybe they can track me down using this ankle device*, he mused.

"What are you going to do with us?" Felicia asked as Baker shoved her back down and strung a fast-tie around her wrists and ankles.

Scrawny man sneered while Baker thought. "I could make a few suggestions—"

Baker cut him off with an icy stare. "Shut up," he growled. "I need to keep these two as bargaining chips just in case things don't work out. Now I've got one more errand to run before I'm finished." As he spoke, he fingered the medallion and Gasper's confidence flagged.

So that's who stole it. Somehow, I've got to alert Balthazar.

Gasper shifted his position to allow Felicia to lean on his shoulder. Despite the pain in his backside, he enjoyed her closeness. "Felicia, do you still have your cell phone?" he whispered.

"No, it was in my pocket, but he took it." Her breath tickled his ear. "I'm scared."

"I know, me to, but God has not given us a spirit of fear,

but a sound mind. We just need to relax and think. He will make a way of escape if we're alert." As he spoke, Baker plopped down at the table and began to study a map and what appeared to be a floor plan.

As the evening dragged on, Felicia's head bobbed and she began to snore.

"If you don't get her to stop, I'm going to have to waste a perfectly good bullet on her," scrawny man said.

"Tape her mouth shut, that'll solve her snoring problem," Baker ordered.

The skinny man stood and yanked a strip of tape and slapped it across her face causing her head to jerk back. "There, now be quiet." As he spoke, he ran his finger along her jawline.

Felicia blinked back her tears.

Gasper reeled at the action. "This place stinks. I don't see how people drink that poison."

The former sheriff let out a sarcastic chuckle. "It don't smell that bad, especially after you've had a couple of shots. What say I give you a shot ... call it your last communion."

Gasper, who had never tasted anything alcoholic, shook his head vigorously. "No, if I'm going to die, I'd rather face my maker with minty fresh breath." That said, smacking his lips. "Hmm, maybe I should have laid off the garlic bread." Felicia's elbow instinctively jerked landing solidly in his ribs.

By the time Baker finished going over his plans, the clock on the wall read midnight. Gasper's stomach growled and he patted his midsection. "Shhh." As if that would quell his hunger pangs.

Chapter Thirty-Five

Sitting around the dinner table and enjoying a Sunday afternoon with the Myers, Ty bristled when his phone buzzed.

"Hello?"

It was Karen.

Hearing her voice sent a cold chill swirling in his stomach. His mind skittered back to the phone call he'd received the night his parents were killed and he gripped the corner of the table for support.

"Any news?" he asked tentatively.

"Yes," her tone lightened. "Listen."

Glenn's voice filled the connection. News of Glenn's recovery sparked a lively discussion around the table with Samantha role playing the courtroom drama her father would invariably lead.

"Your honor," she said in her best Perry Mason voice, "may it please the court that I present my key witness," she paused as all eyes smiled at her over dramatization, "Glenn O'Dell."

Ashton squealed as if he understood the proceedings, much to the delight of his mother and Ty.

It had been four days since Glenn suffered a near-fatal blow to the head. News of his recovery gave Ty encouragement, but the phone call left him disappointed. His memory had not fully covered. With his partner, Deputy Mark Rigby, on vacation, it was up to Ty to get to the truth no matter where it led. After dinner, he excused himself. He still had a job to do and the clock was ticking.

Looking over his notes only brought up more questions; the timeline didn't match, the motive didn't fit and the evidence pointed in different directions. His only hope was to compare his findings with the sheriff's and take the heat for sticking his nose where it didn't belong.

Rather than stopping by the hospital, Ty headed to the police department. After parking his patrol car, he got out and took a nervous walk through the front door. The duty officer glanced up with a weak nod, then returned to the book he was reading.

"Sheriff in?"

Barely acknowledging the question, he jerked his thumb over his shoulder. "Yeah, go ahead in."

Seeing the door closed, Ty knocked.

"Yeah?"

Ty cracked the door open and peered in. "Sheriff ... got a minute?"

Sheriff Carlson eased back in his chair. "What took you so long?"

"Sir, I'm not following you."

Giving him a wave, the sheriff pushed aside a stack of reports he'd been reviewing. "Come in and shut the door."

Ty complied and took a seat.

"Officer Huntley, you're a good cop and I respect you very much."

Ty started to thank his boss but was cut off.

"Yes, Sir."

"It is because of that, I am not suspending you. The way I figure it, you're going to do your own investigation on my time or on yours. Now you didn't come in here just to hear me chew you out, so what do you have?"

Knowing his boss was a fair-minded man, Ty released a tense breath and pulled his notes from his pocket. "Sir, like you said, I've been doing some of my own snooping around."

Carlson nodded, not speaking.

"And nothing adds up."

"Go on," the sheriff said.

"Well, first, let me show you this. It's a shoe print I found in the flower bed. It doesn't match any of the O'Dell's or anyone on the CI unit. Plus, I can personally attest that the suspects do not wear shoes, they wear sandals."

The sheriff dropped the pencil he'd been fingering. "Say what?"

"That's right. Despite the high school's insistence, they never got used to wearing shoes." Ty let that sink in before continuing. "I also interviewed Felicia Beauchamp. She's the foreign exchange teacher and assistant director of the school musical. She is willing to testify that she was with Gasper the entire evening in question. She never left his side during the black-out.

"A black-out?" It was obvious this was news to the sheriff. He sat back and rubbed his chin.

After Ty detailed what happened to the breaker, he stopped at the sheriff's upraised hand.

"Have you taken her statement?"

"No, Sir. Not yet. She's a bit nervous about coming to the police department. I have a gut feeling she might have overstayed her visa and is afraid she'd be sent back."

"Back where?"

"France, she's from—"

"Okay, okay, I get it. We can get around that. Bring her in and let's get her on the record. Anything else?"

Ty shook his head, then remembered. "There is one other thing. Mr. O'Dell has come out of his coma."

Carlson's face brightened. "That's good news. At least your friends won't be facing a murder charge. Has he remembered anything from the attack?"

Ty stood. "No, Sir. I'm going to swing by there on the way home, but unless something has changed, he doesn't have a clue what happened to him."

"That's not good. Keep up the good work and let me know of any new developments." He picked up the next report indicating the meeting was over.

***

The trip to the hospital took only ten minutes. With it being Sunday afternoon, most folks were home either watching the Braves battle for a slot in the playoffs or snoozing. Neither interested Ty. His world was sliced into precious moments with Samantha and Ashton, boring hours on the beat, and working out. Although he kept his spiritual life in balance, he wished he could stop the world and get off for a while. He longed for the times he and his dad would go for weekend campouts. Sitting under the stars, hearing his father's stories of the old days, made his bones ache for just one more day, one more hour, even a minute to ask him for advice. But no, those days were ripped from him by a drunken driver. He had come to terms with the fact that Samm, during her wild days, was only casually involved. The perpetrator of the hit and run was never found, never prosecuted. *One day,* he mused. One day the person responsible for his parent's deaths will stand before God. He had no pity for that person on that day.

Ty pulled to a stop in the hospital parking lot, and got out. As he left his car, he noticed a man walking in the opposite direction. It was Dr. Damian. He had a lilt to his step and whistled a happy tune.

"Good day, doctor." Ty couldn't help remember the near-death experience he had with the man when he traded places with Samm. He often wondered if the doctor ever figured out that it was he who whacked him on the head and locked him in the back of the ambulance.

Dr. Damian's face brightened. "Good afternoon Officer Huntley. I think I just met your pastor. You go to the North Hampton Bible Church, don't you?"

Not knowing where the conversation was going, Ty

answered cautiously. "Yes, why?"

The doctor took a deep breath. It was like a man inhaling for the first time. He savored the moment, then let it out. "Your pastor just guided my steps to the foot of the cross. It was there I laid my burden down."

Stunned, Ty took a step back. "Sir, I'm not following you."

"That's okay, as long as you are following the Savior, and that, my friend is what I chose to do. I must say, as a matter of confession, how deeply sorry I am for my involvement in the matter of Samm and her child."

At the mention of Samantha and Ashton, the hair on the back of Ty's neck arched. "You almost killed her, you know."

Nodding, Dr. Damian's lower lip trembled. "Really, I meant her no harm. If it had not been for you—" his voice trailed off.

"Me?"

The doctor took a halting breath. "Yes, you. You don't think for one moment I didn't recognize the weight difference between you and Miss Myers. Of course, it was you. I had hoped to deliver you to the witch and let you finish her off, but no, you had to go and club me when I wasn't looking." He shrugged. "Well, I guess it all worked out in the end, but I gotta say, it was not for you or me. It was God." Without waiting for Ty's response, Dr. Damian turned slowly and continued his trek to his car, but before he reached it, he called over his shoulder. "Officer Huntley, you might want to look into former sheriff Baker's relationship with Mrs. Littleton. I've got a sinking suspicion that she might be involved with framing your three friends, the wise men."

Ty stopped midstride. "And what would give you that idea."

Shrugging, the doctor gave Ty a knowing look. "I know those two, remember? I was a part of the same coven. Plus, she is their landlady. Connect the dots."

Giving Dr. Damian a tentative nod, Ty thanked him and took a few steps.

As the doctor got into his car, a soft click arrested his movements. Ty caught a glimpse of the man as he held his position, not moving. His hands gripped the steering wheel; his face was as white as paste.

"Dr. Damian?"

"Get away from me. This car is rigged with a bomb."

Hearing the word 'bomb,' Ty dove for cover. A moment later ... the car exploded.

***

Ty squinted at the bright light pouring in from the hospital window. "Welcome back," Samantha's voice was like a gentle stream.

He forced a smile. "Where'd I go?"

"Don't you remember?"

Ty tried to lift his head but stopped as bolts of pain shot through his head. "No, what happened?"

"There was a car bomb. Dr. Damian is..." Samantha choked back her tears.

Shaking his head, Ty pinched his eyes closed. Images of burning metal and glass scraped across his mind. All at once, Dr. Damian's frightened face emerged from a dark place. "I don't understand?"

Pastor Wyatt entered the private hospital room. He'd been keeping vigil ever since Ty was brought in. "You're a very fortunate man, Ty. You could have been killed."

Ty's jaw dropped. "But why would someone want to kill Dr. Damian?"

"I don't know Ty. I talked with him about the Lord just yesterday."

"Yesterday?! What time is it?"

Jacob, who had also been called to the hospital, checked his watch. "It's Monday about ten o'clock."

Ty let out a halting breath. "I feel so bad for Dr. Damian."

Scott drew closer. "I know it sounds bad, but when I talked with him. I was able to share the gospel with him. He trusted Christ an hour before he went to meet him. When we parted, Dr. Damian was as happy a man as I've ever seen. The next thing we know, his car exploded. The police are still investigating, but it appears to be the kind that is activated when a person sits on the seat. It would have been impossible to get him out without getting killed, yourself."

The news had a visceral effect as Ty's face paled. Shaken, he scanned the room. "And to think, I was the last person to speak with him."

Stroking the back of his bandaged hand, Samantha released a pent up breath. "Did he say anything that would indicate he knew his life was in danger?"

Ty shook his head and winced. Being blown off his feet and landing headlong on the concrete left him with a concussion, lacerations and badly burned. Not wanting to tarnish the man's clean slate. Ty waited a beat. "You know, he suggested I look into the possibility that Mrs. Littleton was involvement with framing Gasper."

Samantha's hand clutched her throat. "How? Why?"

"I don't know, but as soon as I get out of here, I am going to look into it. Now, if it's all right with the doctors, I'd like to be released. I need to find Mrs. Littleton and a witness to interview."

Jacob stepped closer. "A witness? Who?"

"Her name is Felicia Beauchamp."

Jacob and the others exchanged quizzical looks. "Miss Beauchamp and Mr. Gasper haven't been seen in about twenty-four hours."

Chapter Thirty-Six

The sun peeked over the horizon robbing earth's residents of the last vestiges of sleep. Not so, however, with Balthazar and Melchior. To them morning was a relief as each man struggled and lost the battle for sleep. Staggering into the kitchen, Melchior pushed the button on the coffee pot. Soon the aroma of the rich, dark coffee filled the room. Since coming to North Hampton, he had developed a love for the brew and this morning was no different. Pulling the handle of the pot out before it finished, he filled a large mug and took a sip. The steaming liquid warmed his chilled spirit and quickened his senses. "Ah, that's better." Peering at Balthazar through blood-shot eyes, he asked, "sleep well?"

Balthazar grunted. "While I'm not giving to drink, I believe I might partake in your habit." Reaching for a mug, he poured it full of the dark brew. After taking a sip, his eyes rounded. "Mmm, that's good. I didn't realize what I've been missing. To answer your question, no. I failed to arrest the elusive sleep fairy. And before you ask, I've already checked, there is no sign of Gasper."

"Do you think we should alert the authorities?" Melchior's question broke the heavy silence which invaded their rented house.

"Yes, I think so, but first, we need to fulfill our duties at the school. It'll be bad enough having to explain why Mr. Gasper and Miss Beauchamp haven't shown up. Missing class would only make matters worse."

"Agreed," Melchior said. He had nearly forgotten about

his teaching responsibilities. He had been so focused on his friend's absence he'd not even prepared a lesson plan. "I guess we'll just have to spend the day reviewing. That wouldn't hurt anyway."

Balthazar nodded. "Yes, these kids today, need as much repetition as possible." Getting up from his chair, he headed to his bedroom to dress.

Ten minutes later, the two men met in the living room. "Shall we?"

"After you," Melchior offed his leader a slight bow before closing the door after him.

***

As the teens gathered around the flag pole, Josh spotted them and ran over. "Have you heard about the police officer and the doctor getting killed? Everyone is talking about it."

The two men nodded. "Yes, we know all about it. The officer's name is Ty Huntley and the other man was Dr. Damian."

Josh's face registered the grief the wise men felt. "That's so sad. We were about to pray for them and their families. Where is Mr. Gasper? I hope he is well."

"He is well and should be along shortly. Let's pray," Balthazar said, keeping his thoughts to himself.

By the time the prayer and praise meeting around the flag pole ended, the students had only minutes to get to class. Breathlessly, Melchior and Balthazar arrived in their respective rooms just as the last bell rang. It wasn't long before they were busy with their students, but all the while, keeping a watchful eye out the window.

No Gasper ... no Felicia.

***

By the time the school day rumors swirled of Mr. Gasper and Miss Beauchamp's alleged romantic escape. Teen girls giggled at the thought of their teacher's misconduct, while guys smiled and elbowed each other. But to Balthazar and Melchior, it was no laughing matter. After being called to the principal's office to explain and having nothing to offer, Davis excused them with a curt wave.

"We need to check on Deputy Huntley and Mr. O'Dell," Balthazar said as they trudged home.

Melchior was already dialing Ty's cell number.

Waiting for the call to go through, Balthazar whispered, "Don't forget to ask him about that ankle bracelet they attached on Gasper's leg while you're at it."

Melchior nodded and stuck a finger in his other ear. "Officer Huntley?"

The female voice on the other end sounded familiar.

"Samantha?"

"Yes, it's me. Ty isn't feeling so well. Haven't you heard?"

Melchior began to pace. "Yes, my dear, and we were worried. Can you give me an update?"

Samantha filled him in with the details before he addressed the real reason for his call.

"Would it be possible for me to have a word with Officer Huntley? It will only take a minute."

A long pause filled the connection. Finally, Ty's voice echoed in the receiver.

"This is Ty, thanks for calling—"

"Deputy, I'm sorry to be so abrupt, but Gasper left with Miss Beauchamp yesterday, and we haven't heard from them since."

The phone fumbled for a moment. Ty could be heard repeating Melchior's message. Finally, Officer Huntley spoke. "Look, Mr. Melchior, the doctors want to keep me a little longer. But as soon as my headache subsides, and I get released, I'll do what I can to find them."

***

It was nearly dusk when the two men arrived home. Tired and hungry, their heavy feet trudged up the steps and were immediately greeted by Gideon. Melchior gave his furry friend the attention he'd longed for and said, "I know, you want to go for a walk, but you'll have to settle for a run in the back yard." Opening the back door, he let him scamper out to do his business.

Settling into a chair, he looked at Balthazar. "Our ranks are thinning. The medallion is missing. Gasper is nowhere to be found. He could be lying in a ditch someplace dead and we sit around waiting, and for what?" The strain was getting to him and it was beginning to show. "What can we do?"

"I know you're weary, so am I, but I believe your skills are needed at the hospital," Balthazar said, gathering his staff. He handed a small bag containing ointments to Melchior and prepared to leave. "I wonder how Master Colt is taking all this? The boy is at such a tender age."

"I don't know. Maybe we can check on the O'Dell's while we're at the hospital. I'm sure they could use the encouragement."

Balthazar nodded. "Good idea, but I think we need to split up. You should go to the hospital and I shall go to the police station."

"And what will you tell them at the police station, my lord? That Gasper is missing, possibly eloped with a lovely young woman?"

Balthazar's eyes burned with holy determination. "I shall tell them nothing, I am going there to retrieve Gasper's staff. We're going to need it..."

***

The moonless night didn't quell the jitters Balthazar felt as he made his way across town to the Police station. Wearing the darkest clothes, he ducked around to the back of the building.

Snap!

What was that? His mind raced through a dozen scenarios.

All at once, Gideon brushed against his leg. "Gideon, what are you doing here?" feeling silly for talking to a dog.

Kneeling down, he gazed into the darkness while he rubbed the dog's neck. "If you were able to follow me here, I wonder who else could?

Maybe I should just walk in and demand they relinquish the staff to me rather than doing all this sleuthing around.

Standing up, he brushed the dirt and leaves from his trousers, straightened his shirt, and inhaled. "Let's do it." His confidence bolstered by Gideon's presence.

***

A twinkle danced in Prince Argos' eyes as he gave permission to Prince Uriel to assist the human servant of the Lord. He took delight in seeing the man of God step out in faith like that of the Apostle Peter. His only fear was that his charge would doubt. That would ruin everything.

Prince Uriel assumed a guarding position between the wise man and the duty officer. As the door opened, he shielded him from hearing the sound and seeing the movement. Balthazar cast a whimsical look at Gideon as they stepped around the man behind the desk, who seemed totally engrossed in reading a novel. Silently, the door leading to the holding cells and the evidence room swung open allowing them to pass through without his notice. Even more surprising was the way the door eased closed as quietly as it opened. The few men who had been apprehended earlier in the day lay still as logs as Balthazar, Gideon, and their angelic guardian tread softly past. When they reached the evidence room, he flicked a glance at Gideon. The dog looked up at him as if to say, "Well, what are you waiting for?"

Holding his breath, Balthazar grabbed the handle. A moment before his fingers touched it, a soft snap sounded and he pulled his hand back. After waiting for a few seconds to pass, his heart slid back down from his throat and he began to breathe again. Turning the handle, he eased the door open and stole a glance. The room was empty except for some shelves, a table, chair and some filing cabinets. Being careful not to knock anything over, Balthazar and his furry companion slipped inside and shut the door. In the dim illumination, his fingers searched for the light switch.

In the silence, the sound reverberated throughout the room.

Once his eyes adjusted, he said, "Well, we'd better get to work. You sniff around for Gasper's staff. I'll look in here."

Gideon lowered his nose and began to follow it wherever the scent led him.

Prince Uriel gave a soft chuckle. He had intentionally delayed the opening of the door to see their reaction. Satisfied the wise men were truly wise. He did his part. Now that he was inside the room, he held his position blocking the video camera so no one could see his charger's clandestine activities. Rather than prolonging Balthazar's search and run the risk of being discovered, Prince Uriel pushed the container holding Gasper's rod forward enough for him to bump into it.

"Well, well. Would you look at this." He whispered through tight lips.

Gideon came over to investigate.

"That's it. Let's get out of here before we are discovered."

Gideon moved his head as if to say, "I agree, let's go."

As they retraced their steps, their unseen guardian went before them, opening and closing doors until they reached the front. Then in one silent move, he closed the front door leaving Balthazar and Gideon standing back in the parking lot with Gasper's staff in hand.

"Can you believe that ... just like in the Bible," he exulted to himself. "I just wish Gasper was here. I would have liked to have heard his embellished version of the story."

"Let's get back to the house so I can embellish the story all I want." Pleased, he mentally patted himself on the back and strode in the direction of home.

As they disappeared, Prince Uriel once again moved into position in front of them. He needed guidance and speed. He needed a car.

Chapter Thirty-Seven

Thirty minutes later, Melchior huffed into the hospital and breathlessly rushed to Ty Huntley's room. He found him sitting up, gauze wrappings hiding half his face and the back of his hands. "You don't look so good, deputy," he said, stepping closer to the bed.

"I don't feel so good either." Ty offered a partial smile, then winced.

"Sorry, I'll try not to make you laugh. What happened?"

Samantha, who'd been sitting close held a cup of ice water with a straw. "I'll answer. It's too painful for him to do much talking. He'd just left the police station and was headed here to check on Mr. O'Dell. He wanted to see if he remembered anything."

Melchior looked at Ty. His eyelids hung half open.

"He met Dr. Damian in the parking lot. They talked for a few minutes. As Ty walked away, that's when it happened. The doctor got in his car and—" Her throat closed as another round of tears took over.

Melchior enfolded her in his arms and allowed her to soak his shirt with her tears. It broke his heart to see such human suffering. But he knew that was a part of the human experience. He and his order had been given the task of relieving such suffering by giving council and bringing about change where possible.

Finally, Samantha released her hold on him. An apologetic smile brightened her face. "Sorry for messing up your shirt," she said, dabbing her puffy eyes.

"I'm glad I was here for you."

Samantha resumed her vigil in silence while Melchior watched Ty sleep.

He fingered his staff, remembering the powers he'd once had. Finally, he began to pace. It had been two thousand years since he'd exercised his abilities. Did he still have all of them? He wondered. Could he depend upon them when he really needed them? Taking a deep breath, he sent up a quick prayer. He knew his powers were to be used expeditiously, not to show off and certainly not to break the law. But this was different. He was using them for good.

Stepping closer he reached into his bag and withdrew a small bottle of ointment. Laying his hand gently on Ty's shoulder, he whispered, "Ty would you be healed?"

Ty blinked, he face registering the oddity of the question. "Of course I want to be healed. Do you have any ideas on how to avoid a skin graft? Because that's what I'm facing."

Melchior's face brightened as he removed the lid. Within moments, the aroma filled the room and Samantha inhaled. "That smells wonderful. What is it?"

"It is a blend of two oils ... lavender and purification." Then he removed the gauze covering Ty's face over his protests. "It's all right. You said you wanted to be healed, didn't you?"

Ty nodded and watched him begin the process.

"Then allow me to begin." Melchior soaked a small swab of gauze with the oils and anointed the places where the skin had bobbled and blistered.

"That feels good—" He stopped mid-sentence. Melchior's eyes were closed and he prayed in an unknown language. When he finished, he raised his staff up and waved it over Ty's body. "In the mighty name of Jesus Christ, I command the infection to depart. Heal our young friend and he shall be healed. Strengthen him in the inner man by Thy might and by

Thy power. Amen and amen."

With his hands still holding Ty's, he drew a deep breath. When he'd finished, he opened his eyes and peered down. "There, that should do it." Looking at Samantha, he continued, "if you will help me, I'd like to see how we did."

The corners of Samantha's mouth turned up into a bright smile. "What do you want me to do?"

"Help me unwrap his hands."

Her jaw dropped, but she obeyed, not speaking.

As the gauze was peeled back, the flesh of Ty's hands appeared as smooth at the day he was born. "It is as I had hoped. No skin graft will be necessary. You are healed."

Ty fingered his smooth flesh. "This is amazing. How did you do that?"

"I give all the glory to our great God and Savior in Who's name I serve. Now I need you to locate our friends Gasper and Felicia while I pay a visit to Mr. O'Dell."

He excused himself and headed down the hall.

After checking with the nurse at the information desk, Melchior quickly made the short walk to Glenn's room. A light tap on the door and he stepped inside. Entering, he was surprised to find Glenn sitting up in bed. The tubes had been removed, but he still appeared to be disoriented.

"Lord Melchior." Colt's sudden outburst at his arrival brought Karen to her feet. "I'm so glad you came, Dad is awake."

Melchior accepted the young boy's enthusiastic hug, followed by Karen's.

"How are you holding up?"

"Oh Mr. Melchior, I'm so glad you came. As you can see, Glenn is awake but groggy."

"Does he remember anything about the night of the attack?" His concern for his beleaguered friend ran deep.

Karen shook her head. "I'm afraid not. His memory hasn't completely returned."

Melchior stroked his chin, a habit he'd developed over the years to help him focus.

"Yes, well, I may be of some assistance in that area. I myself have suffered a bit of a memory loss, but that has passed. Maybe this will help." As he spoke, he carefully lifted a small bottle from his bag.

"What is it?" Colt's eyes rounded with growing interest.

"It is a special blend of oils from rosemary and basil plants. They will enhance your father's memory and restore clarity of thought." The fragrant aroma filled the room and both Colt and his mother inhaled deeply. "That smells great, do you think I could use some to help me with my spelling."

A chuckle percolated in Melchior's chest. "I'm afraid the only thing that will help your spelling is good old fashioned hard work."

Colt feigned disappointment but shrugged it off as his father stared. "And you can count on me to help you win the next Spelling Bee, too."

Karen took her husband's hand and gave it a squeeze. "Oh, Honey, how do you feel?"

"Better than I deserve."

Melchior took another swab of gauze and poured a few drops on it. "If you would permit me, I'd like to annoint you in the name of the Lord and pray."

Karen gave him room. "What is that?"

Giving her a warm smile, he said, "This is jasmine and neroli. They should help trigger his memory and thought processes." Then he turned and lay the gauze on Glenn's upturned forehead and began to pray, again in his own language. When he finished, he lay his staff on Glenn's head and said, "In the name of the Lord, I command the evil presence which has invaded my brother's mind and heart to depart. Give him perfect recall of the night of the attack, but don't allow the fear or guilt to overtake him. Amen and amen."

When he opened his eyes, he leaned closer and peered into

Glenn's eyes. "Can you tell us anything about the night of the attack?"

Glenn peered around, blinking. "Yes, I just got off the phone with a client and heard a noise in the hall. I stepped out to investigate when Sheriff Baker jumped over the railing and slugged me. After that, it's all a blur. I do remember having a long talk with the Lord while I was out."

Melchior patted him on the shoulder. "I think I'll let you two get reacquainted. In the meantime, I have a former sheriff to catch and a lost medallion to find. So it you'll excuse me. Oh, one more thing. There is the matter of Mr. Clavender—"

"I know."

Taken aback, Melchior held his gaze. "You do? How so?"

Glenn pushed himself up and leaned on his elbow. "As I said, the night I was attacked I was on the phone with Mr. Clavender. He is trying to get me to join his scheme to oust the pastor."

"His scheme?" Melchior asked, his mouth gaping.

"Yes, his scheme. He and the former sheriff have been plotting this ever since he lost his job. It seems that Mr. Clavender is a known hit-man for destroying churches. He has a long history of success. I told him I was going to expose him if he didn't stop."

Melchior rubbed his chin. "But that still doesn't explain how Baker knew the medallion was at your house. Did you tell anyone about it?"

Glenn thought for a moment. His face contorted. "Yes, Colt and I took it to the pawnshop to see if they would give us a decent price for it."

"What did they offer you?"

Glancing between his wife and Melchior, Glenn took a dry swallow. "He offered us fifty bucks." He knew Karen's response before it came.

"Fifty dollars? Why didn't you take it?"

Glenn slumped deeper in the bed. "In hindsight, I should

have, it would have saved us a lot of heartaches."

Melchior continued his gaze. "Don't beat yourself up, Glenn. This was all part of God's plan. He had a work to do in your and Karen's hearts, plus, if you sold the medallion to the pawn dealer, we would have never known in whose hands it ended up. At least now we know it was Randy Baker who stole it."

As he excused himself Colt interrupted his retreat. "I'm going with you, remember, I'm one of the wise men, too."

Melchior looked at Karen, then Glenn. "Only with your parent's permission. I wouldn't want to deprive you of some quality dad time."

Glenn nodded with a wink. "Be sure you bring your sling shot. It might come in handy if you meet a witch," he chuckled as Melchior and his young charge reentered the hall.

If he only knew how real his statement was.

***

On the way out of the hospital, he heard his name. Turning, he saw Ty walking behind him. "Officer Huntley, you seemed to have recovered rather well." His voice curled up like smoke from a chimney.

"Yes, thanks to you. I was wondering if you needed a lift."

Again, Melchior touched his chin. If his calculations were correct, Balthazar should be finished at the police station. With a little luck, they should rendezvous back at the house to reconnoiter.

"Officer Huntley, is there a way we could activate that leg bracelet tracking device?"

Ty sighed deeply. "Well, knowing you guys had no way of leaving town anyway, we never actually activated them."

"Is there a way you can activate it now?" he pressed.

Ty shook his head. "That might be a bit tricky since, as you said, you don't know where he is."

Melchior took a sideways glance at Colt. "Tell you what, why don't you just take us to my house. Maybe we can come up with an idea on the way."

Chapter Thirty-Eight

After taking one final look at the floor plan of Mrs. White's former residence, Baker prepared to leave. It was now going on midnight and he was anxious to get moving. Chiding himself for not taking care of this earlier, now that he had the medallion, he knew what he needed to do. Leaving his car parked in a secluded area near the back of the subdivision, he walked the short distance and cautiously entered through an obscure door at the back of the house. Fortunately for him, Mrs. White had chosen to live on a cul-de-sac, which gave him a perfect view of any approaching vehicles. His foray into the uncertain took him less than five minutes and he was back at his hideout in ninety minutes.

Not being familiar with the ancient terminology, Baker found it frustratingly difficult to decipher its code. One thing he learned; the dark being that filled Mrs. White came from an obscure place called Endor.

Glancing through the dim lighting at Gasper, he shouted, "Gasper, I gotta question for you."

Gasper, who'd drifted off to sleep, jerked upright. "Say what?"

"You're a wise man, right?"

Squinting, Gasper tried to focus. "I'm not as wise as you think or I wouldn't be in this position."

"I didn't say you were smart, just asking if you're wise."

Gasper shifted slightly and Felicia sat up. "I suppose you

might say that. What do you want to know?"

"You ever heard of a place called Endor?"

At the very mention of Endor, Gasper felt the blood drain from his face. "Yes, it's a place in Israel, why?"

"I'm asking the questions. Now tell me, does it still exist today?"

He cocked an eyebrow and thought a minute. "I suppose so, but it's probably not at all like it was in Bible times."

Opening his laptop, Baker typed in a few keystrokes and sat back. He scrolled through a few screens skipping several historical and travel sites before he found the one he was looking for. "Ah, here it is, Ein Dor. That's the modern name of a kibbutz located between a hill called Moreh and Mount Tabor. Ever been there?"

Gasper's Adam's apple bobbed as he took a forced swallow. "I don't think I've had the pleasure. Are you sure you want to go there? It sounds like the wild, wild west with Palestinians lobbing missiles all around."

Baker huffed. "I'll be in and out of there in a day. No worries. You wanna come?"

Felicia's breath caught as she saw Gasper giving it a second thought. "No, I think I'll stay here in the good old US of A."

"Suit yourself," Giving him a shrug, he continued studying the ornately inscribed pages. Like a second grader trying to sound out his first multi-syllabled word, Baker began to form the words on a page which showed promise. On the center of the page was a door which, if opened, guided the traveler on a path to a bright horizon. As he stuttered out the incantation, the floor began to shake. Dust from the ceiling filtered through the rafters and smoke from his smoldering cigar mingled with it making the air a corrosive mixture.

Felicia let out a sharp cry.

Scrawny man's jaw hung open as he watched his boss continue. Sweat beaded on his forehead and he mopped his face with a grungy handkerchief. "Boss, do you think that's a good idea," he asked as the table vibrated spilling his hooch.

"Shut up. Can't you see I'm concentrating? Find Gasper's cell, if he has one, and call his two friends. Tell them they need to get out here if they want to see their friends again."

The scrawny man shrugged reluctantly and sauntered over to where Gasper and Felicia sat. "You got a cell?" he asked.

Gasper shook his head. "No, I don't carry one on Sunday."

"Boss, he says he don't carry a cell on Sunday. Want me to look for the girl's?"

No answer.

Her eyes pleading, Felicia whispered, "Help us. We won't turn you in, just cut the tape and distract Baker. We don't want any trouble."

Scrawny man pinched his lips together before speaking. "And get myself shot? You don't know this guy like I do. He'll kill all of us if we try anything." Peering over his hunched shoulder, he continued to whisper. "You see how agitated he is."

Gasper slumped back while the man searched Felicia's handbag.

"You know your friend's cell number?" he asked, looking at Gasper.

"Don't tell him," Felicia said under her breath, but by then, it was too late. Gasper had already spouted off the numbers.

A minute later, scrawny man hung up. "No one answered. The old coots must be asleep," he said.

"Leave them a message," Baker cursed.

"What should I say?"

Baker thought a moment. "Tell them where to find their friends. That should do it."

Scrawny man obeyed, then, with an apology, returned the cell phone to Felicia's bag.

By the time he returned, Baker stood, sweat dripping from his face in large, salty drops. He stared, unblinking. His face turned beet red.

"You all right?" Scrawny man asked.

Baker's focus remained fixed on a cracked mirror which was on the wall near a dirty sink. Drool leaked from the corners of his mouth. He muttered the last phrase in an incantation over and over again. In a breath, a light flashed from the mirror. Voices called out. Their deep-guttural tones invited him to come nearer. Stepping within inches, Baker's breath caught in his throat. Before he could pull back, two wispy hands reached out from the mirror. Their ethereal fingers splayed in an ever-widening grasp around the one reciting the verses. Baker was drawn into their clutches. Closer and closer he came as if drawn by a rope. At the last second, he gasped and pulled away. The voices increased, rattling the windows, threatening to bring down the entire structure. As Baker backpedaled, the spirit took shape and emerged. Its ghastly form spilled into the room like mist off a troubled sea.

"I am the keeper of the door, why have you disturbed me?"

Baker gulped, "I wish to pass through."

"Not before paying. No one is permitted to pass through this door without paying."

The creature's ethereal shape pulsated as if it had a heart, but indeed, this was no human. Its haunting eyes seared into Gasper's consciousness and the creature shrank back.

"What price do you require?" Baker's trembling voice caught the spirit's attention. Then it swept the room as if looking for the answer.

"I'll take him." The demon pointed at the scrawny man cowering in the corner.

Baker laughed. "Him? You can have him. What do I care?"

"Bring him to me," the demonic creature demanded. Its eyes were glowing like embers.

Backing away, scrawny man tried to push himself deeper

against the wall. "No, no!" his muffled protests were covered by the spirit's guttural laughter.

Grabbing him by his shirt, Baker yanked the frightened man to his feet. "Come with me."

Gasper and Felicia watched in horror as Baker dragged the man across the room. His worn boots scuffed the rough-hewn floor in an inane rhythm.

All at once, the spirit turned on the screaming man held in place by Baker's firm grip. Like a mystical python, the spirit claimed its victim and began to squeeze.

Felicia screamed and passed out. Gasper doubled over and lost what little he had in his stomach.

"There, you satisfied?" Baker cried once the lifeless man crumpled to the floor with a sickening thud.

"You may pass, but I require the same payment on your return, so be prepared or you'll pay with your life."

With a nod, Baker snatched the Book of Incantations from the table and stepped closer to the mirror. Then he paused. Taking a quick step toward the still, he turned up the heat. "How 'bout I pay it forward." Looking at Gasper, he chuckled. "I hope by the time your friends get here, you will have passed through this door too. See you on the other side." A moment later, he stepped through the mirror and was gone.

***

Gasper found it hard to swallow as he watched Baker step into the mirror.

Sitting up, Felicia blinked, her expression confused. "Where did he go?"

Gasper pointed with his chin. "You won't believe it if I told you. But I gotta tell ya, this doesn't look good. Before Baker left, he turned up the heat on that container over there. I'm guessing when it reaches a certain point, it will explode. And we'll be blown to kingdom come."

Felicia's lips began to tremble. "Why would he do such a thing? I just can't believe it."

"Believe it."

"I don't want to be blown to kingdom come. I just want to get out of this smelly place."

Gasper knew he had the ability to move through space, but he also knew it might frighten Felicia if she saw him blink out and blink in again. On the other hand, if he didn't do something fast, they both might be traveling through space into the heavenly dimension.

He shifted to look Felicia in the face. "I want you to close your eyes and don't open them until I tell you to. Okay?

A quizzical expression formed. "Look, if you're going to kiss me good-bye, you don't have to be so melodramatic."

Gasper thought about that for a moment. The notion of kissing a woman without being married hadn't occurred to him. Where he'd come from, kissing was reserved for the most intimate settings. He forced a swallow. "Please, just close your eyes, and no peeking."

Felicia cocked her head expectantly and puckered.

Gasper disappeared.

A moment later, he reappeared breathing hard, and carrying a large knife.

At the sound of footsteps, Felicia's eyelids popped open and she gasped. "Gasper, be careful with that," she said, pulling back. "Where'd you get that thing in the first place?"

He swiped the sweat from his upper lip. "Hold still. Let me cut your bindings and we can get out of here before that thing blows."

After taking a few swipes, he realized the blade was too dull to cut the duct-tape in time. Tossing it aside, he scooped Felicia in his arms and dashed through the door. "I should have thought of this in the first place."

They hadn't taken three paces from the structure when the pressure cooker exploded, sending scalding liquid and burning wood in all directions. The blast blew Gasper and Felicia off their feet and buried them in smoldering pieces of roofing and boards.

"Shoo, that was close," Gasper said, as he climbed out from under a large piece of plywood.

"Ooh," Felicia's moan sent his heart into hyper drive. Gasper grabbed a two-by-four which pressed across her chest and threw it aside. Reaching down, he pulled her to her feet.

In a move that took his breath away, she threw her arms around his neck and tugged his lips to hers. "Thank you, thank you, thank you," she repeated as she held him close.

Gasper felt the color drain from his face, then return super-heated. He stood wondering how to respond to such lavished devotion. Finally, he found his voice. "I'm just glad I was here to help you."

For a moment, the two of them stood enjoying the warmth of each other's presence with the burning building as a backdrop.

Finally, Felicia spoke, barely able to suppress a chuckle. "I peeked."

Chapter Thirty-Nine

In the distance, the roar of an engine grew louder until it came to a halt near where Gasper and Felicia stood. Grabbing a burnt two by four, Gasper took a position in front of Felicia. "This might get ugly," he said through clinched teeth.

The vehicle skidded to a stop, sending a cloud of dust in the air. "Gasper," someone called.

It was Ty Huntley.

A figure dashed from the vehicle and pounced on Gasper's chest, knocking him over. "Gideon, what are you doing here?" he asked as he pushed the dog aside.

"I could ask you the same question," Balthazar answered as he and Colt emerged from the car. He was joined by Melchior, who they had picked up as he trudged along the highway.

Gasper's glance switched between his friends. "Am I glad to see you. There for a while, I thought it was the end."

"Tell us what happened," Ty said, pulling a notepad from his pocket.

"It's a long story, but the short version is Randy Baker forced us here at gun point. We've been tied up ever since. Baker had his lackey keep watch while he left a couple of times. When he returned the last time, he brought in a big thick book. He called it the Book of Incantations. He tried reading it, but couldn't make sense of it. He even asked me how to say some of the words. And then, he had the audacity of asking me to accompany him to Endor. I told him, no way, Jose'."

"Endor?" both Balthazar and Melchior asked in tandem.

"Yes, it's pronounced, Ein Dor. It's a kibbutz in Israel. That's what I'm trying to tell you. He broke the code on one of the incantations and a spirit spoke to him." The more Gasper tried to explain what had happened in the shack, the more bizarre it sounded to him as well to his friends.

Finally, he threw his hands up in frustration. "You'd just have to have been there, but I'm telling you, he's gone, puff, ca-putt."

Felicia's head bobbed. "It's true. That demon thing killed Baker's friend, too."

Deputy Huntley stopped taking notes. "It did what?"

"It demanded payment before allowing Baker to pass through the 'Door,' as it was called. Then Baker dragged a guy named RJ across the room kicking and screaming. That thing lunged at him and—" Felicia's voice faded. "That poor man," she sobbed.

"Yeah, and then Baker turned up the heat on his still. He intended to kill us." Sniffing his soiled shirt, he wrinkled up his nose. "I smell like a wino. I can't wait to get a shower."

"Me too," Felicia added after regaining her composure. "But first I need to go back and get my car. It's sitting alongside the road near Blue Ridge."

Melchior, who had been quietly listening, spoke up. "I don't think that would be a good idea. You've already had too much excitement for one day."

Ty nodded. "I agree. You never know what Baker might do when he discovers you're not dead. I'll call a wrecker and have them haul it in tomorrow. In the meantime, we need to get you someplace safe."

Glancing around, Gasper asked, "How did you find us in the first place?"

Ty glanced to Balthazar and Melchior for an explanation.

Melchior extended his arm and held Gasper's staff. "Let's just say your rod and your staff guided us here."

Surprise registered on Gasper's soiled face as Balthazar handed him his staff. "How did you get this?" he asked, clasping it in his hand.

"That, too, is a long story. One we can enjoy over a cup of hot coffee. But first, tell us more about that book Baker was reading."

Gasper and Felicia exchanged questioning looks. "It was big and it had ancient writings in it."

"Yes, and when he left, he took it with him," Felicia explained in her French accent.

As they talked, Colt climbed the steps and began to search through the burnt wreckage of what was once a wooden shack. "Hey, guys. I found something." He held up the page. Suddenly, a board snapped and Colt teetered.

"Colt, your mother will shoot us if you get injured. Now be careful and get out of there. It's dangerous." Gasper said, reaching out and catching the boy by the hand.

Stepping down to the ground, Colt produced the scorched sheet of paper. Driven by curiosity, Balthazar, and the others gathered around Colt.

A sharp click sounded as Ty flicked on his mag-light. "Let's get a better look at this," he said, holding his light so they could read it.

Balthazar leaned closer and began to study the inscriptions. After a long pause, he straightened. "This is a map of a temple … probably the Temple of Endor."

All eyes turned toward him. "I've heard of such a place but doubted its existence. If it is true that Baker was somehow transported to Endor, then with the help of that book, he might discover its whereabouts."

"But if he doesn't have the map, how will he know what to look for?" Gasper asked.

"He's a very resourceful man, but I can assure you of this ... if he finds it, he will unleash the forces of the underworld, and that we cannot permit." His eyes burned with a holy flame.

Ty clicked off his mag-lite and holstered it. "Let's get you people back home. After you've cleaned up, maybe we can form a strategy for moving forward."

Gasper opened the car door for Felicia. "Yes, and maybe you can explain how you disappeared and reappeared," Felicia added.

Balthazar's jaw flung open. "You did what?"

Unable to keep his secret, Gasper explained. "I had to do something. I couldn't just sit there and let Felicia and myself get blown to bits, so I imagined myself outside the building, then I imagined myself back. That's all."

"That's impossible. You didn't have your staff." Melchior couldn't hide his chagrin.

"Actually, I was able to do it once before when I talked with Ty and Samm in the parking lot of the church. I just concentrated on being a few hundred yards away and poof. I was there."

Balthazar gazed at his young friend. "I never thought it possible. This is not something to be taken lightly. I only know of one other person who could think himself to another place and that was the prophet, Elijah."

"That explains why you're not wearing your ankle bracelet," Colt said, reaching down and lifting the damaged device.

All eyes turned to Gasper's leg ... *No bracelet.*

***

As Ty's car rumbled through town, a host of angelic beings hovered all around it. Prince Uriel held his spear pointing forward, parting the cloud of dark hosts which fought against them.

"Glancing at his cohort, he smiled. "Thank you, my fellow warriors. Were it not for your protective shields, Gasper and Felicia would have been scorched to death. Even now, your once glistening shields are marked with the force of the blast."

Prince Selaphiel descended from his lofty post and joined

his fellow warriors. "It looks like you have met the enemy and prevailed."

"Let's just say we have not yet resisted unto blood. We still must defeat the dark force behind this conflict, but I fear he is one of Satan's mightiest warriors. He has not only blinded the minds of those who don't believe, but he has cloaked himself in such thick darkness that my forces have not been able to penetrate."

Prince Selaphiel ran his fingers through his red beard. "Then we may have to invoke the name of the Lord, in order to break through his deception. Only then will we be able to know his devices and how to defeat him."

***

Having to squeeze six people and a dog into a patrol car built for five posed a number of problems. Ty did as much rearranging of his computer equipment as possible, but the main sticking point was where to put Felicia. After much discussion, Balthazar came up with a workable solution.

"Let's put Felicia in the front seat with Colt on her lap." The idea pleased Colt very much. "And the three of us will occupy the back seat."

"Four," Melchior corrected. "Don't forget about Gideon." The dog looked from face to face as if to say, "Okay, who's going to let me sit on their lap."

Gasper grabbed the door handle and opened it to allow Felicia to get in. "He's your dog. He can sit on your lap," looking at Melchior.

Melchior nodded. "Yes, that is so. At least he doesn't smell like a wine cellar."

Taken aback, Gasper sniffed the air, then his clothes. "Good point, maybe I should walk."

"That won't be necessary, Mr. Gasper. I've had worse smelling people in the back seat of my cruiser. Just don't start singing some song about losing your truck, your shotgun, and your hound dog."

Gasper's face registered a question. "I don't get it. Is he referring to my singing?"

Patting his arm, Felicia grinned. "No, Gasper. I think he's talking about you smelling like a drunk."

Standing upright, Gasper began to walk with his arms outstretched. "I assure you, Officer Huntley, I am no drunk. I am as sober as a priest on St. Patty's day."

His attempt to sound Irish brought laughter all around.

"Is he this way all the time?" Felicia asked Balthazar.

Nodding, he stifled a chuckle. "I'm afraid so, my dear. I'm afraid so."

"Worse," added Melchior as he and the others squeezed into the police car.

"Hey, I resemble that comment." Gasper's protests were drowned out by Gideon's bark. Apparently, he too, agreed.

***

By the time they'd reached the outskirts of town, the sun had cleared the tree-lined horizon. Splashes of amber streaks cut across an azure canvas. Mountain ponds steamed as the cooler air kissed the warmer water's lips. The love affair of nature created infant clouds which soon grew until they blocked the very light which conceived them.

Down below, on a narrow strip of blacktop, a police patrol car carrying six uncomfortable people wound its way beneath a canopy of green. Having found Gasper and Felicia, Ty now needed to focus on locating the former sheriff, but first things first. He headed straight to Felicia's apartment. After dropping her off, he drove to the O'Dell's house.

"Can you get in?" Ty asked.

"Yes, Sir. Mom hides a key under a flower pot on the back porch."

"All right, get ready and see if the Myers will take you to school. Maybe when you get home, your dad will have been released from the hospital. I'll call you later today." Ty's appreciation of the young boy grew as he gave him a final hug and dashed around the corner of his house. He hoped one day, Ashton and his children would grow strong in spirit like that of Colt.

Ignoring their grumbling stomachs, Ty headed to the wise men's house. While Gasper showered, he and the others huddled over the page Colt found. Clearly, it was the main clue to where Baker went.

Returning to the kitchen, his hair still wet, Gasper grabbed a slice of breakfast pizza recently delivered. After taking an ample bite, he eyed the loose page. His description of how Baker disappeared chilled the room.

"Are you saying Baker literally stepped through the mirror like it was a gateway?" The lines on Melchior's face deepened.

"That's what I'm saying. First, a demon demanded a blood payment."

"What kind of payment?" It was Balthazar's turn to ask the questions.

"A blood payment. Like I said, it took the guy named RJ."

Ty thought for a minute. "That name sounds familiar. I think I've seen him lurking around town. He was one of Baker's goons."

"Not anymore. That thing sucked the life right out of him. Then, after it had killed him, he told Baker he could pass over, but if he wanted to return, he had to pay again. That's when he turned the heat up on the still. He hoped to kill us."

Chapter Forty

Having been transported instantaneously halfway around the world was an exhilarating experience for Randy Baker ... one that left him bewildered and confused. One minute he was in the shack and the next, he is standing in a small, poorly lit building with a mirror at his back. Turning, he peered into its reflection. All he saw was his own image and whatever was on the opposite side of the room. Apparently, the door through which he stepped had been closed. When he was to return, it would not be empty handed.

With one hand, he leaned against the wall breathing in the dusty air. With the other, he gripped the book. It too, had made the journey, but he noticed in his haste, he'd lost the last page and the back cover. He cursed himself for being so stupid. A drop of salty sweat rolled down his forehead and stung his eye. Looking around, he realized he was in a block building. Its hot stale air closed in around him and within minutes, his shirt was soaked with sweat. It was obvious the building hadn't been occupied in months, maybe years and he hoped it wouldn't be visited too soon.

Voices outside the boarded windows shattered any hope of not being discovered. He flattened himself against the interior wall. Sweat rolled down his face and dripped from his chin. Instinctively, his hand reached for the butt of his weapon. Not knowing the language put him at a disadvantage. It sounded middle-eastern, maybe Arabic. Either way, he was an illegal alien in a foreign nation with no papers, no visa ... no passport.

If caught, he very likely would be shot. He kicked himself for not thinking further ahead. He had no national currency, only US dollars and no idea on how to convert it. It was these kinds of mistakes that could ruin everything he'd worked so hard to accomplish. If it were one of his lackeys, he'd have shot him.

The voices continued for another ten minutes, then began to fade. As Baker's pulse returned to normal, he took a quick glance through a crack in the door. It was broad daylight ... probably noon, he guessed. He quickly ruled out walking across the dusty road to the grungy convenience shop. He needed something to eat and drink, and most of all ... directions. If he waited until nightfall, he would at least have the advantage of darkness on his side. But being an American, dressed in street clothes in the middle of possibly a Palestinian town or worse, an ISIS stronghold, could prove deadly.

Slumping to the concrete floor, he began to reconsider the wisdom of his decision. But what was he to do? He couldn't go back. Even if the shack still existed, he doubted the spirit who opened the door would allow his return, not without a sacrifice. That thing liked blood, fresh, hot, blood ... his blood if he tried to go back. And then there was the explosion. It would have destroyed the mirror along with killing Gasper and his girlfriend. *What a jerk.*

He had to go forward. He had to find the door to the Temple of Endor. If he could do that, he might be able to wield enough power through his medallion that he could command the powers of darkness to submit to him. It was his only hope.

As the shadows grew, so did Baker's hunger and need for water. He had been sweating in that small pill-box for hours and he needed to get up and stretch, but every time he thought he was alone, another pair of men strode by muttering in an indiscernible language. It occurred to him, these were guards on patrol and possibly the building in which he sat was an unoccupied outpost.

Being careful not to make a sound, he crept from corner to

corner peering through cracks and openings in the block wall. On the front side, he noticed a parked car along the narrow street. Down from it, was the convenience store where they sold newspapers, cigarettes, candy, and drinks. Next to it was an automobile shop with a single fuel pump in front. The building in which he hid, was in the middle of a row of other dilapidated structures separated by a narrow alley. To his rear, a courtyard opened containing a small playground complete with teetter-totter, a swing, and a slide. The only thing missing were the children. It suddenly dawned on him. All the time he'd been there, he'd not heard nor seen a child. *Was this a war-zone? Am I caught in the middle of a battle in which I am neither a combatant nor neutral party?*

By now, the heat and dehydration were beginning to play tricks on him. He paced the floor, wishing for darkness, dreading what might be lurking in it when it fell. After returning to his slumped position, he allowed himself to drift into a fitful sleep.

When he awoke, it was pitch black, both inside and out. He breathed a heavy sigh. At least the relentless heat had abated. A light breeze drifted through the cracks on the boarded up windows, making it somewhat bearable. As his eyes adjusted, his breath caught in his throat. A pair of unblinking embers stared at him from across the room. His palms slicked as he involuntarily reached for his revolver.

Holding it with two hands, he pulling back the hammer, took aim and waited. The creature hadn't moved since he'd taken notice of it. That was a good thing, but neither had it retreated. It just stared at him. Finally, the creature made a chuckling sound. At first, he thought it was a baby. *What would a baby be doing in this God-forsaken place?*_Then, the chuckling turned more serious. The laughter turned mocking, and then it spoke. "Are you going to shoot me or just point that thing at me?"

It was a woman, no ... a teenager ... a girl.

***

He had not expected to meet anyone, let alone, a girl. Was she an orphan? A freedom fighter? A sixteen-year old member of the IDF, the Israeli Defense Force? Or just a survivor ... like himself?

"What do you want?" Baker's throat was so dry he could barely form the words.

"I could ask you the same thing. I take it you're hiding. In that case, put the gun away before I shoot you." It suddenly dawned on him, that whoever it was also had a gun.

"If you shoot me, those guys outside will pounce on you like a jackal."

"I have a silencer, stupid."

The statement took Baker by complete surprise. "Are we in Palestine occupied territory?"

"Disputed territory," the girl behind the glowing eyes, said.

"Are we anywhere near a Kibbutz named Endor?"

As silent as a cougar, the girl advanced until Baker could hear her breathing. Still, her stare remained fixed. "Who's asking and why?"

Baker knew lying would get him nowhere. What did he have to lose? "My name is Randy Baker," making sure not to call himself Sheriff Randy Baker. "I'm a researcher. I'm looking for a valuable artifact located in what is called the Temple of Endor. Could you point me in the right direction?" keeping his voice calm.

The girl laughed. "You're a researcher with a gun? I don't think so."

"Okay, okay, but I am looking for an artifact somewhere in Endor."

The girl holstered her weapon. "You're in Tel Kacie, it's about 33 kilometers from there, but you won't get there, at least not alive."

Baker's heart sputtered. "Could you help me get there? I'll

pay you handsomely."

The girl drew close enough that Baker could feel the heat of her body, smell her breath. Something swished his hand and he assumed it was her hair. "What's that?" she asked, eyeing the book.

Baker glanced down at it. "It's my research manual. I keep it to record my discoveries."

Shaking her head unconvincingly, she let a few strands of black hair fall across her face, then she brushed them aside. "You're not a very good liar. Now let me see the money."

His mind raced through a score of options: force the girl at gunpoint, which could backfire big time, show her his US dollars and hope that would satisfy her, or let her in on his little secret. Knowing human nature as he did, he chose the second option. After holstering his weapon, he reached into his pocket and pulled out a wad of bills. He nervously thumbed through the stack and pulled out a hundred-dollar bill. "There's another one just like it once we get to Ein Dor safely." He held the money out.

As soon as she reached to take it, Baker grabbed her hand and yanked her forward. In lightning speed, he whipped his gun out and jammed its barrel at her temple. The girl started to scream, but he clamped his hand over her mouth.

"I'm a man of my word." Stuffing the money down her blouse, Baker assessed his new situation. "Now I'm going to release you, but if you so much as whimper, I swear, I'll shoot you and worry about the consequences later."

The girl nodded.

He slowly released her.

"What's your name," he asked as the girl reached inside her blouse and inspected the money.

"Layla Ali," the girl said, fingering the money.

"You related to Mohammad Ali?" Baker kidded.

Layla returned a blank look.

"Don't worry about it. It was a joke. Now how do you plan

on getting me to Ein Dor?"

"Why do you want to go there, Mr. American? And this time ... I want the truth."

Baker huffed. He couldn't tell the whole truth and nothing but the truth, but he did pull the medallion from around his neck and hold it up. In the dull illumination, it caught a gleam of moonlight and reflected a golden glow. "See this? There are more of these buried in an ancient temple located near the town of Ein Dor. You can have all you can carry, just get me there."

Layla's eyes widened. "It's going to take a few days to arrange things."

As she turned, Baker grabbed her by the arm. "Wait, a few days? I can't sit here and wait while you party on my money."

"Suit yourself," she huffed, handing back his money.

Baker's fingers closed around her arm. "You'd better not be jerking me around. Now tell me, what's your plan, where are you going?"

Yanking her arm from his grasp, she spun around. "I don't know what my plan is, but I know it's going to take a few days and probably a lot more money to convince certain people to let me through."

Giving her a steely look, Baker pulled another hundred dollar bill from his pocket. "Here, don't spend it all in one place."

Layla glared back at him in a way that sent an icy chill through his gut. He'd seen that look before ... in the mirror.

"You can't expect me to just wave my hands and puff, we'll be there."

Baker resisted the urge to tell how he got there and was glad she didn't ask. "You got any food or water, I haven't eaten in a while."

The girls' dark black orbs bore into him. Shaking her head, she reached into a tattered bag which hung around her neck, pulled out a bottle of lukewarm water and a tangerine. “Here, that’ll be twenty bucks, US.”

Baker started to protest but clinched his teeth. Handing her the money, he nodded. “Thanks, now be sure not to mention our little encounter.”

Layla took the money and receded into the darkness as quietly as she appeared leaving Baker to wonder if it were all a hallucination. His only grasp on reality was the tangerine and the water, which he consumed within a minute of her departure.

Chapter Forty-One

Two pizzas later, the wise men and Ty still hadn't decided on their next plan of action. If Baker had escaped to Israel, he was out of their reach. And since he hadn't yet been charged with Glenn's attack, there were no outstanding warrants. It appeared that he had outsmarted them all.

Finally, Balthazar straightened and rubbed his aching back. "Men, it is time we returned to Israel and finish what we started. Had that medallion not fallen from my grasp we would have never found ourselves in this mess."

"But going back could be problematic," Melchior offered in a grim tone.

"I know, but it's the only way. We must stop Baker before he finds the temple and opens the door to the abyss."

"He already has a day's lead on us. He may have reached the temple and is reciting the ancient cipher as we speak," Gasper said.

"That may be so, but we must try. Pack light, we must be going."

"But how? You can't just step on an airplane and expect them to let you out of this country and into Israel without proper documentation. Remember, we live in the twenty-first century. Travel is quite restrictive." Ty's comments stopped Balthazar from leaving the room.

"Wait, I have an idea," Colt said excitedly, gaining everyone's attention.

"Young man, aren't you supposed to be in school?"

Balthazar tried to hide his frustration.

"Nope, it's Columbus Day. There's no school."

"But how'd you get here?"

Colt offered a boyish shrug. "That's easy, I rode my rip stick."

Combined head shaking followed. "So what's your idea?" Gasper's question personalized those of his friends.

"You know Mr. Myers?"

A unison, "yes" followed.

"Well, he's Jewish … he must have relatives living in Israel. Maybe he could—"

"That's a nice thought, Colt," Gasper said in a condescending tone. "But you couldn't expect him to pay our way—"

"I was thinking more like shipping you."

"Shipping us?" Balthazar voiced.

"Yeah, my dad deals in international shipping all the time. He orders stuff from all over the world and when he gets it, if it's broken, he sends it right back. I was thinking he could put you guys in crates and ship you to Israel."

Gasper guffawed.

Balthazar rubbed his chin. "You know, that just might work. If Mr. Myers knows someone in the country, Glenn could ship us there. Then we're on our own."

Ty was already on the phone. "Jacob, I gotta question for you." He waited. "Do you know anyone in Israel?" Ty's face brightened as he listened to Jacob's answer. After he explained their dilemma, the two men held a long conversation considering several options. When he finished, Ty had a pad full of notes. "Okay, I'll tell the guys what you said, thanks. Oh and, give my love to Samantha and Ashton. I'll see them after my shift is over."

The air in the wise men's house scintillated with energy as Ty mapped out their next move. "Guys, how would you like to go back to Israel the same way you came?"

"As clay manikins? No way," Gasper sputtered.

"Just hear me out." The long shift was wearing on Ty and he tried to keep his frustration under control.

"Not particularly as manikins, but in boxes, dressed in full regalia."

Balthazar cocked his head. "I do miss my old garments. They were so much more comfortable than this," holding out his open-collared shirt.

"Yes, and I miss wearing my sword. They won't let us carry them on school grounds. Can you believe that?"

Melchior placed his hand on Gasper's forearm. "And for good reason. If you got carried away with one of your dramatic scenes, you might lop off someone's head."

A chuckle percolated around the table.

"Okay, okay, but surely we can wear them on the plane ... can't we? We could store them in the overhead bin."

"I'm afraid not, my young and impetuous friend," Balthazar said. "If I'm hearing Officer Huntley correctly, Jacob is suggesting that they pack us up in boxes and ship us on a cargo plane. Right?"

Ty nodded. "That's right and he is going to get with Mr. O'Dell to make all the shipping arrangements. In the meantime, Jacob has an uncle living in Jerusalem who is with the Institute in Antiquities. He can receive you and make all the right connections for getting around in the country. And you'd never guess the name of the shipping company Glenn uses."

Ty had everyone's attention.

"It's called Gold Star, as in the star of David ... Gold Star Shipping Company has been flying in and out of Israel for years. It looks like you guys are going to return to Israel, led by a star."

The three wise men exchanged pleased mixed glances. "Just think, Melchior, we are finally going home," Balthazar said whimsically, "But first, we need to tell the administration that we'll be taking a short trip to Israel. Call it continuing education."

***

The assistant principal's reaction to the news that the wise men were taking a short leave of absence was timid. But since it came from their attorney, Jacob Myers, he had little choice but to agree. The second called he received was from Deputy Huntley assuring him that they were no longer suspects and they were, as a matter of fact, being sent on a mission to recover the stolen property.

With their school responsibilities temporarily suspended, Balthazar and the others were able to focus on more important things. They needed documents in the event they were stopped by the authorities. Jacob proved to be extremely efficient in getting the proper papers. Within a day they were ready.

Glenn, after being released from the hospital, was more than ready to get involved. He needed only to make a couple of phone calls to have their departure set for Wednesday. All that remained was to build three crates and deliver them to Hartsfield-Jackson International Airport's Cargo Freight terminals in Atlanta by noon.

The whirlwind of activity hardly left time for good-byes.

Standing inside the O'Dell's garage, the wise men made the final adjustments to their outfits. It was going to be a lengthy trip, but not near as long as the one they took across the desert. But with each man crated separately, they needed to carry a couple bottles of water and some non-perishable snacks.

"I will miss you." Felecia's lower lip trembled as Gasper climbed into his crate. In a move which surprised everyone, she tipped up on her toes and placed a warm kiss directly on his unsuspecting lips.

Wide-eyed, he stood fanning himself. He'd never thought about such things and to have it actually happen took his breath away. Finally, he regained his composure. "Well, that should hold me till I return," he sputtered. As they nailed the lid down, Felicia and the others could hear him singing, "Matchmaker, matchmaker, make me a match, catch me a catch."

Balthazar rolled his eyes. "It's going to be a long trip."

"Where is Colt?" Melchior asked, "I wanted to say good-bye to the young man."

Glenn and Karen looked at each other. "I haven't seen him in a while. I think he's taking your departure rather hard. Even though you promised to come back, I think he thinks you might stay," Karen added.

Before Melchior settled into his crate, he took Karen by the hand and said, "Tell him we'll return with lots of stories."

"I promise," Karen said, wiping a tear. "We'll miss you."

Just before they closed the lid on his container, Jacob leaned in. "Remember, you're ancient artifacts on loan from a museum called Explorations in Antiquities. Once you arrive, my uncle, Simon Levi, will take you to the Israeli Institute in Antiquities. After they've unpacked you and place you on display, you'll have a couple of days before your debut. You'll need to be back there or there will be an international scene. You don't want that."

Melchior took his place in his crate. "Tell me again, how long will we be on display?"

Jacob couldn't hide his chagrin. "Until after the Christmas season."

Gasper's singing stopped. "You mean we'll miss the live nativity?" his muffled protests were drowned out as the FedEx truck arrived.

"I'm afraid so," Jacob chuckled. "But I think you'll not miss it one bit."

***

Thirteen hours later, a cargo plane bearing the Gold Star of David landed in Tel Aviv. After clearing customers, Abram Goldberg, one of the employees entrusted with receiving deliveries for the IIA, the Institute in Antiquities, backed his rented truck up to the loading dock and collected a pallet of crates. The loading chief handed him a clipboard and he quickly scanned the pallet and signed the line at the bottom of the sheet. Then he climbed into the cab and left with his possessions. When he arrived at the IIA receiving dock, he backed his truck up and raised the door. To his surprise, he found a fourth crate. Thinking it to contain items related to the display, he casually returned to the task of unsealing them. Crowbar in hand, he pried open the first lid. He stared down upon Balthazar. Taking an appreciative look at the ancient artifact, he checked his clipboard and moved to the next crate. With care, he cataloged all the items associated with each relic. Each man came equipped with a staff, a sword, and a small pouch. To his surprise, the items in their pouches seemed out of place; a change of clothes, US currency, and an old map. Once he'd finished with the first three, he grabbed his crowbar and pried open the last one. To his surprise, he found a fourth manikin. It was a young shepherd boy.

Colt could barely keep from laughing as Abram's eyes widened and he took in a sharp breath. *I'm going to be in big trouble when the wise men find out I snuck aboard, but I had to.*

"Well, well, well, what have we here?" Simon Levi, Abram's supervisor, asked, eyeing the newly acquired treasures.

"It's replicas of the famous wise men from the Christmas story."

Simon kept a straight face as he inspected the manikins. By now, Balthazar and the others were quite good at holding a position while people gawked. After a while, the short, balding man straightened. "They look authentic enough, if one was to believe such nonsense. Those Christians," he shook his head, "they've got the nerve. Obfuscating Hanukkah and linking it with the Santa Clause and reindeer."

It was all Gasper could do to keep from bursting into laughter.

The supervisor continued studying the ornate robes and fingered Melchior's sword. "Ouch," his sudden outburst nearly caused Melchior to pull back. "That sword is sharp. It's like it hadn't aged a bit."

Simon dragged the fourth manikin into view of the others. "We got a bonus. My nephew included a young shepherd boy to round out the display. It's not as detailed, but he will look good to the thousands of people who come to celebrate the Christian holiday."

Balthazar nearly fell off his pedestal. *How in the name of conscience did Colt smuggle himself on that plane?*

Once the manikins were placed in the display, Simon made one last adjustment to the lighting. Satisfied all was in order, he flipped the lights off, set the alarm and left.

***

In the darkness, Gasper whispered, "Colt what are you doing here?

"I wanted to help."

"Yeah, you're going to help all right, help us get put in jail for kidnapping."

"You didn't kidnap me. I came on my own."

Melchior shifted so he could see him. "But how did you do it and not get caught?"

"Oh, that was easy. I just built a smaller crate and made a label that looked like the ones on your crates. The shippers did the rest."

"Well, what are your parents going to say when they find out you're missing," Balthazar asked, his face a wash of concern.

"I left them a note telling them I went with you to help get that medallion back. Plus, I'm a part of the order of Magi and it's my fault we're in this mess. If I didn't steal the medallion, we wouldn't be here."

Balthazar rubbed his chin. "Now that he's here, we may as well put him to good use. We only have a few days to find Baker and retrieve the medallion and we could use all the help we can get. Colt, do you think you could go over there and bring those Roman display pieces over here?"

Colt's face brightened. "Why?"

"Because if we wise men left our posts, without the proper weight exchange, an alarm will go off."

Satisfied, Colt climbed down and began dragging a Roman guard piece over to where Balthazar stood. After struggling with it for a few minutes, he was able to slide it in place. With Balthazar's help, they exchanged Melchior and Gasper with two other guards which stood near a figurine of King Herod.

"I don't remember King Herod looking so friendly. The last time we saw him, he was quite grouchy." Gasper mused.

"I think grouchy would be putting it lightly. Now let's get going. We have a criminal to catch and a medallion to destroy." Balthazar said, as he led the way to the nearest exit.

Chapter Forty-Two

It had been two days since Randy last spoke with Layla. The few times she did show up, it was when he was asleep and she was only there long enough to leave him a fresh jug of water and some food. His diet had been reduced from steak and potatoes to falafels, hummus, and dried dates. No beer and certainly no *mountain water.*

While he waited, he studied the ornate markings on the pages of the Book of Incantations. From what he guessed, once he found the temple he would need to follow precise instructions to get to the Chamber of Sacrifice and, using his medallion as the key, touch certain stones all the while reciting an ancient chant. It seemed an impossible task, but if he were to unlock the powers reserved for the faithful, he was willing to go all the way, even if it cost him his soul.

As he practiced saying the chant, the room grew darker. The light filtering through the slats on the windows dimmed making it difficult to see. Looking through one of the cracks on the boarded up window, he saw the scorching sun. “So why the gloom?” He wondered out loud.

Leviathan knew the answer. It was he and his hosts who crowded into the small building; pushing out the light, darkening the room. Already, the demons of Greed and Lust had sunk their claws deeply into Baker’s skull. Now it was Pride’s turn. By the time they finished filling his mind, Baker would be putty in their hands.

A guttural laugh percolated in Baker’s throat, jolting him upright. “Who’s there?” His wild eyes searched the darkness.

Standing, he began to pace. "What is happening to me?" he questioned. "I'm beginning to sound like Mrs. White."

He let a cruel grin part his lips. "Yes, Mrs. White ... the White Witch. She thought she was so smart. Hiding in that cave, going to offer a young girl in exchange for being the Dark Lord's mother. How short sighted. When I am finished, I will wield the powers of the underworld. They will bow at my command and if anyone tries to stop me, I will crush them like a bug." Just then, a large, black bug scampered across the floor, but before it reached its destination, Baker lifted his boot and brought it down with a heavy thud. The sound reverberated and the voices outside stopped.

Sweat formed and dripped off Baker's nose as two men approached the door. His hand grabbed the butt of his weapon. He knew he'd probably kill one man ... probably get killed by the other, but he was not going down without a fight.

Suddenly, a face appeared near a stack of crates on the far wall. "Psst." It was Layla. She motioned him to stay down and come to where she was.

Keeping low, he nearly belly crawled to the crates. "Follow me." Her command needed no explanation.

Baker stepped behind the stack of crates and immediately discovered how she'd been able to slip in and out without his notice. A small opening in the wall revealed a passage between buildings. Following her example, he squeezed through and found himself standing in a similar building as the one he'd just left. Behind him, a crashing sound told him he'd vacated the room not a moment too soon.

"Where to next?"

She motioned him to stay quiet ... he obeyed.

Soon the footsteps in the other room grew distant, and both he and Layla started to breathe again.

"There's a car waiting for us at the end of the street. It is loaded with provisions and enough ammunition to start a war but we must hurry. If the authorities find it, they will not stop searching until they find us and kill us."

Wiping the sweat from his brow, Baker peered out the window and then at Layla. "Who's the, they?"

"Does it matter? Neither of us belong here and the sooner we get out of this place, the better. Now sit down and be quiet. We'll make our move as soon as it gets dark." Then she pulled a tunic from her bag. "Here, put this on. At least you'll not stand out like a Jew on Ramadan."

Baker followed her instructions and tugged the rough fabric over his head and sat down. He wanted to ask her why she was hiding in the same place as he, but she sat trance-like, unblinking, and he decided to return to his book.

Whether he drifted off to sleep or had been so engrossed in his study of the book, he wasn't sure, but Layla stood abruptly and dusted off the seat of her pants. "It's time."

Baker stood and waited for the blood to return to his lower extremities. The sharp tingling sensation took his mind off the gnawing hunger he suddenly felt.

Glancing both ways, Layla darted through the rickety door into the alley. Baker followed.

After a heart-pounding minute, she moved again, this time staying close to the dilapidated buildings. The quarter moon did little to light the deep shadows which held most buildings captive. A few quick steps and she moved from shadow to shadow, building to building with Baker close behind. His heavy breathing was the only sound between them.

Finally, they reached the end of the street. Hidden under a tarp was what she called a car. In reality, it was an old army jeep. Its once rugged tires had been worn to nubs like a child's pencil eraser. In the washed-out light, he could vaguely make out a star on the hood.

"Get in," she barked.

"Won't they hear us when you start the engine?"

Layla ignored the question and turned the key. The jeep sputtered, backfired, then stumbled to life. "Nah, they are having too much fun with the girls some of your money paid for."

Baker forced himself to take a dry swallow. He had no idea what she meant by arranging things, now he was beginning to realize her resourcefulness.

With a jerk, the vehicle lurched forward as if she'd never driven a standard transmission. Taking a deep breath, she tried again. This time, the jeep pulled out of the ruts it sat in and she eased the jeep toward the only road leading to and from town. A moment later, shouts exploded behind them followed by gun shots.

"I thought you said the guards were preoccupied."

"They were. But it wasn't forty virgins."

Zip!

A bullet ripped the air open and Baker ducked. He hated being on the receiving end of a gun. He pulled out his weapon when Layla shoved his hand down. "You fire back and you'll bring down the whole camp. Right now, all they think is someone was leaving for a joy-ride. You start shooting and they'll all come after us."

Her logic made sense and he relaxed as the jeep rumbled across the sand-swept road. After fifteen minutes she turned left and took the main road. It led to a town called Maagan which hugged the Sea of Galilee, then she turned right. The route took them along the dark waters where Jesus once walked. He remembered the stories of the life of Jesus from when he was a kid; of Jesus feeding the five thousand, walking on the water and of course, the Easter story. To him, they were just stories, nothing more and he quickly shoved them aside.

Bet Yerah and Kinneret came into view and they drove through the narrow streets without comment. Seeing an Israeli checkpoint, she flicked off the headlights and cut the wheels to the left. Following a rutted cow-path, she guided the jeep around an area of rich farmland. To Baker, it reminded him of Lancaster, Pennsylvania with one distinct difference ... all the homes were enclosed behind high block walls. The occasional military vehicle they passed bore an Israeli flag reminding him of the constant danger they were in.

After stopping to consult her map and once to refuel, she finally broke the silence "There it is, Ein Dor."

It surprised him how quickly they made the journey. In his mind, he figured it would take days, not forty minutes, but there it was ... the kibbutz called Ein Dor. "So this is where she came from," he mused out loud.

"What did you say?"

Baker realized too late his thoughts had been verbalized. "Oh, just a woman I once knew."

Layla shook her head allowing her raven-like hair to shield her eyes. "We're here, now pay me."

"What do you mean, here? You haven't taken me to the Temple of Endor. This is just a sleepy town."

Her orbs burned with an eerie glow from behind strands of black hair. "I'll get you there, but first ... you must pay."

Her words were reminiscent of those spoken by the spirit in the mirror and he wondered.

Chapter Twenty-Three

Earlier Friday morning, Felicia joined the group of courageous teens who met to pray and sing around the flag pole. Having been invited by Gasper on several other occasions, she felt a kindred spirit with the group and even offered a few requests of her own. Most of the time she would join in singing, letting the praise choruses waft across the parking lot, but this morning she was too burdened to sing. Instead, she had some prayer requests. The name Olivia McKinney kept coming to her mind throughout the night, chasing sleep from eyes. For some reason, known only to God, she felt burdened for the women she and Gasper replaced. *Were the rumors true? Was she in some sort of trouble? Was she pregnant? And if so was the child in her womb in danger?*

When Josh asked for prayer requests, her hand shot up. "Yes, Miss Beauchamp?"

It always amused Felicia when a student, not five years her junior, called her Miss Beauchamp. Nodding tentatively, she stepped to the center of the circle. "Yes, I have three." Glancing around she scanned the group wishing Gasper was there to lend his support. But he had a job to do and so did she. "You remember Miss McKinney?" A smattering of 'yes's followed. "Well, her name came to mind last night and I sense she has a need." Quizzical expressions formed on many faces, while others exchanged 'I told you so,' looks. "I also want you to pray for Mr. Balthazar, Mr. Melchior, and Mr. Gasper. While I'm not at liberty to disclose their whereabouts, I know they would appreciate your continued prayers." Heads nodded, some girls sniffed back tears, grim-faced guys squared their shoulders, their jaws set. "And I want you to pray for tonight's performance. We have a big job ahead of us and some of the performers are feeling a bit squeamish."

Madi, the junior who would play Hodel, nodded her thanks for not mentioning her name and for being concerned for her health.

As the group knelt to pray, a myriad of silver wings formed an impenetrable wall around them. Standing with his sword unsheathed, Prince Leo held his gaze at the dark forces pouring forth from the school like smoke from a furnace. The gathering wicked beings ascended skyward turning the sky-blue ceiling into an ominous green. The wind whipped up sending debris into the rapidly cooling air. Teachers and students shivered as they scrambled from their cars and buses to the school entrance.

Despite the chaos outside their circle, the devoted Christian teens continued to pray, lifting up holy hands and declaring the name of the Lord. Above the cacophony, Josh's voice rose in clear tones.

"Lord, would You reach out and touch Miss McKinney. Protect her from harm and evil. If she doesn't know You as her Lord and Savior, draw her to Yourself by Your grace and save her in Jesus' name. We also plead for our teachers who are following Your leadership. If they are in danger, protect them. If they are facing spiritual wickedness, give them a double portion of Your spirit and give them the victory. And we pray for the upcoming performance. Help everyone to remember their lines and do their best for Your honor and glory."

Others repeated the prayer in various renditions until the five-minute school bell sounded. Finally, the group grabbed each other's hands and lifted their united voices in one last chorus.

As the teens scattered in a dozen directions, Prince Leo

relaxed his stance. A flutter of activity caught his eye and he looked at the messenger sent from the throne of grace.

"News, my lord."

Prince Leo turned to face the ever young spirit who held a position far below his station. Returning his crisp salute, he waited for the messenger to deliver his report. "News? So quickly?"

"Yes, Prince Argos cleared the way and I was able to make the journey unhindered."

"And your message is?"

"The Almighty has heard and accepted the prayers of the young people. Miss McKinney's life has been spared and has come to the light of the glorious gospel even as we speak."

Prince Leo lowered himself to one knee. Hands raised, he lifted his resonant voice heavenward praising the God of salvation. A moment later, he was joined by his cohort and the fleet-footed messenger.

***

By six-forty-five, the auditorium buzzed with excitement as parents, teachers and the invited public squeezed into the recently constructed building. As the near capacity crowd gathered for the night's opening performance, the main topic of discussion was not *Fiddler on the Roof,* it was the news of Principal Davis' arrest. Having watched the police frog-march Richard Davis to a waiting patrol car, Felicia wondered what kind of reaction it would have on her student actors. The effect was nil, and even supportive of the police action. She agreed.

Behind the drawn curtains, Madi and Clayton paced the backstage like two caged cats. Madi repeated her opening lines, while Clayton hummed a scale in an attempt to stretch out his vocal cords. It didn't help that he was suffering from a post-nasal drip limiting his range and causing his voice to sound strained.

"Where is Mr. Gasper? He's supposed to be my backup."

Madi's brown eyes warmed. She had played the leading

role opposite him in several productions and had grown to know how to cover for his memory lapses, but singing his part was not possible. "Do your best and it will be okay. Just stay focused on staying in character."

Clayton nodded. He looked quite pitiful in his turn of the century garb, but he owned his character. Even off stage, he carried himself as if he really was Tevye, the father of three husband-hungry daughters.

All at once, the lights dimmed and Felicia rushed across the stage. "Okay, this is it. Everyone take your places. The assistant principal is about to make a few announcements and then it's all up to you."

The young people grew sober and waited. This was their night.

As the lights came on and the curtains rose, Felicia crossed her fingers and wished Gasper was there.

Chapter Forty-Four

Having reached the street through a rear exit, the wise men and Colt navigated their way to the nearest corner. Even at that late hour, the streets of Jerusalem bustled with foot traffic and cars. Down the block from where they stood, loud music blared from a disco bar, and scantily clad women called to passersby.

"Looks like not much has changed," Balthazar said, averting his sight.

Nodding, Melchior took up a position between him and Colt. "Yes, things have changed ... they've gotten worse."

After hailing a cab, Balthazar instructed the driver to take them to the Ein Dor kibbutz.

"Ein Dor? That's 153 kilometers from here. It'll cost ya."

"How much?" Gasper asked, his hands held out, expressively.

The taxi driver tapped into his phone a few numbers and waited. "That'll be 200 shekels."

Gasper glanced at his friends and mouthed the words. "How much is that in US?"

The taxi driver shook his head and stared at his fare with suspicion. "More than you have. You sure you don't want me to take you to Circa Ola?"

The wise men exchanged confused looks. "No, we want to go to—"

"I know, I know. I heard ya the first time. It ain't gonna happen. Now, if you'll pardon me, I've got paying fares waiting." He slammed his little car into gear and sped off, leaving the wise men to wonder how wise it was to be in Israel without their camels.

"It will take us days to get there at this rate. And we don't have a star to guide us," Gasper grumbled as they trudged along the road leading from the city.

"Are you going to start complaining again? We haven't been in this country two hours and you've already started." Melchior's admonition temporarily ended Gasper's diatribe.

In the distance, a pair of headlights appeared around a corner followed by the roar of an engine. The car slowed to a stop and Simon jumped out.

"Mr. Levi, what a pleasant surprise." Balthazar couldn't hide his shock.

"No need to be alarmed. Your friend Mr. O'Dell informed me all about your little escapade. Now get in, we must hurry."

***

As the wise men rode through the streets of Jerusalem, they stared wide-eyed at the changes.

"I hardly recognize the place, it has changed so much," Balthazar said as he watched the high rise buildings race past his window.

"Herod's Temple, his lavished palace, all the beautiful mansions which once lined the streets ... gone, all gone," Gasper mused. "What happened?"

Simon checked his rear view mirror. "You really don't know, do you?"

"No." They said in harmony.

"We've been gone for a long time," Melchior added with a wry smile.

As Simon guided the car east, then north through the Galilee region heading toward Ein Dor, he gave the wise men a brief summary of Israel's history. When he finished, the wise men were even more confused and astounded than before.

His eyebrows knit, Balthazar looked at his friends. "That

means all the prophecies about Israel's dispersion and regathering are true."

Smiling, Simon continued, "That's right, since A.D. 70 to May 14th, 1948, after nearly two thousand years of being scattered all over the world, we Jews have returned and Israel became a nation again. Nowhere in history has it been said, that a lost nation has been found, but it is so, as you can see." His face beamed with joy.

"Tell us about the Six-Day war," Gasper pressed.

Simon rolled up his sleeve and revealed an ugly scare. "It was June, 1967. Israel had roughly 75,000 troops, nearly 1000 tanks, and an air force of 175 jets. But we were outnumbered five to one against an Arab army of 900 combat jets, 5000 tanks and a half million men. After two days of being pounded, we retaliated with the ferocity of a lion robbed of her whelps. In four days we broke the backs of the Egyptians, Syrians, and the Arab league. I took a bullet in the arm in the process."

"You will chase your enemies, and they will fall before you. Five will chase a hundred, a hundred will put to flight ten thousand and your enemies shall fall before you. For I the Lord will have respect unto you and will multiply you and establish my covenant with you. Leviticus 26:7-9," Melchior said.

A bright smile parted Simon's lips. "Yes, that about sums it up, and it's been that way ever since. With US backing and supplying us with the most up-to-date weaponry, we have been able to hold off the tide of Islamic hatred and Palestine encroachment. But we live with the constant threat of annihilation."

Leaning forward, Balthazar placed his hand on Simon's shoulder. "My friend, you are leaving out one key element."

Simon glanced back. "What's that?"

"God's protection. The Almighty had kept his covenant with Israel. He has promised to bless this nation above all other nations and to make it the head, not the tail. But first,

Israel must suffer greatly."

"You know this to be true?" Simon gripped the wheel tighter.

"Yes. We are not only wise men, but we are men of the Word. Your scripture prophesied all the disasters and Israel's regathering, which you just listed. Since God has kept his word in the past, He will surely keep what is yet to be revealed."

"And what is that, my friends?"

Balthazar looked at the others. What awaited his beloved land was Daniel's seventieth in which nearly the entire nation would be killed. Only then would the remnant turn in repentance to their Messiah. It was a message the nation needed to hear. It was a message Simon needed to hear, but was there time? They had just passed the gate leading into Ein Dor, and they had a mission.

After passing the Riding Stables, they traveled in silence toward the hill of Endor. Finally, they reached an area with a historical marker stating the hill's biblical claim to fame. The story of the Witch of Endor, found in I Samuel 28, is one of the most mysterious witch stories of all time. Saul, after destroying all the mediums in Israel, found himself in dire straits. He was surrounded by a Philistine army much larger than his fledgling nation was prepared to face and he hadn't heard from the Lord. In desperation, he disguised himself and sought the counsel of a witch ... the witch of Endor. After conjuring up a spirit whom she identified as Samuel, the Witch of Endor became so frightened that it is impossible to doubt the story's authenticity. The old prophet asked King Saul, 'why have you disturbed me?' To which he replied, 'The Philistines are attacking us and I haven't heard from the Lord.' Samuel's chilling answer has been the subject of theological debate for the last twenty-five centuries. He said, 'Tomorrow, about this time, you and your sons will be with me.' Since then, the story has been told and retold until it had grown to legendary proportions like that of Paul Bunyan and Babe, his

Blue Ox. Nevertheless, the prophecy came true, just as Samuel had predicted.

"So where is the Temple of Endor?" Gasper asked the question that was on all their minds.

Simon parked the car and got out, followed by the others. Colt quickly dashed into the darkness and ducked behind a large Olive tree. The three wise men grinned at each other.

"Too much water," Gasper chuckled.

As their eyes adjusted to the darkness, Balthazar gazed heavenward. Above them stretched a blanket of velvet peppered with tiny holes through which a countless number of dazzling lights glistened. He took in the scene and thought about the last time he and his friends were there. Suddenly, it all came back to him; the parched air, the unrelenting desert, the deep silence. It was like he'd traveled back in time ... to his time and he thought of his wife ... and son.

Simon's gravelly voice called him back to reality. "Well, first of all, it's nearly midnight. We can't see anything in this darkness. We'll have to get some rooms and wait until morning before we can scout around."

Balthazar rubbed his chin. "On the other hand, we've already lost several days. For all we know, Baker has found the door and is working on trying to decipher the code."

"Not without this." Gasper held up the last page from the Book of Incantations.

Out of the corner of his eye, Balthazar caught movement. At first, he thought it was Colt playing a trick, but then a shadow grew larger.

***

Gasper's breath caught in his throat as Randy Baker's hulking frame came into view followed by a petite woman. More than seeing the gun leveled at his chest, what caught his attention was the woman's black orbs. Her focus seemed to pierce right through him ... into his soul.

"I guess my little surprise in the shack didn't go over very well," he said with a smirk. His eyes narrowed as he peered at Gasper. "Your blood will be required of you when I'm done here."

A chill wrapped its icy fingers around Gasper's heart and squeezed. Knowing that Baker would stop at nothing to get what he wanted, Gasper stepped between Baker and Balthazar. With his tucked hands behind his back, he spoke in an even tone. "If you ask me, that was the worst batch of hooch I've ever tasted. I think you overcooked it." As he spoke, he passed the rolled page to Balthazar hoping he would know what to do with it.

Baker chuckled. "Real funny. Now where's that page you stole from me?"

"What page?"

"Don't play stupid. You wouldn't be here if you didn't steal that page from me. Now where is it?

"I believe you have it all wrong. You were in such a hurry to get out of there, you left it behind."

Baker wagged the statement aside with the barrel of the gun. "Doesn't matter. You have it and I want it."

Gasper brought his empty hands in front of him and held them in surrender. "No, actually, I don't have it."

By then, Balthazar had taken it and passed it to Simon. Using the larger man to block his escape, Simon backed away and dashed behind a boulder. Not knowing the lay of the land, he stumbled across a field of standing wheat, but the soft soil slowed his progress.

It didn't take Baker long to figure out what had happened. "After him!" he shouted.

An instant later, the woman charged into the darkness, her weapon drawn and ready.

Gasper and the others held their breath, hoping Simon got away in the dark, looking for an opportunity when Baker was distracted to take the initiative.

***

It had been a long time since he'd felt such fear, but Simon knew the risks. He had to protect this page from falling into the hands of these people even if it cost him his life, but age and failing health were his enemies as much as the people with guns. Heavy breathing sounded. A quick glance over his shoulder revealed the woman accomplice advancing quickly. Not being used to running, Simon quickly tired. The footsteps grew louder. Wishing he'd thought to bring his gun, he plunged deeper into the night looking for a place to hide. If he didn't stop to catch his breath soon, he would collapse. By the time he'd reached the far end of the field, his lungs screamed for oxygen and his heart jackhammered against his ribs. All at once, a metal building emerged from the gloom and he ducked behind it. Slamming up against the corrugated metal, he forced his lungs, heaving. With seconds to spare, he jammed the roll under the metal frame and kicked dirt over the opening. Then, with sweat blurring his vision, he turned and scampered for a stand of trees.

Bang, bang!

The air reverberated with the force of two shots. Heat seared Simon's shoulder and he tumbled forward. Gasping for air, he tried to reach the safety of the tree, but the female pursuer pounced upon him like a wild animal.

"Where is it?" She tore at his bloody shirt.

"Where is what?" Simon fought to keep the panic from his voice despite the pain which clawed at his muscles.

The woman rolled him over and held the gun at his head while her other hand rummaged through his pockets.

"Why were you running?" she demanded.

"I was scared. They forced me to take them here, I know nothing." He lied.

Layla grabbed his wounded shoulder and jammed her thumb into the wound. He screamed. "It's in the metal shed. Please don't kill me."

She shoved him to the ground and dashed back to the shed.

After scouring all around the shed, she shot the lock and threw the door back. "Empty." She cursed.

Returning to Simon, she grabbed him by the collar and dragged him back to the car and tossed him down.

"Did you get it?" Baker demanded.

"No, he said he hid it in the shed, but it's too dark to see anything."

Baker released a string of expletives. "Didn't you think to pack a flashlight?"

Layla cut her eyes in his direction, clearly annoyed at his tone. "Yes, I packed a flashlight. I just didn't have it with me when I chased that jerk across the wheat field. If you didn't act like John Wayne, we could have been better prepared, but no."

Baker took a step in her direction, but she backed up and aimed her gun at his chest, stopping him cold.

Hands held in surrender, he took a step back. "Okay, okay, I was just going to get it. In the meantime, don't let these people out of your sight."

"Yeah, right," she spat as Baker strode off.

As they waited, the warbling sound of a Siren began to grow louder. Layla cursed again and tucked her gun in her belt. Turning on her heels, she ran after Baker. "This isn't over," she hollered over her shoulder.

The moment she left, Melchior grabbed Simon and helped him get to his car. "We'd better get out of here." Touching the bloody wound, he clinched his jaw and inhaled deeply.

Gasper jumped in behind the wheel and started the engine, followed by Balthazar.

As they sped off, Balthazar glanced around. "Where's Colt?"

Gasper took a quick count. "This is bad, really bad," he said as he shoved the car in gear and rounded a corner moments before the local police arrived. "We can't go back ... not with a wounded man in the car. We have to find someplace to hide until tomorrow night. And Simon needs medical attention."

Simon sat up and released a sigh. "That won't be necessary." Looking at Melchior, he smiled. "Thank you. Whatever you did was close to miraculous."

Melchior returned his smile as he wiped his bloody hands on a towel. "It wasn't me. I was just the vessel through which God's healing power flowed."

Shaking his head, he continued to hold his gaze. "Well, that may be so, but I still say thank you. Turning his attention to the road ahead, he pointed. "Turn right at the next road and pull into the driveway on the right."

"What's there?" Balthazar asked.

Releasing a chuckle, Simon rubbed his stiff shoulder. "Funny thing about our building codes. We can build a building, but as long as it is not finished, we don't have to pay taxes on it. I own that building up ahead. It's got a working refrigerator and a stash of food. So we can rest there until tomorrow. Then we can go back and hunt for the young man."

After pulling around to the back of the building, Gasper shut off the engine allowing the silence to close in. Leaning his head on the steering wheel, he sighed heavily. "This is not at all as I expected."

Chapter Forty-Five

Glenn closed the garage door and trudged into the house. It was his first day home after being released from the hospital and he was feeling the effects. He, Karen and Jacob had successfully shipped the wise men off and all he wanted to do now was to sit and rest a while.

"I wish Colt was here to say good-bye to his friends before they left," Karen said, bringing her husband a cup of coffee and sitting it on the end table next to him.

He lifted the cup and sipped thoughtfully. "You know, it's not like him to be so quiet. Usually, he's so inquisitive, always asking questions."

"Yes, but he's gotten so close to Gasper and the others, maybe you should take him camping to get his mind off his friends."

Glenn's face brightened. "That's a great idea. Call him down and let's gather around the Bible. We can pray for the wise men's safe arrival and discuss plans for tomorrow."

Karen was already on her feet. "Colt ..."

No answer.

"Colt," she called, this time with more urgency. "Could you come down, your dad and I want to talk with you." She waited.

"That's funny, maybe he wasn't feeling well. You know how that medallion thing affected him." Glenn's voice carried an edge of uncertainty.

"I'll check on him." Taking two steps at a time, Karen dashed up the stairs. A moment later, her scream brought

Glenn to his feet.

Sensing her concern, he forced his legs to push himself up the stairs and enter Colt's room.

"He's gone." She buried her face in his chest as she clutched a sloppily written note.

Still holding his wife, Glenn slumped to the empty bed and read the note.

"Dear Mom and Dad, you don't know this, but I am a member of the Brotherhood of Wise Men. I have sworn to defend the honor of the Brotherhood and I couldn't let them leave without me. So I sneaked aboard the truck. I love you and will miss you.
Love, Colt."

Karen sobbed while Glenn remanded stoic. "I thought something was going on when I saw him with a hammer. I assumed he was just trying to help out." Glenn's voice broke.

Finally, he cleared his throat and looked at his wife. "Honey, I have a confession to make."

She pulled away, her face showing the strain of the last week.

"All the time I was unconscious, I heard you praying—"

"I know, that's all I did."

"Yes, and I heard Colt. He wanted to know why God let this happen. He sounded so pitiful. That's when I saw Him."

"Saw who?" her eyes rounding.

"Him ... the Lord. I knew in an instant why He let this happen. I'd been so preoccupied that I crowded out not only you and Colt, but also the Lord. But He wasn't mad or angry. He just looked at me with those warm, loving eyes. He offered me grace ... and another chance."

Dabbing her tears with a corner of the sheet, Karen took a raggedy breath. "What did you do?"

Tears streaked down Glenn's face and he brushed them away. "I yielded ... surrendered. I told the Lord what I'm telling you now; my priorities are now God and family, church and lastly, work."

Karen had heard his short termed promises before, but not like this. This was different ... it was heartfelt ... real. She threw her arms around his neck and drew him close. "I'm going to hold you to it, but most of all, I'll going to support you in whatever decisions you make."

Glenn pulled a folded piece of paper from his pocket. "I was going to show you this later, but I guess this is as good a time as any. I just wish Colt was here to hear it."

Karen bit the corner of her lip in anticipation.

He read. "I'm going to sell my rental properties starting with the bookstore. Mr. and Mrs. Powell have been wanting to buy it since I hired them as managers. They will be much better at running it than me, anyway. Next, I'm going to give my percentage of ownership of the department store over to my uncle. The only thing I'm keeping is the shipping company."

Another round of tears rushed Karen's eyes and she hugged her husband close. "I have a confession to make too."

Glenn pulled away. His mind chafed at what she might tell him. Had she been having an affair because of his inattention? Was she and Colt about to leave him? Was he about to lose his family just at the time he was getting his life back together? He braced himself for the worst.

Taking a shaky breath, Karen began. "I'm afraid I'm as guilty for your misplaced priorities as you are."

Her words slammed into Glenn like a freight train.

"How? Why? I don't understand."

Hand raised, she stifled his questions. "Please, let me continue." She sucked in another breath. "You see, it was my constant nagging for a bigger house, newer car and a dozen other little things that drove you to work all the time. I thought those things would make me happy, but all they did was leave me feeling empty ... wanting more. What I really needed was a closer walk with the Lord and a loving relationship with you. Instead, I drove you away along with God. For the last two years, I've been faking it at church ... covering for your actions when, in fact, I was the one responsible for them. At least some of them," she added.

Glenn knew it was true, but he loved buying things too. The Christmas display, the yard ornaments, the relentless chase for the Year of the Season Award. It was his pride which drove him, not his wife. "Well, that's all behind us now. We are tooling way back on our spending except for one thing."

Her forehead wrinkling, Karen asked, "What?" her tone dubious.

"Giving money to the church. I'm way behind on my tithing, and then there is the mission's fund. I understand the pastor has had to solicit money from people outside the church to build the children's home in Haiti. That shouldn't be necessary. Once I get caught up on my giving, and with the help of my shipping company, they will have all the supplies they need to finish the project."

Karen's eyes glistened and they knelt next to Colt's bed and sealed their commitment with prayer. Then they turned their attention to Colt and the wise men.

***

Standing nearby, a smile stretched across Prince Uriel's broad face. Taking a quick look sideways, he took in Prince Selaphiel's satisfied expression. He spoke in a low tone. "When Glenn fell under Baker's attack, I had no idea what the Good Shepherd had in mind or what He was trying to accomplish. But I knew there must have been a higher purpose."

Prince Selaphiel shifted from one foot to the other as he and Uriel guarded their human charges. "Yes, my experience at watching the Almighty work is this, His ways are past finding out. O the depth of the wisdom and the knowledge of our Creator, they are unsearchable. None can know the mind of Jehovah, nor give Him council. For of Him, and through Him and to Him, are all things: to Him be the glory forever. Amen."

"But what of Colt?" Prince Selaphiel asked.

Prince Uriel lifted his gaze to a higher plain where his commander stood. "I've asked the same question of Prince Argos."

"And?"

"And he informed me since the wise men and Master Colt have left his jurisdiction they have come under the authority of Michael the Archangel."

Prince Selaphiel relaxed his stance. "Then they are in good hands. Prince Michael is one of the mightiest of his order."

"That is so, yet even he, when contending with the devil over the body of Moses, didn't bring an accusation against him, but rebuked him in the name of the Lord."

Holding Selaphiel's gaze, Prince Uriel's tone grew dark. "I'm sorry my lord, I underestimated the one with whom we are dealing. Obviously, we are in a spiritual battle. One with eternal consequences."

Chapter Forty-Six

Staying back behind the adults, Colt let the older men do the talking when Baker and his female accomplice got the drop on them. He had never seen Baker so angry and feared something terrible would happen. Hoping to get a good shot at the former sheriff, he pulled his slingshot from his back pocket and loaded it with a round, smooth stone. But before he could fire, Simon spun and dashed into the darkness. Without thinking, he took off after the man as Baker shouted an order. His feet carried him swiftly through the tall stalks, but as he neared Simon, he realized someone else was also chasing them. Suddenly, a metal shed appeared and he watched Simon bury the rolled page under the edge of the building before dashing off.

Gunshots erupted causing his legs to turn to rubber. He wanted to run, but not knowing which way to go, he backed into the shadows and curled into a tight ball. He'd never even been shot at by an air gun, let alone a real one, but seeing Simon fall turned his stomach and he nearly wretched.

Knowing he had only seconds to spare, he dug in the soil and found the paper. Snatching it, he sprang into a shadow just before the woman came crashing through the wheat. From his vantage point, he watched her rough up the older man and then go to the metal building and shoot the lock. The moment she disappeared in the shed, he ran in the opposite direction hoping to find his friends.

By the time he realized he'd been running in the wrong

direction, it was too late. From a distance, he saw the two cars speed off in the opposite direction, leaving him all alone. Slumping down on the ground, Colt fingered the paper and wished he'd never come. Soon, tears soaked his dirt-smudged face and he cried himself to sleep.

***

Michael, the Archangel, crossed his arms across his massive chest. Having watched the events of the night unfold, he directed his forces to set up a hedge of protection around the young boy and the older men. He knew a powerful demon was at work seeking access to the abyss and using Randy Baker to do its bidding, but what form it had taken had not yet been revealed to him.

Nodding to Prince Ethanes, one of his most trusted princes, he said, "Send a messenger to the All-knowing One. Ask Him to reveal with whom we are contending."

"Yes, my lord," the prince answered smartly. With a quick bow, he backed away. An instant later, a flash of light split the night sky and he was gone.

Turning his attention to the boy, Michael summoned Prince Laina. "I have a job for you."

Prince Laina, one of the least in the armies of God, was not unaccustomed to small jobs. It had been his privilege to enter the physical realm and carry out special missions which the larger, mightier angels couldn't do without frightening the earthly beings to death. It was he who touched Daniel and strengthened him. That one touch helped one of God's most beloved prophets receive instructions concerning the distant future of the world's kingdoms, and of the end of the age.

On another occasion, he touched John the Revelator. Prince Laina cracked a smile. "You remember what happened on that assignment, don't you?"

The mighty prince joined him in his amusement. "Yes, the frightened man was so grateful for your aide that he fell on his face and began to worship you."

"And I was so bothered that I quickly lifted him to his feet, saying, 'See that you don't do it: for I am your fellow servant. I have been sent to you and your brethren the prophets, and those who obey the sayings written in this book. Please, I implore you ... worship God!' But I especially enjoyed my assignment to the Apostle Peter. He couldn't believe his eyes when I showed up to help him escape. I actually had to nudge him with my foot to get him moving." The two angels shared the moment, chuckling.

Prince Michael shifted to face his understudy. "You did well to remind John of such things. Oh that Lucifer had your insight. He would have absorbed that worship and even rewarded the Revelator with great riches just as he offered the Messiah. After forty days of fasting, the evil one tempted the Lord's anointed and would have given him authority over the entire world if he fell down and worshiped him. It was then, I sent you to minister to the Anointed one."

A silver moment slipped past the two before Prince Laina spoke again. "It is sad, is it not, that in these days, so much is made of angles?"

"Yes, there is such confusion. The mortals have actually come to believe when their loved ones pass on, they turn into an angel. What a demotion. If they only knew their position in Christ ... sons of God, joint-heirs with the One who sits on the throne. Why settle for being an angel, when they could be a child of the Most High?"

Prince Laina's shoulders firmed. "And it is an honor to serve these blessed ones along their troubled way."

Michael dipped his head allowing the rays of celestial light to dance off his golden crown. "Now, go in the strength of the Lord."

Chapter Forty-Seven

It had been a sleepless night for the wise men as each man replayed their near death experience. How could they have been so blind as to not expect any resistance from the enemy? Once again, they had relied upon human wisdom and instinct to guide them. It nearly cost them their lives. Already, Simon received a severe gunshot. Fortunately, Melchior's powers of healing had returned and he was able to restore him to health. But they had lost Colt. Losing the last page from the book was one thing, losing Colt was a blow that none of the wise men could sustain. Could Colt and the last page have fallen into the hands of these killers? If so, would they show him mercy? Knowing the grudge Baker had against the little guy nearly drove them nuts. How could they return home to face Glenn and Karen without their son?

Huddling close, Balthazar faced his friends. "Men, we must once again repent of our foolishness. We are here without God's protection and power and we have paid dearly. Simon was nearly killed and Colt and the page are probably in the hands of sheriff Baker. We need God's help."

For the next thirty minutes each man poured out their hearts; confessing their dependence upon the flesh and trust in human instrumentality. Finally, they turned their attention to Simon. Balthazar led the way to the throne of grace. "And Lord God, maker of heaven and earth, savior of men, lover of our souls. We plead for Mr. Levi's soul. He is so blind, his heart hardened by the deceitfulness of the world. Open his eyes to the truth that Jesus is his Messiah, the Redeemer. We know Jacob's week of trouble is near at hand. Your beloved nation will soon suffer greatly. Many will die and go to a Christless eternity. It is our duty to warn those with whom we come in contact. Thank you for sparing Simon's life, give us an opportunity to tell him what he doesn't want to hear and soften his heart to receive it."

He paused. The battle for men's souls took much energy and he leaned back, exhausted.

Gasper picked up the mantle of prayer and continued. "And Lord, you know where Colt is. Send your protective angels to shield him from harm. Return him to our care and to his parents loving arms." He choked back a sob at the thought of losing his young friend and his prayers dissolved into tears.

"O Lord, our Lord, how majestic is your name in all the earth! You have set your glory above the heavens. When I consider your heavens, the work of your fingers, the moon, and stars which you have ordained; what is man that you are mindful of him? You have made him a little lower than the angels and crowned him with glory and honor, and have given him dominion over the works of your hands; and put all things under his feet. It is in this truth we claim the victory you won on the cross and in the empty tomb. We claim dominion over those powers of darkness; to subdue kingdoms, work righteousness, obtain promises, stop the mouths of lions, to quench the violence of fire, escape the edge of the sword, to be strong and fight valiantly, and turn the enemies back." Melchior wiped the sweat from his brow, took a sip of water, then continued. "You have brought us here for such a time as this. Grant us your wisdom to complete our mission. In Jesus' name, Amen"

When they finished, the first gentle rays of golden sunlight tickled the receding fringes of night sending the darkness scurrying to its hiding place. Standing, Balthazar stretched and gave an ample yawn. "Where is Simon?"

***

Sometime in the night, Simon slipped from the unfinished building and quietly backed the car down the driveway before getting into it and starting the engine. While he lay wounded after being shot, he remembered seeing the young boy who'd accompanied the wise men, sneak out and retrieve the page he'd buried under the shed. He had to find the boy if it were possible and bring him back.

Hoping the people with the guns had gone, he searched the area, finding only footprints, but no child. His heart ached for the boy's mother. He too knew the pain of losing a son ... he had lost two. War is no respecter of persons, it claims those it wants; sons, daughters, fathers, mothers. "Oh God," he cried in anguish. "Why have you dealt so harshly with these people?" It had been years since Simon prayed ... longer since he'd thought about God. Was it too late to call upon the God of his childhood? Would the God who parted the Red Sea and delivered his ancestors from all their troubles respond to a prodigal such as him? Indeed, the regathering of Israel was a miracle. Their very existence was a witness to the world that Israel's God was a promise-keeping God. But what about those other promises? Jehovah the Suffering Servant, the Righteous Branch, the Ruling King? None of it made sense. How could God be all those things at the same time? As he returned to the block building where his guests waited, he determined one thing ... to find the answers to his questions or die trying.

***

As the sound of an engine grew louder, Balthazar and the others took up defensive positions. If it were the local police that was one thing, if it was Baker ... that was another. To his relief, it was Mr. Levi.

"Where have you been? We've been worried sick," Balthazar asked flatly.

Simon shrugged. "I've been looking for the young man. What's his name, Colt?"

Balthazar relaxed his stance. "Obviously, you didn't find

him. What of the page?"

Simon shook his head. "I searched where I buried it. Either the boy found it and escaped. Or that woman did. Either way, both are missing. By the look of the footprints, I feel confident the boy got away. But I couldn't find him ... I looked all night."

***

The cool morning breeze whispered across the tops of the wheat causing them the undulate like the ocean, and Colt woke with a jolt. Staring at him from across the clearing was a young girl about his age. She was dressed in a pair of tattered jeans and a flannel shirt. Her raven hair was tied in two ponytails. On her feet, she wore a pair of old tennis shoes.

"You're not from here, are you?" Her English was good, but had a European flavor to it.

Colt looked down at his rumpled clothes. "How'd you guess?"

She gave him a casual shrug. "No one is from here, actually. Everyone in this kibbutz is from somewhere else. Where are you from?"

Feeling rather conspicuous, Colt decided to tell the truth. "I'm from Georgia."

"Georgia as in near Russia?"

Colt tried to remember his geography. "No, Georgia as in, 'Georgia, Georgia, the whole day through, just an old sweet song, keeps Georgia on my mind.'" His poor rendition of Ray Charles' defining song, made the girl chuckle.

"Don't quit your day job, kid."

Colt felt his face heat.

"Really, what are you doing here? I heard gun shots last night and we were told to be on the watch for Palestinians. You don't look like a Palestine though."

"What's a Palestine look like anyway," he asked.

She jammed her hands in her pockets and scuffed the ground. "Oh, they usually wear the latest beau monde in terrorism; black turbine, black shirt, and black pants. It's a real fashion statement."

Not understanding her French, and not wanting an explanation, Colt moved on. "My friends were looking for the Temple of Endor and were attacked by a couple of people with guns. That's when the shooting began. I got separated from my friends when the local police arrived. They left before I could catch up."

The girl seemed satisfied and slumped to the ground and sat Indian style. "Why were they interested in the old temple?"

Colt's shoulders rose and fell. For a moment, he considered showing her the single sheet of paper which might have cost Mr. Levi his life, but then decided to give her the verbal version. "My friends believe the people with the guns want to unleash the powers of the underworld."

Instead of laughing, the girl sat and stared back at him.

Colt shifted uncomfortably. "What'd I say?" he asked after a prolonged minute.

"I saw a guy with a Palestinian girl yesterday snooping around the temple ruins. It looked like he was trying to find something, so I hid and watched. He kept opening a big black book and recited something over and over again."

"What did the girl do?" Colt couldn't help his growing interest.

"She acted really weird, almost like she was enjoying the whole spectacle. Finally, the old guy and girl stomped off in a huff. I lost sight of them when my mudder called."

"I wonder what they were looking for."

The girl shook her head. "Don't know, that place has been abandoned for hundreds of years. Archeologist and treasure hunters have stripped it clean so I doubt there is anything of any value left to find. You gotta name?"

Colt stood and crossed the open area between them and extended his hand. "My name is Colt O'Dell, what's yours?"

"Mudder says I'm not supposed to touch a boy until I'm

betrothed, so put your hand away. My name is Sasha."

Feeling his face redden, Colt tucked his hand in his pants pocket and scuffed the ground. "I've never heard that rule. Do your parents have a lot of rules?"

Nodding, Sasha sighed. "Yeah, like no work on the Sabbath, wash your hands after you touch unclean things, memorize large portions of the Torah before my twelfth birthday."

"What happens on your twelfth birthday?"

Sasha shrugged her shoulders. "It's called a Bet Mitzvah. The priest will ask me a bunch of questions, I answer them, then we eat. We like to eat. We even have weeklong celebrations just so we can eat."

"Is that why you live on a farm?"

Sasha's smile revealed a perfect set of teeth, her eyes sparkled like sapphires and Colt felt his heart skip a notch.

"Yes, you might say so. It seems the whole Jewish calendar revolves around remembering our suffering, celebrating our deliverance and feasting."

"Sounds fun."

"Yeah," Sasha said. An impish twinkle danced in her eyes. "Stick your hand out."

"Say what?" Colt asked.

"I said, stick your hand out."

"Why?" he asked, following her request.

Giving him a girlish giggle, she grabbed his hand and tugged him forward. "Follow me." She began running.

Colt's legs barely had time to respond as she pulled him through the wheat field. "Where you taking me?" he asked through gasps of air.

"Home, I want you to meet my mudder and poppa."

***

Hand in hand, Sasha and Colt emerged from the wheat field, panting. "I thought you weren't supposed to touch a boy until you were betrothed."

Sasha laughed. "You really are gullible, aren't you?"

Colt released her hand and rubbed it on his jeans.

"Sasha."

A voice sailed across the field and he wheeled around.

"Who's your friend?"

It was Sasha's mother. She towered over him, her hands on her hips, her dark brown eyes scrutinizing him.

Sasha tugged him closer to her mother. "This is Colt, he's from Georgia."

"Georgia, Russia?" her tone rose in a Jewish twist.

"No, Georgia as in, 'Georgia, Georgia, the whole day through, just an old sweet song, keeps Georgia on my mind.'" Sasha extended her hands dramatically as if on stage. She winked at Colt and said, "There, that's how you do it."

Colt shook his head. "Don't quit your day job."

Sasha's mother burst into a hearty laugh. "Did she tell you she couldn't touch a boy until she was betrothed?"

Colt's face flattened. "How'd ya know?"

The woman engulfed him in an overt hug. "You've got a lot to learn about my Sasha. She's got a vivid imagination. Now, come inside, you must be starving."

Colt fingered the rolled up sheet of paper, shoved it deeper under his shirt and wondered if he could trust his new friends ... could he trust himself?

Chapter Forty-Eight

Having gotten so close to his prize and failing to get it only made the former sheriff more agitated. He and Layla spent the night in their hostel room ... he paced, she slept. Finally, when he'd worn himself out, he flopped on the bed without taking off his clothes and fell asleep, but his mind kept working. Visions of dark, smoke-filled tunnels formed in his mind and he saw himself running down one corridor, turning a corner and dashing down another. He sensed a presence behind him ... chasing him ... reaching out ethereal fingers ... trying to grab him. A door appeared before him and he clawed at its surface looking for a handle. Moments before the presence caught him, he yanked the door open, jumped in, and pulled it closed. Panting, hands on his knees, he narrowed his eyelids and tried to see into the muted light. Suddenly, he jolted upright, staring back at him were thousands of red glowing orbs.

"Baker." Hearing his name whispered sent chicken-flesh crawling down his back. Fearing for his life, he grasped for the door handle. It was not there. The voices grew louder. The faces of the spirits pressed in around him; their gaping mouths widened as if to swallow him alive. Closer, ever closer they came.

Gasping for air, Baker's eyes sprang open and he sat upright. Sitting two feet from him was Layla. Her piercing gaze sent cold chills over his body.

"What did you see?" she demanded.

Baker shoved her back. "Wouldn't you like to know."

"You saw it didn't you ... the temple."

"Yes," he shuttered at the memory. "But I wasn't alone. There are things down there, evil things."

"That's why you came, isn't it? To gain their power. I heard you reading from that book. I know what you're up to." Her tone turned cold, her unblinking eyes never left him. "I can help you."

Baker stood and walked over to the coffee pot which contained last night's brew. He sniffed it and wrinkled his nose. Pouring a mug full, he took a sip. The bitter taste assaulted his tongue, but despite its wicked flavor, he forced down a few gulps. Turning, he asked, "What do you know about the underworld?"

Layla shifted on the bed. "More than you know."

A light knock on the door interrupted their conversation. "You order room service?" he asked through pinched lips.

Layla got up and peeked through the tattered curtain. "Open the door."

"Say what?"

"I said, open the door," she spat.

Baker complied.

A moment later, a man dressed in black slipped inside. The barrel-chested man carrying an AK-47, peered through a slit in the curtain, as two other men carrying an assortment of weapons burst through the door and shut the door behind them.

"Your friends?" Baker demanded.

Layla nodded. "Call them my backup plan just in case you don't keep your part of the bargain."

"Hey, I'll keep my part, but you'll have to share yours with these guys. They're not a part of the deal. Do they speak English?"

She shook her head.

"Then tell them they can get their own room or sleep outside."

Layla's eyelids narrowed to slits, then she spoke in a language he was not familiar with.

"What did you tell them?"

"I told them to set up a perimeter and stay out of sight."

Satisfied, Baker kicked off his shoes and stretched out on the bed. Within minutes, the room reverberated with his snoring.

Layla reversed a chair, straddled it and peered down at the sleeping man through slanted eyes.

***

The following morning broke bright and clear with not a cloud in sight.

Baker stood and stretched. Glancing around, he noticed Layla was not in her bed, neither was she in the shower. He pulled back the curtain and saw their jeep still in its place and wondered where she'd gone.

Suddenly, the door creaked open and Layla strode in.

"Where've you been?"

Layla perched on the corner of the bed. "My friends needed food. I went and got them some."

"From the restaurant?"

"No. I'm not stupid. That would be too conspicuous. I went to that convenience store down the way and filled a couple of bags."

"How'd you pay for it?"

"I didn't."

Baker decided not to ask any more questions.

After breakfast in the hostel common area, Baker returned to his room. He had his fill of falafels. What he really wanted was a good strong shot of whiskey, but unfortunately, this kibbutz was dry, meaning, no alcohol; no beer, no whiskey, and especially no *mountain water.* His body craved sleep, but his greed drove him to study the Book of Incantations. If only he could figure out the pronunciations of some of the words, he would feel more in control.

Sitting in a trance like pose, he remembered how Mrs. White showed her coven how to open their minds to the spirit world. With him, sometimes it worked, sometimes it didn't. Maybe he was too much a doubter of anything spiritual; however, he was becoming a believer, at least in the dark side of the supernatural. Already, the talons of several evil spirits gouged deep crevices in his mind. Many had taken root and controlled parts of him, yet there was room for more. Sighing deeply, he willed his mind open and allowed himself to drift.

Suddenly, he saw a face ... one that was familiar. *Layla.*

He jolted upright. Once again, she sat within inches of his face, her fingers touching the top button of his shirt. Her breath wafted over him as if she were trying to invade his body. "What are you doing?" he asked, reeling back.

Layla's eyelids hung half open. She moaned and slumped to the floor.

Thinking she'd passed out, Baker scooped her up and laid her on the bed. The demon of Lust rammed its claws deeper, but he had more important things to think about. He wanted power, not pleasure.

Slap!

His palm stung from the force of his hand against her cheek. Layla's eyes fluttered open. Heaving a deep breath, she bolted upright. "Get off of me you creep." Her voice cut like a knife.

"It's not like it looks," Baker said apologetically.

"I don't care what it looks like. Get off and let me breathe."

"What were you doing so close to my face?" Baker demanded, taking in short gulps.

"You were sitting dead still and you were muttering something."

"What'd I say?"

"How should I know, I don't speak Aramaic."

"Aramaic? How'd you know it was Aramaic and not some

other language?"

Layla leaned forward on her elbow. "I don't know I just said that. I once heard an old Jewish guy talking and it sounded kinda like that."

Baker stood and began to pace. "Do you think you could find someone like that?"

Shaking her head, she looked at him. "No, not here. This is a Jewish kibbutz, not Jerusalem. Maybe we should make a quick trip to Jerusalem and find someone who could read your book."

"And widen the circle? I already have one too many people involved in this—" he clamped his mouth shut as Layla gaped at him. "Sorry, we're a team, but to involve someone else is risky. What if they blab?"

Layla slumped back on the bed while Baker continued to pace. Finally, he stopped. "I'm going back to the temple ruins, maybe I missed something."

"What about those wise men? Won't they be there?"

"Look, I can't very well hunt for that missing page in the dark and I can't open the door without it. So if you don't mind getting your sorry butt out of bed and come with me, maybe we'll both get what we want." His voice boomed.

An impish grin parted Layla's lips. It seemed she knew she'd pushed his buttons. "All right already, don't get in a huff." Jamming her gun in the small of her back, she tugged her shirt down over it and grabbed her bag. "Ready." She glared at Baker.

Baker glared back. "After you ..."

Chapter Forty-Nine

After having eaten his fill of scrambled eggs, toast, and fresh fruits, Colt washed it down with a cold glass of milk. He wiped his lips with his sleeve and got a dower look from Sasha's 'mudder', as she called her. By now, he had told his new friends all about him being a stowaway on a cargo plane. Sasha's eyes grew big as a stopwatch. His story expanded in proportion to her gaping mouth. He liked the way she cocked her head and got a dreamy look on her angelic face whenever he spoke about America. She had an imagination as wild as his ... he liked that, too.

"I've never met a stowaway, especially one from America. And I've never been on an airplane for that matter. What was it like?" She rattled off a string of questions faster than he could answer them.

Colt tried to put a positive spin on running away from home, but in the end, he had to admit he missed his folks. Wiping a tear from his cheek, he took a shaky breath. "I didn't know until later that the wise men were staying through Christmas. That's a long time."

Sasha's mudder enfolded him in a warm embrace. "Well, you are welcome to stay with us, if you need a place, but you'll need to work. This is a kibbutz, you know."

"What's a kibbutz, anyway?" he asked, glancing from face to face.

Sasha giggled. She'd never encountered anyone who'd not heard of a kibbutz. "It means *group*, in Hebrew. It is a community where we voluntarily share everything equally. We all work together and then sell the harvest. At the end of the season, we divide the profits."

Colt's eyebrows hiked up. "It kinda sounds like communism."

Sasha's mudder broke into laughter.

Sasha's face reddened. Crossing her arms, she huffed. Her punchy lip was meant to manipulate, and it worked.

His hands raised in surrender, Colt felt his face heat. "Sorry, I didn't mean to make you mad."

"That's all right Sasha," her mudder said. "While we wait for his friends to return, why don't you show your new friend how us *communists* work."

Uncrossing her arms, she let a devilish smile replace her angry expression. "That's a great idea. Come Colt," she said, extending her hand. "I've got a bucket with your name on it."

"Wha, what am I going to put in it?"

Handing him a large metal bucket, she grabbed one more along with a couple of straw hats and a pair of gloves. "Today we're picking blueberries. Once you've filled your bucket, you can eat lunch. The sooner you fill it ... the sooner you eat." She gave him an impish grin. "So don't eat the harvest. It'll take you longer to fill your bucket and you might get sick."

Colt gulped and looked at Sasha's mudder.

"She's right, now run along. I'm planning on a hearty lunch."

Snatching Colt by his free hand, she tugged him outside. The screen door slapped against its frame as she led him to the field where a group of people hunkered over the low-growing bushes. "When you're finished with that row, start on the next one. After lunch, if your friends haven't arrived. You and I are going to sneak off and do some exploring." An interesting glint twinkled in her eyes inviting him to stare.

The idea of exploring raised Colt's dampened spirits. "Exploring? Where?"

Sasha glanced from side to side conspiratorially. Lowering

her voice, she said, "The Temple of Endor. Now let's get to work."

Following her example, Colt began picking. The plunk of blueberries on the bottom of the bucket was a new sound to Colt and he liked it. At first, it was slow going, but the more he did, the faster he became.

"Don't skip any," Sasha's voice sounded from the other side of the row. "And don't eat any. It'll spoil your lunch. Mudder expects you to have a full bucket and an empty stomach, so let's get going ... I'm hungry." Her bossiness didn't offend him, but he guessed she'd gotten it good and natural from her mudder.

Colt grinned and kept working. *All these people think about is eating.*

***

The sun beat down upon a group of people with a vengeance as they bent over rows of blueberry bushes. Every once in a while, Colt would stand up straight and work his blueberry-stained fingers into the small of his back. Glad for the straw hat Sasha had given him, he wished she'd given him the extra pair of gloves he saw on the shelf near the door. By now, his fingers were not only blue, but bloody as the small limbs and sharp leaves snagged his exposed flesh.

Once the novelty of hearing the constant plunk of berries falling to the bottom of the bucket had worn off, it became a test of his endurance. Sasha, who was much better at the task, moved with fluid skill from one bush to another. Her constant humming kept his mind off the pain in his back.

"What's that tune you keep humming?" His curiosity could withstand it no longer. Getting her to talk was much better than hearing the same tune over and over again.

Sasha stopped humming and looked up. "Oh, that? It's called, 'When the girl you love is loving.'"

Colt's face reddened. He suddenly dreaded what else she'd say.

She continued, "if girls are good when they meet men, with matrimonial views, they're sure to find a husband, though of course, I can't say whose!' Heard enough, or shall I sing more?"

Colt tugged his hat over his eyes and kept working. By the time the sun had reached its zenith, his shirt was soaked with sweat, and his bucket was only three-fourths full. All at once, Sasha broke through the row, her bucket heaping.

"Here." She tipped her bucket near his, filling it to the top. "Now let's eat," she said. Turning, she scampered toward the house.

By now, Colt was as hungry as Sasha. Following her lead, he took off and raced her to the house, holding his bucket out and being careful not to dump his morning's labor.

Just about the time they reached the house, Sasha's mudder stepped from the kitchen door with a wash bowl in her hands. "Wash," she announced.

At her one-word command, Sasha and Colt skidded to a stop. They placed their buckets at her feet as if they were an offering them to a god, then backed away. The water from the hose was ice cold and sent a welcomed chill over Colt's steaming body. After scrubbing their hands and faces, the older woman handed them a couple of towels. "Be sure to dry behind your ears."

"Yes, mudder," they said in harmony.

While they finished cleaning up, Sasha's mom disappeared into the house and returned with a large picnic basket, a knowing smile tugging at the corners of her mouth. "Sneak off ... humph. Just don't be late for supper. I'm fixing something special."

Colt sniffed the basket. The aroma of fresh baked bread kicked his appetite into overdrive. "What if I'm still too full from lunch?"

"Don't worry, you won't be. I'm sure after you two get done exploring, you'll be as hungry as a rabbi after the Day of

Atonement." The imagery didn't escape Colt and he laughed out loud.

With one hand, Sasha grabbed the handle of the basket. "Come along Colt. I've got the coolest place for a picnic." Clasping his hand, she tugged him in the direction of the Temple of Endor.

Chapter Fifty

Having prepared a breakfast of fresh fruit, cheese, flatbread, and black coffee, Gasper finally took a seat next to Simon and bowed his head. Balthazar prayed the traditional Jewish prayer thanking God for his provision and protection with the added thanks for healing Mr. Levi.

As plates and bowls drifted around the table, the conversation soon turned to speculation concerning Colt and how best to find him without running into sheriff Baker and his trigger-happy friend.

"I suggest we keep it simple," Gasper suggested. "We go back to where we last saw Colt and begin a widening circle until we cross his tracks and follow them."

"But what if Baker is doing the same thing?" Melchior asked.

"He's a night stalker, not a daytime hunter. If we do it this morning or afternoon, we'll have a better chance of picking up his trail and not running into Baker." Gasper's logic made sense and by the time breakfast concluded it was decided they'd leave within the hour.

***

"Melchior," Simon called him aside while Balthazar and Gasper cleaned up. "Could I have a word with you?"

Melchior nodded. "Yes, care for a walk? If I sit, I might fall asleep."

After the long sleepless night, it sounded like a good idea to Simon as well. As if old friends, Melchior curled his arm through Simon's and guided him from the house and down the long driveway.

With their heels crunching the gravel like an unruly child chewing with his mouth open, the two men walked until they were far enough from the house so as not to be heard. "What is on your mind, my friend?"

Simon slowed his pace. "You said something last night that got me thinking."

"We spoke of many things. To which one are you referring?"

"You said in your prayer that God has brought you here for such a time as this, that he would give you the wisdom to compete your mission. What is your mission? If I might ask."

Melchior laced his fingers behind his back. "Our primary mission was to retrieve a certain medallion that once belonged to the Witch of Endor. I'm sure you know the story. Mr. Baker stole it. We are here to get it back and destroy it."

"The story of the witch had been widely exaggerated, but this medallion ... I've not heard about that."

"It was in her hand the day she—" Melchior stopped mid-sentence. His story was too long and too involved to go into detail. Plus, he sensed this was not Simon's real need. "Well, suffice it to say, it is an important artifact. But our mission has changed," he continued.

Simon's forehead wrinkled. Clearly interested, he asked, "Changed? How so?"

Melchior inhaled and let it out slowly. "Well, I'd say our mission is to find Colt and ..." He paused and sent up a quick prayer.

"You were saying?"

"And show you the truth about your Messiah."

"You mean the one in whose name you prayed?"

Melchior nodded. "Yes, that name. His name is Jesus or Yeshua. As you know, that is the same name for Joshua which means Jehovah Saves."

Simon ran his hand through his thinning hair. "I just can't make sense of it. How can the Messiah spoken of throughout scripture be both servant, sacrifice and king?"

His question couldn't have been more succinct. It had been debated down through the centuries. "You are familiar with the ceremony of the two goats? One is the scapegoat the other is the sacrifice."

"I am," Simon confessed.

"Well, since God is not in the practice of resurrecting animals, he had to use two to teach one truth. The twenty-second psalm provided a vivid description of what would happen to the sacrificial lamb. In verse one it says, 'My God, my God, why hast Thou forsaken me?'. Verse seven and eight paint the scene ... 'All they that see me, laugh me to scorn: they shoot out the lip, they shake the head, saying, he trusted in the LORD that he would deliver him: let him deliver him, seeing he delights in him.' These are the exact words used the day of Jesus' crucifixion. The psalm continues by describing his physical suffering. 'My strength is dried up like a potsherd; my tongue cleaves to my mouth.' This speaks of Messiah's thirst. It even describes how he would die ... on a Roman cross. 'They pierced my hands and feet, they parted my garments among them and cast lots upon my vesture.' This entire psalm describes in painful detail what happened on that day, which, I might add was Passover." The significance was not lost on Simon.

Continuing, Melchior said, "The thirty-fourth psalm says not a bone was broken. Psalm forty-one speaks of His betrayal by Judas Iscariot. Psalm sixty-nine refers to the gall and vinegar they offered him to drink. Simon, you can't escape the fact, that Yeshua fulfilled every prophetic word about the suffering servant, and yet in Psalm sixteen, verse ten, it says, in the King James, 'For Thou wilt not leave my soul in hell; neither wilt Thou suffer Thine Holy One to see corruption.' Obviously, this was written by King David, but He died and saw corruption. This man saw no corruption. On the day of First-Fruits, He came forth. You see, God demonstrated his love for us in that while we were sinners, Christ, the anointed one, died for us and was resurrected the third day according to prophetic scripture."

For a long moment, Simon walked in silence, his chin buried in his chest. It was all true ... the psalms didn't lie. It was all there, why hadn't he seen it? Tears welled and rolled down his cheeks. "What shall I do that I might gain the smile of God?"

Melchior stopped, clutched Simon's arm and turned him around. "You know what we just did?"

Simon shook his head. "No, what?"

"We repented. We were going one way and we made a complete reversal. That is what you must do. Stop trusting in the Law and the Prophets, and trust in the One of whom they speak. The One who died and lives again ... His name is Yeshua Ha Masha, meaning—"

Simon waved him off. "I know what it means. I just don't know if I'm ready to accept it."

"Accept it ... accept Him?"

Simon's mind stood on a knife's edge. Finally, he spoke. "You're right. Jesus is the Messiah ... He has to be."

"That's not enough for you to admit it. You must claim Him as your Lord and your Savior ... place your eternal destiny in His nail-scarred hands."

Simon stared into Melchior's eyes long and hard. "If I do that, will I still be a Jew?"

Melchior's lips parted into a bright smile. "Yes, my friend, and more. You will have fulfilled the purpose for which you were born; having a Jewish Savior to take you into His kingdom."

Together, they knelt on the rocky surface and prayed a simple prayer. Within minutes, one wandering Jew helped another wandering Jew find the way, the truth, and the life.

***

Above the two kneeling figures, innumerable hosts of angelic beings folded their wings and bowed their noble heads as God himself sang the song of the redeemed. He needed no instrumentation, no backup singers, no orchestrated track to follow. This was His song and none other could voice the joy He and He alone felt when one of His chosen people accepted Him who paid the ultimate price for them.

As the heavens reverberated with joy, the myriads of angels surrounding the throne could hold their silver tongues no longer. In one magnificent chorus, their joyful songs spilled down the golden streets like a mighty torrent, summoning the saints of all ages beckoning them to lend their ethereal voices. Together, they lifted up the name of Jesus and praised the One who lived, died, and lives forevermore.

Chapter Fifty-One

By the time Sasha and Colt had reached the grassy knoll overlooking the fertile valley surrounding Ein Dor, it was past noon and Colt's stomach gnawed at his ribs. "When are we going to eat?" he asked between breaths.

Sasha glanced over his shoulder. Her black hair swayed like a pony's tail in the light breeze. She turned and caught him staring. "Any minute, we're almost there."

"I thought we were going to the temple ruins. We're a long ways away from there."

Sasha took a couple more steps, stopped and plopped down Indian style. "We're here." Her smile changed everything.

Colt scanned the vista. At his feet spread a patchwork of greens and golden browns. They had reached the top of the only hill in the entire region; the hill of Ein Dor. From their vantage point, they had a commanding view in all directions.

"This is the hill of Ein Dor. Now let's eat." She said in a mischievous tone. Then she dug in the basket and began taking out fresh bread, sliced cheese, freshly cut fruit and a couple bottles of sparkling water. "You pray ... that's the man's job."

Colt gulped. He'd prayed over a meal at home, but never on a picnic, and never with a girl. As he tried to figure out what to say, he heard Sasha's impish giggle.

"Out loud," she whispered.

"I'm going to. I was just thinking of the right words," he whispered as if not wanting to disturb the sanctity of the moment.

"Just say anything, I'm starved."

Colt cleared his throat. "Thank you, Lord for the food and for the hands that prepared it. Bless my mom and dad, and bless Sasha and her mudder and pop pa and—"

"Okay, that's enough thanking, let's eat," she interrupted.

Undeterred, Colt pressed on. "And bless the wise men and help us to get home soon. In Jesus name, Amen. Now let's eat."

Colt looked up and found Sasha staring wide-eyed at him. "What did you say?"

"I said, let's eat."

She twisted open a bottle of water and took a long gulp. "No, before that."

Colt wracked his brain. "About going home?"

She handed him some bread and cheese and some sliced meat. "You ended your prayer in that name ... Heshem."

Colt took a bit and chewed thoughtfully. "Yeah, that's how we pray, in Jes—"

Her hand flew up. "Don't say it. It's, it's—" she let her voice fade.

Confusion fogged Colt's brain. They were having such a good time talking and laughing at each other's bad jokes all the way to the top of the hill. Now a curtain as thick as the veil in the temple hung between them. They ate in silence and Colt's heart ached. Finally, Colt broke the lull. "Have you heard the story of the wise men?"

Sasha shook her head. A few strands of silky black hair shaded her face.

"No, tell me." Some of her playful tone returned.

"Well, I told you how I got here, but I didn't say much about the three men I came with. They are the real wise men from the Bible."

Sasha's eyes darkened. "I've not heard about that. We only read the Torah."

"Yes, well, have you read in Numbers twenty-four, verse seventeen, where it tells us about the star of Jacob?"

"I have, it says, 'I shall see him, but not now: there shall come a star out of Jacob, and a scepter shall come out of Israel.'"

Colt's expression brightened. "The book of Micah chapter five actually names the city where he would be born. "But you, Bethlehem, Ephratah, although you are small in Judah, yet out of you shall he come forth whose past is from everlasting."

Sasha's nose wrinkled. "That's not exactly how it reads in the Torah, but it's close. What's that got to do with your wise men friends?"

"The wise men followed that star from the East all the way to Bethlehem to worship the new-born king."

Sasha stood and brushed the crumbs from her lap and scanned the valley. "They worshipped a king?" her voice hiked up an octave. "You can't worship a king. The first commandment says, 'you shall have no other gods before me. How could they do such a thing?" her face flushed.

"Well, what if the king was also God? Have you heard the name, Immanuel?"

She crossed her arms and huffed. "No."

"It means, 'God with us.'"

"So, how can God be with us. He is too holy. He lives in the heaven of heavens. Not down here."

Colt could feel the tension building between them, but he had to try to share his faith. "Can I tell you my favorite verse in the whole Bible?"

Sasha's shoulders lowered and her face softened. "Yeah, go ahead."

After clearing his throat, he began in typical Sunday School fashion. "For God so loved the world that he gave his only begotten son, that whoever believes in him will not perish, but have everlasting life."

"That was beautiful."

Colt nodded, his voice softening. "Yes, it is."

"But I still think you have a bigger imagination than me, and mine is pretty big."

Her contagious laughter captivated Colt's attention. Rather than further offending her, he followed her lead. "What kind of things do you like to imagine?"

After packing up the picnic basket and shaking it out, Sasha glanced up. "You know why I brought you here?"

"I thought it was to explore the Temple of Endor, but we're a long ways from it. So, no."

Smiling, Sasha stomped her foot. Rather than a dull thud, he heard a hollow echo. "You're standing on it."

Eyes widening. "We're what?"

"You're standing on it."

Colt yanked the old page from his shirt, Colt began to study it.

"What's that?" Sasha's voice hiked up.

"It's the last page from a book called, The Book of Incantations. It's why that nasty woman shot Mr. Levi. It's a map leading to a special door."

Sasha grabbed the map and turned it around. Walking her fingers across the images she studied the scene and returned to inspect the map. "Follow me." Leaving the basket where it sat, she dashed in the direction of a series of collapsed rocks. The closer they came into view, the more defined the edges of the rocks became until it was obvious these were once the supports of an ancient structure.

"What is this place?" Colt's voice echoed.

"This is the outer court of the Temple of Endor," she said, swirling around like a ballerina.

"But I thought it was back there," pointing down range.

"Nope, that's just an old synagogue. Our city fathers put a historic sign there to keep unwanted visitors from overrunning our home and ruining our way of life."

***

Layla shut off the jeep's engine and got out followed by Baker and her three friends. They immediately took up guarding positions. She walked past the historical marker and scanned the rubble. "Something's not right. This doesn't look at all like the pictures in that book."

Baker stepped next to her and scanned the area. "It looks too young. Like maybe it's only a couple hundred years old, not thousands. You think this is the right place?"

Shaking her head, she narrowed her eyes. "I think it's a red herring, a fool's errand." She had enough of his tales of gold. "I'm outta here."

"Stop!" Baker's tone carried a deadly edge. She turned and faced his 45 caliber, Beretta. "Take another step and you will join this historic site."

Movement arrested his attention as three men trained their weapons on him. Still holding his gaze, he watched her focus shift over his shoulder. In the distance, two figures labored up a hill.

"Look," she said, pointing at the distant objects.

Not trusting her, Baker steadied his weapon and took a quick glance over his shoulder. "Well, well, well. If it's not my little buddy."

Layla peered into a pair of binoculars. "Your buddy?"

Baker tucked his gun in its holster. "Yeah, my little buddy. His name is Colt O'Dell and I have a score to settle with him. I'd bet dollars to donuts, he's the thief who got the last page of the book."

After lowering her binoculars, Layla took a few paces in the direction of their jeep.

"Hold up. Let's lay back and watch to see where they're going. I don't want to give our position away just yet."

Layla slowed her pace and watched Sasha and Colt march across the countryside until they disappeared.

"Okay, let's go," Baker said. "But let's keep our distance."

Following at a distance, Baker and Layla and her band of

cut-throats stayed low and tracked Sasha and Colt. Suddenly, Baker raised his hand.

"Why are we stopping?"

Baker raised a pair of binoculars to his face. "They're stopping for a picnic." He handed her the binoculars and she peered through them for a moment.

"Let's take them."

"And what, act like Yogi Bear and Boo Boo come to steal their picnic basket? No, we wait."

"Wait," Layla huffed. "First you're in a hurry, now you want to wait."

"Yes, we wait for them to make their move, then we make ours."

Layla plopped down on the ground and pulled a granola bar from her bag, opened it and began to eat it.

"Got one of those for me?"

She cocked her head and gave him a sideways glance. Pulling a second bar from her bag, she tossed it in his direction. "Here big boy, enjoy your picnic."

For the next forty-five minutes, they waited. Finally, Baker took another look through his binoculars.

"What do ya see?"

"They're studying a piece of paper ... could be the page they stole from me. Let's come around the backside and see if we can get a closer look."

Staying low, Baker and the others crept closer until they were within earshot.

"This is the outer court of the Temple of Endor," the girl said. Then spun in a dramatic circle.

"But I thought it was back there." Colt's voice echoed down the hill.

"Nope, that's just an old synagogue. Our city fathers put a historic sign there to keep unwanted visitors from overrunning our home and ruining our way of life."

As Colt studied the map, Baker stepped from behind a

large stone.

"I'll take that." Baker leveled his gun at Colt, who stood like a deer in the headlights.

"Run Sasha!"

Seeing people with guns, Sasha leaped behind a stone pillar and zigzagged through the maze of debris. "After her," Baker yelled.

As Baker turned, Colt launched a golf ball sized rock directly at him. It struck him in the chest knocking him off his feet. A moment later, Colt ducked inside a dark opening and disappeared down a long black tunnel. His eyes stabbed the darkness. His tennis shoes slapped wildly on the wet surface. In an instant, his mind was carried back to the Witch's cave. The further he went, the deeper the sense of dread. *This is not a good place.*

Temporarily dazed, Baker rolled to his knees as shots rang out. He hoped they were far enough away from civilization that no one heard. After a moment, he regained his equilibrium and stood. His ribs ached like he'd been kicked. "I'm going to kill that kid the next time I see him," he cursed.

Layla emerged breathing hard. She tossed Sasha to the ground.

"Now we're getting somewhere." Baker eyed the girl. "What's your name?"

"Sasha." Her voice squawked.

"Well, Sasha, it looks like you and Layla are going to get acquainted real quick." Then he grabbed her by the shirt and dragged her closer to the opening. "Colt, Colt O'Dell, I have your little friend out here. Now come out and I'll not have to hurt her."

Baker waited.

Colt waited, too.

Chapter Fifty-Two

The echo of gunfire rolled across the valley and Simon turned in search of its source. "That sounds like gun shots."

Gasper and the others followed his gaze as he stared at the distant hill.

"By my calculations, that hill is about two miles to our north. Do you think it has anything to do with your young friend?" he asked as he and the others breathlessly hurried away from the area marked Temple of Endor.

"I don't know, but the sound of that gun was similar to the one last night and I fear it does. Let's go and check it out."

Simon was the first to reach the car and had it running by the time Melchior got in. "Hold on, this might get rough." Taking a rutted cow path, he pointed his vehicle in the direction of the hill and accelerated.

"Look," exclaimed Gasper pointed at an aging jeep. "It's got Palestinian tags," he said as they passed it. "Why would a jeep from the disputed area be in Galilee?"

Balthazar watched it as they went by. "That's the same jeep I saw last night. It's gotta be Baker's and the woman's. Men, it's time we prepare to defend ourselves."

Rather than getting too close and giving away the element of surprise, Simon cut the engine and let the car drift the rest of the way before pressing the brake. Then he opened the glove compartment and pulled out a 9mm STEN and checked the magazine before ratcheting back the chamber.

Melchior wiped the sweat from his forehead and grabbed his staff and handed Balthazar his without speaking. Gasper did the same. "I don't know how effective our swords will be against guns, but that's all we have."

"That's not completely accurate. We have God's protection and our cause is just," Simon added.

Grim-faced, the four men crept single file up the rocky terrain following Simon's lead. As they entered an area encircled with fallen rocks, movement caught Simon's attention and he stopped.

Three armed men appeared. All wore black, all were hooded.

Simon aimed and fired, missing.

The first man fired his weapon and hit his mark.

***

At the sound of gunfire, Layla released Sasha and took cover. Sasha, seized the moment and leaped behind a large stone, then scampered to safety. From her angle, she watched the events unfold. She wanted to run and get the authorities, but something kept her there. Biting back tears, she told herself not to cry. Violence and death were a part of life in Israel. She had to be strong, for herself ... for Colt.

By now, Baker was long gone as was Colt. Staying low, she kept her distance as Balthazar and Gasper continued up the hill. Knowing Colt was somewhere inside the ancient Temple of Endor, she feared for his life. Her only hope was to stay out of sight and wait for her chance. Finding a fist sized stone, she inched forward.

***

Balthazar, holding his staff in both hands, braced himself for the next bullet. The second man fired, but the bullet veered high. Another hooded man lunged at Gasper, slicing the air with a machete. Gasper drew his sword and the two men began a dueling match. He turned and saw a third man battling Melchior who stood his ground valiantly. With his staff held like a shield, he blocked the spray of bullets from the man's weapon.

Seconds stretched as the scene unfolded in slow motion.

Pointing his staff at his attacker, Balthazar lifted him from the ground and swung him around like a fish at the end of a pole. The muscular man landed hard against a large boulder, knocking him out. With his immediate threat eliminated, he raced to Melchior's side, lifted his staff and took aim. A burst of energy sprang from his staff and struck the man with such force that he tumbled backward over a cliff and wasn't seen again.

The swish of Gasper's sword slicing through the air and the crack of the two blades clashing held Balthazar's attention. Gasper's opponent proved to be more resilient than he had expected. The man was light on his feet and skipped out of reach of Gasper's superior blade, but he was able to take advantage of him with his shorter machete. Suddenly, the man lunged and his weapon caught Gasper under the arm piercing muscle. He cried out and staggered back. The black-clad man was upon him in a heartbeat. Rearing back, he prepared to slice Gasper's throat, when a bolt of energy from Balthazar's staff struck him. Dazed, he lost his footing and collapsed.

Seeing their fallen comrade, Balthazar and Melchior grabbed him and dragged him to safety.

"Where's Simon?" Melchior asked.

Balthazar scanned the area. "I don't know. Do what you can for Gasper," Balthazar said and took off in the direction of where he last saw Simon.

Melchior pulled back Gasper's bloody shirt. "This doesn't look good."

"Can't you heal me?"

Melchior nodded. "I can, but—"

"But what?"

Melchior pulled back his robe revealing a bloody hole in his chest. Gasper sucked in a sharp breath. "Melchior, what happened?"

He slumped to the ground and coughed. Blood leaked from the corner of his mouth. Color drained from his face, and his breathing was labored. Speaking in a weak voice, he said, "The bullet meant for Simon—" Too weak to finish his sentence he laid his head back.

"But Melchior, don't worry about me ... heal yourself."

"No, not this time. I used much of my strength healing Simon the last time. I can save you, but then—" he coughed and wiped blood with the back of his hand.

"Melchior, listen ..."

"No, you listen. You have Felicia to return to. I've got nothing."

"You have your Gideon."

"What's a dog compared to your ... life ... your ... friendship." Then he laid his trembling hand on Gasper's bloody wound, muttered some words and inhaled. All at once, the gaping wound closed, leaving only a scar.

A shutter rolled over Melchior's body and he gasped.

"Melchior, Melchior." Gasper desperately tried to revive his old friend.

Slowly, Melchior opened his eyes. "Do you see them?" his voice a mere whisper.

Gasper flicked his eyes around. "Who? Who, Melchior?"

A smile deepened the line on his face. "All around us, our friends, the ones who have guarded and guided us through our long journey."

"But I don't see anyone."

"That's all right. You will ... someday. But for now, they are here to guide me ... home."

The tone of his voice changed as if to say he'd already arrived.

Chapter Fifty-Three

Gasper buried his face in Melchior's chest. Between sobs, he listened for a pulse, a breath ... but nothing. After a long moment, he realized his friend was gone. Hearing someone call, he looked up. It wasn't Balthazar. It was a girl. She stood on a boulder, her face smudged with dirt, her hair askew ... she'd been crying.

"Where did you come from?" Gasper called out.

She pointed.

His eyes followed.

Balthazar stood, his staff extended toward the woman from the preceding night. She held a gun at Simon's head.

"Balthazar, do something," she cried in a tight whisper.

His staff held so tightly that his knuckles glowed white, Balthazar strained as if giving birth. "I tried, something is stopping me."

Gasper stood and took a step.

"That's close enough," the woman yelled. "Tell your friend to surrender or this man dies."

"Don't do it." Simon's voice shook, but his face remained calm. "They'll kill all of us. I know these kinds of people."

"Shut up!"

He continued, "I'm ready to face my God, thanks to Melchior, but these people ..."

Thwack!

Layla cracked his head with the butt of her gun and let his body slump to the ground. Then she took aim at Balthazar. The instant she squeezed the trigger, Balthazar dove for cover and the bullet zinged past them.

***

Ducking behind a fallen marble column, Balthazar looked up and the woman was gone. "Where's Melchior?" he whispered. Gasper shook his head. "He's gone. He used what little strength he had left to heal me." Gasper's throat constricted and he took a halting breath.

Gasper peered around. "Who was that girl?"

Balthazar shook his head. "I don't know."

"Why couldn't you throw the woman aside like you did that man?"

"I don't know that either. There was something stopping me. That woman's eyes were demonic—" Balthazar's shoulders went rigid. "I feel there is more to that woman than meets the eye. Do you have Melchior's staff?"

Thankfully, Gasper had the presence of mind to grab it. "Yes, why?"

"Toss both yours and his to me."

Gasper did so, without question.

"If one shall prevail against a foe, two shall withstand them; and a threefold cord is not easily broken." Using his belt, he tied the three staves together. At once, they began to meld into one. Balthazar pushed himself to his feet and shook it. Suddenly, the ground rumbled beneath their feet. "We go in the power of the Almighty."

***

With the heavier staff in his gnarled hands, Balthazar moved into position. The dark entrance through which the woman and Baker disappeared loomed ominously higher up the hill. He took a hard swallow. "After me." On his hands and feet, he crawled over the rock-strewn hillside until he'd reached the mouth of the tunnel. Taking a deep breath, he plunged into the darkness followed with Gasper close at his heels.

Once inside, it took a few minutes for their eyes to adjust.

Heavy breathing echoed deeper and Balthazar followed it not knowing if it were friend or foe. Down the narrow tunnel they plunged. Holding his staff with one end pointed ahead, Balthazar shook it and a warm glow illuminated and burst from its cloven end. The orange glow illuminated the low ceiling as moisture slicked walls and stony floor. The deeper they pressed, the deeper the darkness grew until even the light from his staff was nearly obscured. All at once, they came to an intersection with corridors veering off to the right and left.

"Which way?" Gasper kept his voice low.

Unsure, Balthazar glanced both directions. Darkness swallowed each tunnel making it impossible to tell which way they should go. "Let's go right," he said after much deliberation.

"You go right, I'll go left," Gasper whispered.

"Left? Why?"

"I don't know, I just have a feeling."

"But you don't have any way of lighting the way."

Gasper's jaw muscle twitched. "Darkness can be as much an advantage as a liability." Turning, he disappeared down the blackened corridor.

Cautiously, Balthazar proceeded deeper in the opposite direction. His trek took him through a series of turns until he'd lost all sense of direction. The few chambers he'd discovered appeared to be empty and he continued. All at once, voices echoed in his direction. With slick fingers, he pulled his sword from its scabbard and waited.

***

Inch by slippery inch, Gasper moved through the black hall. Using his hands, he felt along the rock surface of the tunnel. Suddenly, the wall ended and he felt around. It was the frame to a chamber. Blindly, he stepped inside and was immediately attacked. Two hands clamped around his throat and dug into his exposed flesh. Struggling to fight off his unseen attacker, he thrashed around like a wild bull. Backing up, he slammed himself against the wall. Someone groaned. A female voice echoed in the inky blackness. Leaning forward, Gasper threw his attacker over his shoulder. She landed on the stone floor with a thud. Thinking she was the woman with the gun, he pounced on her. As he reared back to land a solid punch, he heard a slight whimper. "Are you that little girl?"

A weak, "Yes," squeaked from her throat.

"Why did you jump me? I'm one of the good guys." Gasper said, keeping his voice to a whisper.

"I thought you were that evil woman or that big guy."

Rubbing his clawed neck, Gasper thought of the time he and Samantha thrashed around down in the witch's cave. "Well I'm not. Do you know which way they went?"

"No, I've been wandering around down here looking for Colt. He dashed in here when those people showed up. They want the map."

"I know, and we're here to stop them."

A shoe scuffed on the stone floor outside their hiding place and they froze. An unseen figure inched past them. By the breathing, Gasper sensed whoever it was, was large. Holding their breath, they waited until he passed. Counting to ten, Gasper stepped into the hall.

Smack!

Chapter Fifty-Four

Using a penlight, Baker searched each chamber of the dilapidated temple. Over the centuries, the support beams had weakened allowing parts of the walls and ceiling to collapse making it difficult to navigate the unknown terrain. With the limited light from his penlight, he often stumbled over an unseen rock. Moving deeper, he followed what he remembered of the temple's floor plan, but without the last page, he knew he could wander for hours and not find the Chamber of Sacrifice. With the wise men hot on his trail, he desperately needed to get his hands on the map. He plunged further ahead until the scuffle of feet and the sounds of two people struggling stopped his progress. Someone was fighting. *Could it be Layla? Had she found the boy? Or was it the kid with the slingshot?* Bile crept up his throat. That boy messed up his plans one time too many, now he was going to pay.

After flicking off his light, he inched along the wall. The faint whisper from a young voice came from somewhere in the darkness. He moved with stealth past a chamber he'd already cleared, then he stopped and waited. Movement to his left brought his gun to eye level.

Thud!

Someone stepped right in front of him. Feeling the hair stand on the back of his neck, he brought the butt of his gun down on whoever it was.

A sharp snap echoed followed by a narrow beam. Gasper's face came into sight and Baker sat back on his haunches.

"Well, well, well. If it's not one of the stupid wise men. You guys keep showing up at the darnedest times. I will remedy that at the first opportunity. Meanwhile, we have a runt to catch and you're the bait." Shoving him forward, Baker and his prisoner shuffled deeper into the Temple. Unseen, by Baker, Sasha peered at the two figures.

As the ruffle of feet faded, Sasha backed up the hall, hoping to find help.

***

Jamming his gun in his ribs, Baker forced Gasper down the corridor until they entered a large chamber. With a cigarette lighter, he lit several torches which hung at right angles from the walls, and within minutes, orange glows flickered from each torch. Glancing around, Baker realized the dimly illuminated room was home to a massive throne. Chiseled in the walls were niches with busts of former rulers, Baker assumed. On the opposite side and directly across from the throne, was a blank wall with etchings. Baker shoved Gasper to the floor. "Don't move or I'll kill ya," he said, then began to inspect his surroundings. "Look what I found, even without that stupid map." He slammed the Book of Incantations on the flat surface of what appeared to be an altar and flipped it open. Frustrated, that he still needed the last page, he returned to Gasper. "Okay, it's time for you to pay your debt to society. I'm going to stand over there in that corner and I want you to call to your friends. You say the wrong thing and *bang,* you're dead. Got it?"

Gasper nodded, closed his eyes, and disappeared.

***

In the gray darkness, Colt wandered from one inky hall to another. The deeper he went, the more confused he got, but the voices which echoed after him, kept him moving. Finally, exhausted and thirsty, he climbed a flight of steps leading to a shadowed door and crouched down. From his vantage point, he watched Baker lumber by. He also caught a glimpse of the woman with the gun. He feared what would happen to his friends if she found them. By now, he'd used up his supply of round stones, the last one when he hit sheriff Baker in the chest. He knew Baker would be gunning for him and dreaded what would happen if he found him. *Where is Sasha?* He chided himself for running away when she needed him. Being only eleven and inexperienced when it came to matters of the heart, he wondered about the feelings he had for her. *Was it just a boyish crush? Or was it more? Was a boy his age capable of love ... real love?* If only he could talk to his dad and mom. Bowing his head, he lifted up Sasha before the Lord. Not only for her as a person, but her as a sinner in need of grace.

His prayer was interrupted by someone breathing.

They were close ... very close.

His eyes popped open.

Sasha knelt inches from his face. "What are you doing?" she whispered.

"Praying."

"You can do that?"

"Yeah, why?"

"We kids don't pray, at least not until we have had our Mitzvah."

Colt wanted to know more, but under the circumstances, thought it best not to get into a theological debate.

Suddenly, shots echoed throughout the temple followed by shouts. Baker's voice bellowed and cursed Gasper's name. The foundations of the temple trembled, sending dust and debris trickling into the air. Sasha moved closer.

"We need to get out of here," he whispered.

Sasha nodded and clutched his hand.

Colt's heart skipped a beat or two removing all doubts about his feelings.

***

Colt and Sasha had not moved three paces before Layla

appeared out of nowhere. "Hold it right there." Leveling her weapon at the two frightened children, her voice cut through the dusty air with a deadly edge. "Turn around and move." Shoving them forward, she began calling Baker's name. "We got 'em," she hollered. Her voice faded into the moisture-laden air and a light clicked on.

"In here." The big man stood in the large chamber. "Let's have that map kid," Baker demanded, his breath came in short puffs. His meaty hand gripped Colt's shirt and yanked it open. A smirk played on his lips as Colt's face reddened. "Now there." Eyeing Layla, he nodded. "I've got no more use for these vermin. Take them down the hall and, well, you know what to do with them."

She leered at the two kids. "With pleasure." She pointed her weapon toward the entrance and shoved Colt and Sasha into the murky corridor. "And don't try anything funny."

Turning the corner, she herded them into an empty chamber. Colt knew they were about to leave this life. He knew where he was going, but Sasha? That was another thing. As Layla backed up and took aim, Colt pinched his eyes shut. *Oh, Lord, spare us, if not for my sake, spare Sasha's life so she can believe on You.* His prayer was simple. He just hoped his faith was strong enough.

***

Unseen by Layla, Balthazar plunged his staff forward. The force of its energy thrust her to the stone floor. She tumbled and rolled, releasing a demonic cry. In an instant, she was on her feet. Balthazar aimed the staff at her and shoved. She flew against the opposite wall and slumped down.

"Run," he commanded, but Colt held his ground. Reaching down, he picked up a golf ball size rock and loaded his slingshot. Pulling back, he let the stone fly, but to his amazement, the rock passed through her body, striking the wall behind her.

At once, the woman's angry glared bore down upon him.

"Run, I said." This time, Colt grabbed Sasha's hand and yanked her into the corridor. Together, they scampered over fallen support beams, rocks, and debris as they blindly picked their way through the corridors.

Back in the chamber, Balthazar continued battling the woman. It was obvious, this was no ordinary adversary. He saw the stone fly through her body, looked into her eye sockets and saw two glowing embers. Suddenly, she stood and began to grow in proportion. Her voice turned ominous and she called for the bats to descend upon the figure before her. Balthazar stood his ground.

"Bats, I hate bats." Gasper's whispered complaint brought a smile to Balthazar's rugged face as his friend sprang into the chamber.

"What took you so long?"

"I made a wrong turn."

"Well, don't just stand there, do something," Balthazar yelled as the creatures swooped down.

Gasper grabbed a torch from the wall and blew upon it. The embers burst into flames, illuminating the scene. Using two hands, he began swinging it while Balthazar continued doing battle with the woman.

Using the end of his staff, Balthazar pointed it at her and tugged it to his right, then left. The spirit woman dangled in mid-air, then fell to the floor. He thrust again, but her power continued to grow.

"Baker must be reading from the book," Gasper yelled over the flutter of leather wings.

Looking at the demonic creature, Balthazar spoke directly to her. "Three cords are not easily broken." He swung the staff in a great arch. "I rebuke you in the name of the Lord Jesus Christ and the blood of the eternal covenant." The demon released a scream that turned his blood to ice. As Balthazar's strength flagged, Gasper tossed the burning torch at the being that threatened them. Immediately, flames engulfed it, licking at its ethereal garments. Within minutes, all that was left was a smoldering pile of ash.

Balthazar nudged the smoldering embers with the end of his staff. “She’s gone, but Baker has the medallion and the last page. We must hurry.”

Chapter Fifty-Five

The flutter of leathery wings chasing Colt and Sasha beat in his ears like an adolescent in a room full of drums. Black corridors beckoned, but without any way of getting their bearings, they were at the mercy of wherever their feet took them. Ducking beneath a low-hanging outcropping, Colt slipped and fell. “Ouch!” He splattered on the slick floor. Clambering to his feet, he watched as a beady-eyed creature flew low and snagged Sasha’s hair.

Her scream shot a jolt of adrenaline through his veins.

Unable to free herself from the deranged creature, Sasha flailed her hands wildly. “Get it off of me.” Her muffled cries were nearly drowned out by the screeches of the bats.

Caring nothing for his own safety, Colt pulled his pocketknife from his pocket and slashed a clump of her hair. “Sorry,” he said sheepishly.

Sasha shrugged. “That’s okay, I’m just glad to have that thing out of my hair.”

Still holding the bat with its entangled claws, he slung it down. It smacked the floor with a dull thud. “There, that’ll teach that critter for messing with my girl.” The words slipped out before he could stop them.

Sasha’s face reddened in the dim illumination and she giggled. “Let’s get out of here.”

“Wait.” Colt listened. “This way.” Hand in hand, they dashed toward a light which promised an escape. A moment later, they found themselves face to face with sheriff Baker ... again. But rather than taking aim at them, he stood transfixed.

The whites of his eyes glowed and his pupils were like black orbs. He stared ahead, unblinking.

A glint of light caught Colt's eye and he turned. The golden medallion which Baker stole from him was in the center of a circle. Like a zombie, Baker moved past them and began touching the pointers on the pentagram. First one, then another; all the while reciting something in a foreign language. Knowing the danger of what might happen if the man succeeded in opening the door to the abyss; Colt reloaded his slingshot, took aim and fired. The stone flew straight and struck Baker in the back of the head. He turned on him with rage.

"You," he cursed. "I'll kill you for that." Reaching for his weapon, he pulled it his from its holster and aimed.

***

In an instant, the room burst into blinding light. Balthazar stood in the midst of the chamber, his staff held out.

The deafening blast of Baker's weapon shook the room. Dazed, Balthazar staggered backward.

"No," Gasper screamed, as he rushed into the chamber. Baker's wicked laughter echoed off the slimy walls.

Touching the last of the points on the pentagram, Baker grabbed the handle and swung the door open. Searing heat immediately engulfed the room, scorching anything it touched.

Gasping for air, Colt and Sasha sprang for the door, barely making it out before the flames consumed them.

Still holding the bradded staves as a shield against the blazing heat, Balthazar slumped to the floor. Gasper huddled over him waiting for the end to come. Amidst the roar of flames, Balthazar whispered in a raspy voice, "Finish the mission," Then he sagged back.

For a long moment, Gasper couldn't tell if his old friend was dead or alive, but he had his orders. Clutching him under the arms, he dragged Balthazar to the backside of the throne where the flames would not reach him. Then he stood. Bracing himself against the onslaught, he pressed himself forward.

Voices of the condemned lashed out of the flames. Spirits moaned in agony crying out for relief. None came. None would ever come. If Gasper didn't slam the door shut soon, it wouldn't be long before those same spirits would find their way to the opening and flood out. Who knew what havoc they would wreak, if released.

As Gasper dragged himself closer, he noticed Baker. He was standing with his arms outstretched, calling for the spirits of the underworld to obey. They laughed and mocked. "Jesus we know, and Paul we know, but who are you?"

Cursing, Baker grabbed the medallion and held it up like a badge of honor. The spirits continued their scorn.

"Out of my way," a large spirit demanded. It bore down upon Baker like a locomotive. Its teeth dripping with ooze, its eyes bulging and its claws reaching out to pounce on the trembling man.

Baker filled his lungs and screamed in an ancient language. The looming figure stopped as if it hit a thick wall.

"I command you to yield to my authority."

The spirit backed away.

"Bow, I say."

Gasper watched in horror as the spirits yielded to his commands. He knew, if he didn't act fast, all would be lost. Grabbing the three-fold staff, he raced across the room. Hellish flames licked at his garments with every step, yet he pressed on. *This must have been what it was like to be Shadrach, Meshach, and Abednego when they were thrown into the fiery furnace.* Feeling the presence of the Lord, he plunged the end of the staff into Baker's chest and shoved. Baker clung to the door; flames wrapping their scalding fingers around his ankles and legs. His eyes grew wild and he fought with a fanaticism that shook Gasper to the core.

Still clutching the medallion, Baker cursed and snarled like a rabid wolf. As the two men battled, each one pushed with their might until the sheriff lost his footing and stumbled. In an instant, Gasper grabbed the medallion from his fingers and tossed it into the flaming river below. Baker reached out to capture the medallion as it sailed over his head, but missed. Cursing, he dove after it and was immediately engulfed in the inferno.

The looming spirit tried to push past Gasper as Baker disappeared in the flames, but he pulled back, and like a whale hunter, tossed the staff like a harpoon into the spirit's chest. "The Lord rebuke you," he cried over the hiss of flames and cries of the condemned.

The staff struck a death-blow to the creature. Clutching its chest, it tumbled back in the flames. The voices grew in intensity with one familiar one rising above the babble. Gasper's heart slammed against his ribs. *No Mrs. White, or whoever you are. Not this time.* With what strength remained, he slammed the door closed.

Breathing heavily, Gasper leaned against the door and wiped the sweat from his brow. Only then did he remember his fallen comrade.

"Balthazar," he hollered.

Closing the distance, he knelt and lifted his mentor, his friend. The older man's eyes fluttered open. A weak smile parted his lips. "I was just dreaming of home," his voice barely above a whisper.

Gasper dabbed the blood from the corner of Balthazar's mouth. "Balthazar, you can't leave me. I still have much to learn."

Balthazar clutched Gasper's hand close to his chest. "You have come a long way since we started our journey."

"But the order? We are all that's left."

"No, Gasper. You have Colt to train. He is your focus now."

"But, but ..."

Balthazar held up a finger. "We all must leave this life

sometime." His voice grew weak. "We have had the privilege of hanging around longer than most. But I am tired, I want to go home ... son."

Gasper sat bolt upright. "Son?"

Balthazar gave him a weak smile. "Yes, actually ... grandson. You see, your father, my son was so impetuous. He never wanted to listen to me. He didn't want to learn the disciplines of the order. And so he struck out on his own ..." His tone was etched in anger, pain ... and grief. "Like the Prodigal Son, he demanded his portion and soon left. Sources told me he went to India and married. Years later, I got word that he had a son of his own, but I was too stubborn to go after him. Call it foolish, call it pride. But then you appeared. You were so much like your father." His eyes twinkled with joy. "I knew it the moment I saw you." By then, his tone had softened. A silver stream flowed down his cheeks.

Gasper tried to speak, but his throat closed. "My father, one of the Magi?"

"Yes, he had such potential. I see that in you. He was a good man, but of course, that's all in the past. I doubt you could even find a distant relative now. Yours is to move forward, to live in the present, not looking over your shoulders in regret."

Unable to stop the tears, Gasper let them roll down his cheeks. "But our staves ... they're gone."

Shaking his head, Balthazar's eyes wander to the door. "No, there is power in the three-fold stave and as long as you have them, you will always have us. Remember our pledge."

Clutching his hand, he began, but stopped as Colt's small hand joined theirs.

"Now we can begin," Colt said. "We pledge our lives and our sacred honor to each other, and choose to follow where the God of Heaven leads us that we may fulfill His will. So say we all."

"So say we all," Gasper added.

Chapter Fifty-Six

Seeing the Book of Incantations laying on the altar, Gasper grabbed the bradded stave and touched the end to the open book. A bolt of lightning shot out, igniting the yellowed pages. Within minutes, the ancient tomb was engulfed in flames. Its ashes fluttered upward forming a thick, black cloud. Suddenly, the cloud took shape. A deep, throaty voice called out of the blackness. Staring wide-eyed, Colt, Sasha, and Gasper backed away from Balthazar's limp body as the spirit took form.

"I am Beelzebub, the lord of the book. Why have you released me?"

Too frightened to speak, Gasper grabbed Colt and Sasha by the hands and sprang for the door. Struggling to breathe in the thick atmosphere that surrounded them, they dashed through the inky corridors, while the dark shadow chased them, demanding them to stop.

They didn't.

Amidst the chaos, the floor beneath their feet began to break apart. Large crevices appeared causing them to leap from one stone platform to another. Billows of rich, dark smoke filled the tunnel; stinging their eyes, scorching their throats, making them stumble along blindly.

"We'll never get out of here in time," Colt croaked.

"Yes, we will," Gasper answered. Lifting the stave high over his head, he let its light illuminate the way. "That way," he called and leaped forward.

With every fearful step, the tunnel behind them collapsed.

There was no turning back. There was no saving Balthazar. He had already departed to the land that was fairer than day. His fight had ended, he had finished his course. By now, he was hearing the Savior's kind words, "Welcome home my child. Well done. Enter into the joy of thy Lord."

The thought of Melchior and Balthazar's deaths filled Gasper with mixed emotions. He would miss his friends sorely, but to deny them their long-awaited reunion with loved ones, to prolong their needed rest, was too much to ask of any man. Even a Magi, even Balthazar and Melchior.

Balthazar's final words, "Yours is to move forward, to live in the present, not the past," clung tenaciously to the fringes of his mind. He still had a job to do. He had Colt, he had Felicia. Her face came into clearer focus at the thought of her name.

As a faint light grew brighter, so did his hope, they would escape unharmed, despite the falling ceiling and rippling floor. Panting for air, he tugged the two young people forward. All at once, the earth shook with a violence that stopped him mid run. Maybe Beelzebub wasn't going to let them escape, maybe their time had come, after all.

Suddenly, Sasha yanked her hand free.

Turning, Gasper called to her as she ran back into the shadows.

"Sasha, where are you going?" Fear laced Colt's voice.

Gasper stood, torn between running or staying. Holding his staff out, he saw Sasha standing, her arms outstretched, her angelic face glowing with a radiance defined only in terms of brilliance. The light burned away all vestiges of evil, of darkness, of demonic presence.

She filled her lungs and declared. "The Lord God Almighty liveth and commands everyone, everywhere to bow the knee, whether it is in heaven, or earth or things under the earth."

The sound of her commanding voice silenced the tortured spirits. Holding her arms extended, she held her position ...

waiting. Then it started ... the voices of the disembodied began their agonized pleas. "Have you come to destroy us before our time, Prince Laina? Please, we adjure thee by him who sits on the throne. Do not send us into the abyss. Bury us in this mountain and we will trouble you no longer." The conjoined voices echoed through the halls and corridors of the condemned Temple of Endor, pleading, crying. Finally, they joined in forced subjection acclaiming Jesus as King of kings and Lord of lords.

Satisfied, Sasha spoke one word. It came with such controlled power, that Gasper thought it would bring down the mountain upon them before they escaped. "Go!"

Turning, Gasper clasped Colt's hand and sprang for the entrance.

"But Sasha, we can't leave her." Colt's tear-filled voice ripped at Gasper's heart. He knew the truth, but it had not been made clear to his young charge ... yet. That was lesson number one.

As they cleared the mouth of the tunnel, the earth shook as if giving birth ... or death.

Blinded by the sun's rays, the two survivors stumbled down the rocky hill until they reached the place where Simon Levi still lay. His breath was labored, yet he clung tenaciously to life. Placing his hands on the stricken man, Gasper closed his eyes and inhaled. Simon's eyelids fluttered open and he gasped a long awaited breath. "We must keep going," Gasper said before the man could thank him.

Together they ran and stumbled downward until they reached level ground. Hands on their knees, Gasper, Simon and Colt panted until the earth stopped misbehaving. Collapsing, Colt repeated Sasha's name. It was obvious to Gasper, that it was more than a youthful infatuation with the wispy girl. She had meant the world to him and Gasper ached for his young charge.

Minutes turned to hours as the three figures lay on the

grassy field. They had lost much, yet they had gained more. They had faced the enemy of their souls and had overcome.

As the sun retreated after a full day of punishing earth's inhabitants and cool shadows offered their soft caresses. Gasper pushed himself up on wobbly legs. "We need to be going, Colt."

Too spent to argue, Colt stood. "Sasha's mudder will be expecting us. Says she's prepared a big meal. I wouldn't want to disappoint her. Plus, we need to explain what happened. She'll be devastated."

Gasper nodded grimly.

***

Plodding past the hill where he and Sasha shared a picnic lunch, Colt stopped and wiped the tears from his face. "This is so hard," he agonized, his shaky voice cracking with emotion.

Gasper laid his hand on the boy's shoulder and gave it a gentle squeeze. Turning south, they cut through the wheat field. He again paused and surveyed the place where he'd spent the night. Sighing, Colt scanned the sheaves of wheat which remained packed down. He wondered if they would ever recover, he wondered if he would ever recover. Finally, they emerged near the blueberry field. The barren limbs reached out as if to say, "Thank you for unburdening us of our fruit." He sniffed a tear back and kept walking.

When they reached the end of the field, Sasha's house rose to meet them. Candles in every window welcomed them with a warm glow. A rotund figure graced the back door and a tender voice sailed across the yard.

"Colt, is that you?"

"Yes, mudder. It's me, and I have brought along some friends."

"Yes, I can see that. Come in, come in. We have such a feast waiting for you."

It seemed odd to Colt that Sasha's mother didn't act the least unnerved not to see her daughter.

Stepping into the house where just a few hours ago, he had enjoyed a hearty meal, much laughter and the tantalizing smiles from Sasha. Colt was overwhelmed with a sense of loss.

"What is wrong, my child?" Sasha's mudder was at his side in an instant. Gasper and Simon held their breath ... waiting ... praying.

Colt took a hiccupping breath. "I'm sorry, Ma'am, but Sasha—" his words morphed into sobs and she enfolded him in her arms. Arms that had been empty far too long.

"Oh, you poor child. Sasha has been missing for a long time." She heaved a deep sigh.

"But, but—"

"Yes, I know. You thought you met your soul mate. But I assure you. You were entertaining an angel."

"But you spoke with her, you fed her. We laughed together ... I don't understand." His voice cracked.

"No, child. We didn't do all those things. I'm afraid someone has played a mischievous trick on you."

Gasper uncrossed his arms, stepped closer and laid his hand on the boy's slumping shoulder. "She is right. We are told in scripture to show kindness to strangers: for in so doing we may be entertaining angels and not know it."

The idea of Sasha being an angel brightened Colt's tear stained face. After a few minutes, a low chuckle percolated in his chest and grew to a belly laugh. "You mean to say, I had lunch with an angel? And ran through the wheat field and even fought off demons with a real angel? Wow! Mudder and papa will never believe it."

***

Prince Laina stepped through the crystalline veil between celestial with the physical and nodded to Michael, the Archangel.

"You have had a busy day," the mighty prince said with a chuckle.

Prince Laina gave him an impish smile. "Yes ... yes, I

have, but very productive."

As he spoke, two men in white robes stepped closer. Behind them, the host of the redeemed gathered.

The Archangel crossed his arms and acknowledged them with a smile. Returning his gaze to Prince Laina, he continued, "But you nearly ruined everything with that stunt you pulled with the blueberries and picnic. The boy grew quite fond of you."

His comment brought knowing smiles to the two onlooker's faces.

Nodding, Prince Laina considered his words carefully. A sparkle of delight danced in the smaller angel's startling blue eyes. "His heart is still young, he will heal. But I can assure you, he will never forget the lesson he learned. And if my instincts are correct, he will meet his Sasha and live happily ever after."

"Yes, I think you're right" Michael, the Archangel said, as they gathered and peered down at the three figures trudging down the hill they fought so hard to climb hours before.

Balthazar laid his hand on the mighty angel's shoulder. He turned. "My friend, Melchior and I would like to thank you for all you did throughout those trying days."

Michael tipped his head. "We serve a mighty God. It was an honor to assist you in your endeavor."

A voice called out from among the great cloud of witnesses who'd been following the events on earth with great interest.

Balthazar turned. It was Balshinar … his son.

"Father," the eternally younger man ran toward him and knelt. Joyful tears soaked his gleaming face.

Balthazar helped his son to stand, then embarrassed him for the first time since they parted centuries ago. "My son, I am so glad you found your way."

"Not my way, *His* way," he said, looking at the Lord upon His throne. As father and son glided up the golden strand,

Prince Laina asked, “Shall I guide them home, my lord?”

The towering angel shifted his gaze southward. “They are not expected home until Christmas, right?”

Prince Laina nodded. “Yes.”

“Good, I have an idea.”

A billowy cloud enfolded the two angels as the night deepened.

Postlude

The light breeze carried children's laughter across a manicured lawn. A massive oak tree swayed with the rhythm of a rope swing hanging from its mighty limb. Looking up from his notes, Gasper smiled. It was the first nice day after a string of gloomy days, and he couldn't stand to be cooped up any longer. The Adirondack chair provided him with a comfortable place to sit and an ideal position to write. With gnarled fingers, he tugged a tattered Afghan higher up his lap to keep the chill from penetrating his tired bones.

Setting his pencil aside, Gasper fingered a stack of pages. He had just finished putting the final touches on a story he'd started many years ago. He leaned back, admiring his work. At his feet, Gideon the Fourth rested in the sun. He too seemed to be enjoying the change. Melchior's original companion had long since gone to his resting place, but not before Siring the next generation of Gideons. Since then, Gasper had named the first born of each successive litter after his mentor's dog. It was his way of honoring his memory.

It had been nearly thirty years since those wild days in which he and his friends faced down the White Witch and her demonic minions. Thirty years to grow old, thirty years to teach the wisdom of the ages to those who would listen, thirty years to marry the woman of his dreams, thirty years to watch his children, and grandchildren grow up and grow wise.

Sitting on the veranda of their palatial home in North Hampton, Georgia, Gasper watched his and Felicia's grandchildren play with the neighbor's kids. Colt O'Dell and his wife, Sasha, had built a happy home. Colt's consulting firm provided him with enough business to keep him out of trouble and in good standing with his church. As a lay-pastor of one of the churches started by North Hampton Bible Church, Pastor Colt divided his time between preaching, giving wise counsel to those serious enough to take it, and directing the annual Live Nativity where he doubled as a wise man.

"What are you doing, Granddaddy?" It always delighted him when one of his grandchildren asked him a question. His answer usually involved him playing a verbal shell game with the inquisitive child.

Looking at her angelic face, he leaned down, lifted her to his lap and kissed her rosy cheek. She giggled as his grizzled beard tickled her neck and she scrunched closer. "Bel, I just finished writing a story about four wise men and how they defeated a wicked witch."

Bel's nose wrinkled. "I don't like witches, they're yucky."

"How do you know that, have you ever met one?"

Finger to her chin, Bel thought a moment. "Yes." Her childish voice sparkled with enthusiasm.

"You have? When?"

"Joey says Mrs. Huddleston is a witch."

"Oh? And why would he call your Kindergarten teacher a witch?"

"'Cause she has a wart right on her nose."

Bel's honesty was a refreshing breeze. Squeezing her tightly, he let a deep chuckle bubble in his chest. "Well, having a wart on your nose doesn't make you a witch. But we don't want to talk about that. What we want to focus on is being wise."

The golden-haired girl nodded absentmindedly. Pointing at his staff, she asked, "Why do you always carry that stick?"

As he reached for it, Mel, Bel's twin, scampered up. Her inquisitive eyes missed nothing. "Here, Granddaddy," she said, grabbing the bulky staff. As she did, she waved it in the air. Then, with an impish giggle, she pointed it at her sister. "Rise," her tone turned dark.

Bel's jaw dropped, as she rose an inch from the porch.

His eyes bulging, Gasper snatched the staff from her hands. "Mel, how many times have I told you not to fool around with this?"

Mel offered her best pooch lip knowing its manipulative effect. Gasper relaxed his grip. "I guess you have been listening to too many of my stories."

The two girls exchanged questioning looks. "Tell us another one, Granddaddy," they said in harmony.

A wispy shadow crossed over the trio as Felicia stepped from the house. Her meticulously maintained figure, silvery tight-cropped hair, and deep brown eyes still sent Gasper's heart aflutter. "Are these two munchkins interrupting you, Gasper?"

His weathered face wrinkled into a smile. "No, my dear. I was just about to tell them a story."

Taking a seat next to her husband of nearly thirty years, Felicia laced her fingers in his. "Which one, this time? You've told them all, multiple times."

It was true. He had told his children and grandchildren all but one, and it lay dormant in the back of his mind. His secret was known only to one other person and he guarded it well. Now that Gasper was nearing the end of his earthly pilgrimage, he reconsidered his decision.

Lifting his pencil, he turned to a blank page and began writing ...

Discussion Questions

Which character did you find yourself drawn to?

What flaws in my characters did you see reflected in your own life?

Was there a moment in which you found yourself lost in the story?

In what way did you see a clear connection between the Messiah of in the Psalms and the Lord Jesus Christ's sacrificial death in Calvary?

Have you made Jesus the Lord of your life?

What issues are there in your life in which you need wise counsel?

When God's Word addresses those issues, would you be willing to obey it, even if it was painful?

Do you know someone with whom you could share this story of hope and redemption?

After reading this story, what singular truth stood out in your mind?

Acknowledgments

Growing up in a home where my mother read stories out loud to me and my four siblings stoked my imagination, so it goes without saying, I love hearing my wife read my stories. She is my Alpha and Beta reader and I thank her for her patience and insight.

I also want to thank Elaine Day for her encouraging comments when she said; "This book has real potential. I really did enjoy reading it and wish you the best!!

The Chase Newton Series

by Bryan M. Powell

The Order

Follow investigative reporter Chase Newton as he goes undercover in search of the truth. What he finds puts him and those he cares for in mortal danger. Fast-paced and high- energy describes this first of three mystery and action thrillers.

The Oath

The president and vice president have been attacked. The vice president survived, but he is a hunted man. The man who was sworn in is an impostor and Chase must get a DNA from him to prove who the real president is.

The Outsider

After a thousand years of peace, the world is suddenly thrown into chaos as Satan is loosed from his prison. These action-packed stories will hold you breathless and capture your imagination until the exciting conclusion.

The Jared Russell Series

by Bryan M. Powell

Sisters of the Veil

Jared Russell, a former Marine turned architect, must navigate the minefield of hatred and prejudice to find the meaning of love and forgiveness.

ISBN - 978151057994

Power Play - #8 on Amazon Political Fiction

Jared and Fatemah Russell go Beirut, Lebanon, to establish the Harbor House, a refuge for converted Muslims and find themselves caught in a Middle East conflict of global proportions.

ISBN – 9781511402750

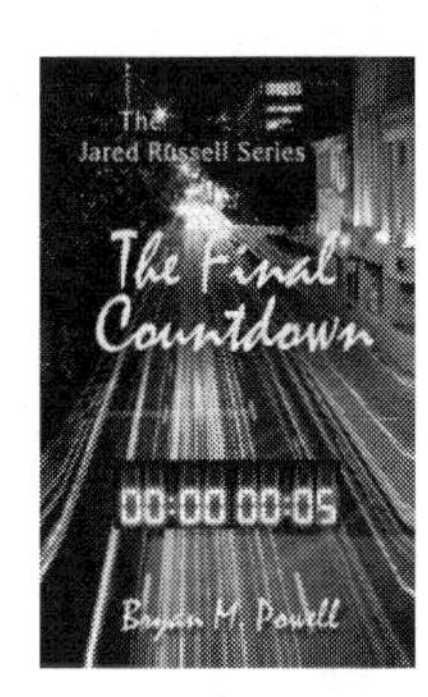

The Final Countdown – #25 on Amazon

The clock is ticking and Jared once again finds himself battling against forces beyond his control. Can he and his friends unravel the mystery in time to stop two radical Muslims from perpetrating a horrible crime against our country?

ISBN – 978153297825

Non-Fiction Series

by Bryan M. Powell

Seeing Jesus a Three Dimensional Look at Worship

Seeing Jesus is a thought providing and compelling expose' on what is true worship.

ISBN -9781511540582

Show Us the Father

A thirty-day devotional showing how Jesus demonstrated His Father's character and qualities.

ISBN -9781517633905

Faith, Family, and a Lot of Hard Work

Born the year Stock-Market crashed, Mr. Gillis grew up in South Georgia with a 3rd grade education. After being challenged to get the best job in the company, he worked hard and got a degree from the University of Georgia and Moody Bible Institute in Finance. By mid-life, he owed 14 companies. **ISBN -9781467580182**

About the Author

Novelist Bryan M. Powell is the author of 8 Christian Fiction novels, 2 Inspirational Books and 1 Memoir he co-authored. Working within a Christian ministry for over forty-two years, Bryan is uniquely qualified to write about Christian topics. His novels have been published by Tate Publishing, Lightening Source, Create Space, Kindle Direct Publishing and Vabella Publishing. His latest novel, The Witch and the Wise Men, held the #23 slot on Amazon's best seller's list.

In addition to his novels, Bryan's short stories and other works appeared in *The North Georgia Writer* (PCWG's publication), *Relief Notes* (A Christian Authors Guild's book, released in 2014), and in the *Georgia Backroads* magazine.
Bryan is a member of the following organizations: American Christian Fiction Writers (ACFW), The Christian Author's Guild (President, 2016), The Paulding County Writers' Guild (PCWG), and the local chapter of ACFW, the New Life Writers Group.

www.facebook.com/authorbryanpowell
www.authorbryanpowell.wordpress.com
authorbryanpowell@reagan.com

Page 27

Made in the USA
Lexington, KY
12 November 2019